BOOK ONE

DEREK SHUPERT

Grid Down

Cover design by Derek Shupert

Cover art by Christian Bentulan

This book is a work of fiction. The names, characters, places, and incidents are products of the writer's imagination or have been used fictionally and are not to be constructed as real. Any resemblance to person, living or dead, actual events, locales or organizations is entirely coincidental.

For information contact :

Derek Shupert

www.derekshupert.com

First Edition

ISBN : 9798450040707

ALSO BY DEREK SHUPERT

AGE OF COLLAPSE SERIES:

GRID DOWN

BRINK OF EXTINCTION SERIES:

SUDDEN IMPACT

STAY ALIVE

GET HOME

SURVIVE THE FALL SERIES:

POWERLESS WORLD

MADNESS RISING

DARK ROADS

TOTAL COLLAPSE

FIGHT BACK

THE COMPLETE SURVIVE THE FALL BOX SET

THE COMPLETE UNDEAD APOCALYPSE SERIES:

THE COMPLETE UNDEAD APOCALYPSE BOX SET

THE COMPLETE DEAD STATE SERIES:

DEAD STATE: CATALYST (PREQUEL)

DEAD STATE: FALLOUT

DEAD STATE: SURVIVAL ROAD

DEAD STATE: EXECUTIONER

DEAD STATE: IMMUNE

DEAD STATE: EVOLVED

THE COMPLETE DEAD STATE SERIES BOX SET

THE HUNTRESS BANE SERIES:
THE HUNTRESS BANE (SHORT STORY)
TAINTED HUNTER
CRIMSON THIRST

THE COMPLETE BALLISTIC MECH SERIES:
DIVISION
INFERNO
EXTINCTION
PAYBACK

STAND ALONE
SENTRY SQUAD

DEDICATION

I wouldn't be able to write without those who support me. I thank you for your encouragement and being there for me.

To those that read my books, I thank you for your support.

PREFACE

The Age of Collapse series takes place in Houston, TX, and surrounding areas. In the spirit of telling a compelling story, some aspects of the real towns and cities have been altered. Thank you for understanding the authors creative freedom.

PROLOGUE

ALEX

The endless wave of threats showed no signs of stopping. Alex Ryder was a dead man walking.

Alex's hands trembled and throbbed. Both knuckles were swollen from the brawl he'd been in the day before. It hurt to make a fist and to do simple tasks, but he powered through.

The side of his face ached. A tooth in the back of his mouth felt loose. The shiner and bloody nose he'd received from the brute who'd attacked him in the prison's cafeteria added to the meld of pain. The shiv the brute had pulled had only grazed Alex's bicep. The wound stung but paled in comparison to the beating and constant barrage of inmates looking to take him out. He'd have to stay on high alert from now on if he hoped to complete his four-year stint.

The prison guards had all but vanished within the low-lit corridors of the Huntsville prison. Alex hadn't noticed their exodus, and feared the worst. He'd kept to himself, focused on keeping a low profile and doing his assigned tasks without tarnishing his already spotty record any more than it had been. He hadn't started any fights or made any trouble, but seemed to be the center of a number of skirmishes within the prison. The frequent attacks made him believe he'd been targeted for the job him and Trey, his associate on the outside, had done that landed him inside the pen.

A handful of other inmates, and himself, worked in the on-site laundry facility without any supervision at the moment. The four other convicts peered his way, staring at him with malevolent eyes. The men had various tattoos and satanic imagery covering their bodies and skulls—pentagrams, the numbers 666, and swastikas with a picture of a bluebird, and double lightning bolts rounded out the markings.

Each member of the Aryan Brotherhood fanned out from the large, commercial washing machines and dryers and checked the halls.

The sharp noise created from each old, rickety machine in the recesses of the prison drowned out any outside sounds. A loud scream or yell wouldn't be heard, or so he'd been told from other inmates.

Alex turned away from the open door of the washing machine, where he'd shoveled the bed sheets and white prison garb they wore, and faced the men. He squinted and glanced at each of the bald, surly thugs who had a variety of tattoos covering their skulls. Two stood at the openings of both halls that led into the space, keeping a look out.

"I have no beef with the Brotherhood," Alex said, shifting his gaze from the other two men who advanced on him. "I'd think real hard about going through with this if I were you, Davidson. More guards could come back at any moment."

"How are we looking?" the short, stocky, bald man asked the other men keeping watch. They each gave a thumbs up and continued watching the halls.

"You're right, Ryder. We don't have a beef with you, but Mr. Vargas has placed a bounty on your head and we aim to collect it. I wouldn't worry about the guards either. We'll have time to handle what's needed here before anyone shows up."

A portion of the guards had been paid off it seemed. That didn't bode well for him, seeing as he had twenty months or so left on his stint.

Alex balled his hands into tight fists. The bones in his fingers radiated pain. He took a step back, pushing the wide, rolling cart out of his way. "That hasn't worked out too well for the other handful of convicts who have tried to take me out. I'm still here and they're either in the infirmary or in solitary confinement. Think about it."

Davidson reached inside the pocket of his white pants and pulled out what looked to be a shiv. He glanced to his taller, plump partner who parroted the move. Both men advanced.

"I've thought about it and the amount of money hanging over your head is too good to pass up." Davidson repositioned his hold on the handle of the shiv. "We can do this the hard or easy way. I'm good with whatever. If you'd like for it to be quick, tell me where your partner took the money you two stole and the Brothers will grant you a quick death. If not, others could get hurt, like that daughter of yours."

Alex worked his way around behind the rolling cart, using it as a barrier between him and the Brotherhood. He eyed both men, waiting for them to attack, or for help to show up. "I don't know where Trey is or the money for that matter. We went our separate ways that night and I haven't seen or heard from him since."

A scowl formed on Davidson's face. His wrinkled brows slanted inward. He flashed his clenched teeth, then glanced at his plump partner. "Get him, Zane, and be quick about it. Looks like we're going to do this the hard, painful way."

Here we go.

The overweight ogre stomped toward the rolling cart. His nostrils flared under the dull, yellow lights that hung overhead. The shiv tucked in his fat hand squeezed the handle tighter as he closed in.

Alex shifted his gaze to Davidson, then back to Zane. He kept a firm grip on the top edge of the cart, rolling it back with him. His hands hurt from holding the cart so tight and from moving it around like he was, but Alex had little choice.

The back wall lined with running machines flanked him, offering ten feet or so of open space to maneuver. A closed door across the way that led to a storage room caught his eye, but Alex would be hard-pressed to make it in time.

Zane reached for the top of the cart. His sausage fingers took hold. He was strong as an ox and about as dumb as a bag of tools. He wrenched the rolling cart toward him, overpowering Alex with little effort.

"You don't want to do this, big man," Alex said in an unsteady voice, bringing his arms up in front of him as uncertainty and fear took hold. "You can still stop and leave. It's not too late."

"Get him now and let's finish this," Davidson shouted at his lackey's back.

Zane rushed Alex, blade up and at the ready.

The lights crashed.

Blinding darkness swallowed the space.

The hum and rattling noise of the washing machines and dryers stopped. An eerie silence took hold.

"What the hell happened to the lights?" Davidson shouted at his crew.

"No clue," another gruff voice replied. "The power crashed or something."

The chatter among the other Brotherhood members loomed within the blackness. No visible light could be seen. The vague outline of the men melded with the darkness, making it that much harder to track them.

Alex backed away from Zane, listening for his footfalls as he searched for a way out of the dire situation.

A light flickered into existence. A mixture of yellow and blue lingered. Davidson held the Zippo lighter up, turned toward his men, then faced Zane. He pointed at his minion with the shiv up. "Don't lose track of Ryder. We need—"

Alex made for the storage room.

Zane moved quickly for an overweight man who didn't exercise much in the yard. He grabbed Alex by the scruff of his white prison-issued shirt and jerked him back.

Alex stumbled backward, turned, and faced the towering giant. The flicker of light from the Zippo cast his wide frame in a dark shadow, revealing only a scant portion of his rounded head and gritted teeth. Alex hammered Zane's thick forearm, then his wrist.

His hold on Alex's shirt lessened. He swung with the shiv at Alex's side.

"Don't kill him, you moron. We need him alive for now," Davidson said, huffing. "We can stick him once he gives up the information on the money and his friend."

Alex blocked Zane's attempt with his forearm, then jabbed the giant in the throat.

Zane dropped the shiv. Both hands reached for his throat as he struggled to breathe. He backed away, wheezing.

Alex bent down and scooped up the shiv, then hammered Zane's balls with his foot. A painful howl fled the big man's bearded mouth as he dropped to his knees, cradling his jewels.

Footfalls hammered the concrete nearby.

Each report echoed louder.

Alex punished the side of Zane's head with his balled fist, knocking him to the floor. The big man crumbled to his side. Alex turned on the heels of his shoes and confronted Davidson.

The blade in Davidson's hand slashed upward, slicing through the fabric of Alex's shirt. The flame whipping about from the top of the lighter framed the stocky neo-Nazi in a manic rage. Spit spewed from his clenched jaw. He came at Alex once more. "I'm going to enjoy gutting you like a fish once we have what we need."

"Not going to happen." Alex leaned to the side, then ducked under Davidson's arm as he tried to find any point of his body to make contact with. He stood, then rammed his knee in the agitated convict's gut, ripping the air from his lungs.

Davidson struggled to breathe, gasping. He doubled over and dropped the lighter. The casing pinged off the concrete, but the flame didn't diminish. The shiv stayed glued to his hand, fingers bound over the handle.

The two other members of the Brotherhood fled their posts and vanished beyond the darkness lurking in the halls.

Alex towered over Davidson, blade in hand. His chest heaved. Adrenaline surged throughout his body. The pain and discomfort waned as he thought of the threats the Brotherhood had spilt.

"Go ahead and shank me," Davidson said, hunched over with his head trained at the floor. "You do it, and you'll never get out of here and see that sweet girl of yours ever again. Not that you'll survive much longer."

Davidson's arm sprung upward.

Alex kicked his arm away, knocking the shiv to the floor. He bound his fingers into the depraved thug's clothing, then wrenched him up until they were eye to eye.

"You're right," Alex replied, contemplating sticking the neo-Nazi in the gut with the blade, but surviving and getting out was priority one now. Besides, he wasn't a cold-blooded killer, despite what he'd told the thugs. "I told you that you didn't want to do this. You should've listened."

"Eat crap." Davidson spat in Alex's face. "You won't survive the day in here. You're as good as dead, Ryder."

The thick spit clung to the side of Alex's face. He brushed the back of his hand across his cheek, wiping away the fluid. "We'll see about that and what gets done to you and the other Brothers when they find out you failed. No loose ends, I'd imagine."

Davidson lifted his arm.

Alex punched him in the face twice, sending him hard to the ground. Davidson writhed on the floor, cupping his nose and mouth with his hands.

A clicking sound and footfalls echoed in the dark silence, heading toward him.

Alex glanced to the far side of the laundry facility, unsure who was coming. He had to get out of there and to the outside. If he found Trey maybe he could settle matters before it was too late.

CHAPTER ONE

ALEX

FOUR MONTHS EARLIER

The straw that broke the camel's back. That's what it felt like being fired and facing a mountain of problems alone.

The mound of bills covered the rounded kitchen table. The dark red ink stamped on each late notice and final warning. Alex had been working hard to keep things afloat, and provide for his teenage daughter as best he could, but life didn't care, and couldn't be bothered by the stress he battled.

Alex shifted his gaze to the bottle of whiskey next to the shot glass he cradled. He'd been pounding the spirit for the better part of the day.

The brown-tinted liquor had been depleted halfway. The missing spirit resided in his gut, working on staying his frayed nerves. If he didn't stop, the remainder would vanish and he'd have to replace it.

His fingers spun the shot glass around as he thought of his deceased wife, Stacy, and their last moments together before she lost her battle with cancer. His eyes watered. He gulped down the whiskey, then slammed the glass on the tabletop.

The ticking of the clock on the wall near the swinging door leading to the living room played in the background. Alex glanced over to the white-faced clock and sighed. It was past three. His daughter, Wendy, would be home from school soon. He needed to gather himself and not let her see him in such a way.

The back of Alex's hand wiped the wetness from both eyes. He cleared his throat and sat up straight in the chair. The whiskey bottle and shot glass wouldn't leave his sight and tempted the struggling single father to take one final drink to curb the pain.

No. I can't.

The back door to the modest two-story home opened.

Alex shook his head and focused his thoughts as best he could. He kept his head pointed at the table.

The door slammed shut.

A dense thud hit the floor at his back.

"You're home early," Wendy said, moving about behind him. "I thought you were working a double shift today?"

The dread in her tone made the weight pressing down on Alex's shoulders that much heavier. Wendy had a hard time hiding her feelings and conveyed it through the tone of her voice.

Alex ran his hand over his face, not wanting to disappoint her again. "Um, yeah. They decided they didn't need me to work the double after all and sent me home."

"Oh, really?"

The cabinet door squeaked open behind him. A clatter arose.

"Yep." Alex adjusted his backside in the chair, then ran his fingers through his hair. He had no desire to burden her with adult problems. "How was school today?"

Wendy sighed, then trudged across the linoleum floor to the fridge with a glass in hand. She sat it down on the counter, grabbed the handle to the refrigerator, then wrenched it open. “It was school and a pain in the ass like it is every day you ask me. Hasn’t changed and probably won’t.”

The long strands of her red hair were bound up in a ponytail. The back of her neck glistened with sweat from the humidity that plagued Houston. The cool air rushed from the open refrigerator door, brushing against her.

Wendy stood motionless in front of the appliance, silent.

Alex nodded, then folded his arms across his broad chest. “I’d enjoy your time in school. I’d give anything to go back to being a senior in high school and doing science and history instead of messing with bills and such.”

“Yeah, well, sitting around and getting plastered does sound tempting,” Wendy shot back, rummaging through what few groceries sat on the shelves. “You seem to be a pro at that, especially since Mom passed. I do believe that bottle had a ton more in it the other day than it does now.”

“Can we not do this now?” Alex shook his head. “You have no clue what it’s—”

“I guess I don’t want anything to drink.” Wendy stood, then slammed the door. She turned and faced Alex. A scowl formed on her face as she grumbled under her breath.

Alex hated the tension between them. It had only mounted after Stacy passed and created a wall that he couldn’t circumvent. They struggled to connect. It added to the stress he battled daily. “I’ll go to the store and pick up some groceries soon. I know we’re running a bit low on things.”

Wendy rolled her eyes and marched past the table. "I'd sober up a bit before you do. Maybe splash some water on your face and gurgle mouthwash."

The whiskey bottle and glass wouldn't leave his view. Alex pushed the chair back, grabbed the neck of the thick bottle, and hauled it to the cabinet next to the fridge. "Do you have any homework that needs to be done? Did you get that report for history finished and turned in?"

Wendy retrieved her bag from the floor, tossed the straps over her shoulder, and marched past Alex. "The report was for English and due last week. I turned it in already."

Alex shoved the bottle toward the back corner of the empty cabinet, then shut the door. "Oh, okay. Make sure and complete the other work you have. We need to end the year on a high note so those grades look good for college."

"I get it completed every day." Wendy pushed her way through the swinging door.

"I love you, sweetheart."

Wendy paused, tilted her head to the side, and kept moving without a rebuttal.

The door swung back and forth.

Alex leaned against the counter, sighed, and rubbed his jaw. He didn't know how to fix their relationship and hoped it wasn't to the point of being too far gone.

The phone in his back pocket vibrated against the edge of the counter. Alex leaned forward and dug it out. He thumbed the power button and glanced at the bright screen.

Trey had sent a text—short and cryptic.

Need to talk. You free?

Alex hadn't spoken with him for a number of years— not since Alex had gotten his life on track and put some distance between him and the lowlife. Trey had done more harm than good to his family and Alex had vowed to steer clear of the criminal.

A question mark popped up under the previous message. Alex wanted to ignore the text, but knew Trey would keep messaging until he received a response.

The ends of his fingers mashed the digital keys on the phone.

A knock sounded from the back door.

Alex looked away from the phone to the window. A man stood on the other side, hunched over and waving. It was Trey.

The last thing Alex wanted was company, especially from the likes of him. If they hadn't made eye contact, he would've hidden until Trey left.

The bright screen faded away. Alex pocketed the device and walked to the back door.

Trey stood and took a step back. Both hands plunged into the front pockets of his jeans as Alex opened the door.

"What's up, brother?" Trey smiled from ear to ear. "Sorry for dropping in on you like this. I got impatient and decided to just come up to the house."

Alex kept the door cracked and popped his head out. He peered over his shoulder at the swinging door leading to the living room—watching for Wendy. "What do you want, Trey? I thought I was clear the last time we spoke. You're not supposed to be coming around here."

Trey rubbed under his nose, then nodded. His hands shook. Both eyes had a glossy sheen to them. "Yeah, yeah. I know, but I wanted to run something by you. It won't take but a minute or so." He took a step forward.

"Not going to happen." Alex stayed planted in the open space of the doorway, blocking his path. "You need to leave, now." He leaned back and closed the door.

Trey wedged his boot in the gap, stopping it from shutting. "Come on, Alex. Five minutes is all I'm asking for. That's it. If you don't like what I'm saying, I'll leave. I think you will like it, considering the pickle you're in."

Pickle?

"What do you mean by pickle?" Alex raised his brow.

Trey craned his neck and looked over Alex's shoulder to the table, then to the swinging door. "I know you've been struggling since Stacy passed in more ways than one. You might've cut ties with me, but I never did with you."

Alex and Trey had a number of friends in common. Any of them could've let his woes slip at any point. "We're fine. Thanks."

Trey held his ground and refused to budge. "I didn't want to have to use this card, but you do owe me, remember? The money I lent you back in the day and told you not to bother with paying it back? I said if and when I needed a favor, I'd come calling. Well, today is that day."

"Yeah. I haven't forgotten about that." Alex regretted taking the money. He'd made a deal with the devil when he had.

Trey stared at Alex, leaning against the door. A coy smile formed. "You'll like what I have to say. It'll settle our debt. Plus, it'll help you out, financially."

"You've got five minutes."

"Perfect."

Alex glanced to the far side of the kitchen, then stepped out of the way of the back door. "Keep your voice down."

"I take it Wendy's home?" Trey walked around the kitchen, glancing at the cluttered tabletop filled with bills and other paperwork.

"She is and I'd rather her not know you're here." Alex closed the door, then faced Trey.

Trey grabbed the shot glass and sniffed. “You’re still pounding the whiskey, huh? I’m more of a vodka man.”

Alex stormed to the table, reaching for Trey’s arm. “I’d appreciate it if you got to whatever the hell it is you want.”

Trey dropped the past due bills, tossed his hands skyward, then backed away. “That’s a lot of red, bud. But I have a way to help with that. Consider me your guardian angel.”

We’ll see about that. Alex took the shot glass to the sink, then turned around to face Trey. “You’ve got four minutes.”

“Enough fluff. Right to business.” Trey walked around the far side of the table. He grabbed the back of the chair, fingers worming their way under the metal loop at the top. He leaned forward, eyeing Alex. “I’ve got a job coming up tonight and I need a wheel man. It won’t take too long and it’ll be the easiest money you’ve made in a long while. Drive the car. Get paid. Simple as that.”

“It’s never that simple with you,” Alex shot back, tapping his foot against the floor. The palms of both hands rested on the edge of the sink, and his fingers gripped under the counter.

“This time, it will be for you.” Trey’s hands released the top of the chair. “Drive for me tonight, settle our debt, make some good money, and I’ll be out of your hair after this. You won’t ever see me again. Promise.”

Alex didn’t want to venture to the dark depths of his past life, but mounting bills and an eviction notice looming on the horizon challenged his moral compass. “How much paper am I looking at?”

“Enough to put a good-sized dent in that sea of dead trees cluttering your tabletop,” Trey answered, pointing to the various letters. “Five large at least.”

“And I only have to drive?” Alex asked. “Nothing more?”

"Yep. The only thing you need to know is where to drive to, wait, then drive back," Trey answered. "Like I said, simple as that."

Alex eyed the bills for a hot second. A part of him tried to resist, but having no job, and a lengthy rap sheet, made it harder to just pick up more work in a pinch. He contemplated asking his folks for more help, but they'd done so much already, and he couldn't drain any more money from them. "Fine, but after this, we're squared, and don't even think about screwing me over."

Trey smiled, then rubbed his hands together. "After this, we're square and done. You'll get your cut after we get back."

"You better hope I do." The stairs in the living room creaked. Alex pushed away from the counter, then made for the back door. "Wendy is heading this way. You need to bounce."

"Be ready. I'll text you the meetup point later." Trey slipped through the open door, then vanished down the walk and around the corner of the house.

Alex shut the door and deflated against the window. He watched the swinging door, second-guessing if he had made the right call or not.

CHAPTER TWO

ALEX

Wendy and their life were his main priorities.

Alex told himself that over and over while driving to the rendezvous point Trey had texted an hour ago. It helped Alex justify sliding back into the life he'd sworn he'd never return to. A means to an end. After the job was completed, he'd be done for good, and done with Trey.

The air outside felt balmy, thick, and wet. The humidity was horrible, but it always was in Houston. Beads of sweat raced down the length of Alex's face. The cracked driver side window funneled the tepid air inside the older model Toyota Camry he drove.

A battery of thoughts ran through Alex's head, bouncing from one thing to another. He wondered what Trey had planned that night and also worried about Wendy and what she'd think of him reverting back to his old, destructive ways.

The back of his hand wiped the sweat from his moist brow. He closed the window and turned the air conditioning on. The unit rattled and sounded worse for wear, but he had grown tired of stewing in the seat.

Alex thumbed the power button on his phone and double-checked the address Trey had sent. It was close. Maybe another mile or so up the deserted street that had little to no traffic that late at night.

Lights flashed at the back of the Camry. Alex flitted his gaze to the rearview mirror, concerned that the police somehow knew he had mischievous plans in mind. His heart skipped a beat. He held a bated breath.

The vehicle closed in fast on his bumper, pulled into the other lane, and flew past him. Alex peered at the small blue Ford Ranger that drove away at max speed.

A sigh of relief left his mouth. His clammy palms adjusted on the steering wheel. He shifted his backside in the uncomfortable seat, then shook his head.

The hue from the green light at the upcoming intersection changed to yellow, then red. Alex stopped shy of the white painted line, turned his blinker on, then hooked around the curb.

The Camry rolled down the vacant street at a modest pace. He glanced at the address on the phone, then to the buildings that lined both sides of the road.

Alex knew the area somewhat, but hadn't been down that way for some time, especially at night. He drove a bit farther and spotted a black-clad figure next to the corner of a brick building on the east side of the street.

The figure walked across the sidewalk toward the curb, hauling a black duffle bag in his hand. Alex pulled over and came to a stop next to the man dressed in black.

The passenger side door opened. The interior light sprung to life. Trey stooped, then dropped into the passenger side seat. He shoved the duffle bag onto the floorboard between his boots.

"Right on time. Another reason why I wanted you on this." Trey slammed the car door shut.

The interior light died.

Alex punched the gas, driving away from the curb. "Where are we going?"

"Head toward the highway, then get on 45." Trey pulled his phone from the back pant pocket of his jeans. He tapped the screen. The light shone on his sweaty, dingy face. He squinted and brought the phone closer, then huffed. "Son of a bitch."

"What's wrong?" Alex asked, watching the side streets they passed and the speedometer to make sure he wasn't speeding.

Trey pursed his lips and mashed the keys on the screen. He dropped the phone to his lap, then ran his gloved hand through his long, black oily hair. "The other guy I had lined up to give me a hand backed out. Had an emergency or something."

Alex glanced his way. "We're still on, right? I didn't come out in the middle of the night to not get paid."

"We're still on." Trey looked at Alex, then asked, "How would you like to make another five large? Ten grand for a quick job isn't bad. That amount of money would sure solve a bunch of problems."

"Was there even another player, or are you jerking my leg?" Alex drove through the green light, then under the bridge. He made a wide arch and hit the access road that led to the on-ramp.

Trey nodded. "There was. He was going to meet us there. I'm not messing with you. I had no intention of you doing anything other than driving, but things have changed."

Alex shook his head, then glanced out of the driver side window as they merged onto the highway. "Why am I getting the feeling that you're playing me here? I told you back at the house, you mess with me and it'll be the last thing you ever do."

"I'm not happy about this either, and I'm not jerking your chain," Trey replied with his hands up. "I shot you straight earlier, but here we are. I need you with me on this as backup. I'll do all the talking and heavy lifting. You just watch my back."

The rattling of the air conditioning unit grew louder. The noise grated on Alex's last nerve. The depths of stress swallowed him a little more with each moment he went along with Trey's plan. "I want fifteen large or I can pull over and let you out right here on the highway. Your call."

Trey snickered under his breath. "Who's trying to take advantage of who now?"

"You came to me, not the other way around. If you don't like it, say the word and I'll drop you off. Easy as that."

"I imagine you like having my feet to the fire, don't you?" Trey asked, resting his elbow on the armrest attached to the door.

"I don't like anything about this, and I'm only here because of the money," Alex shot back. "Do we have a deal?"

Trey mulled it over for a moment, then said, "We do."

"What's the job anyway? I'm not hurting or killing anyone and neither are you. I just needed to get that out and make sure we're clear on that."

"Agreed. I don't plan on that either, and we shouldn't have to worry about running into anyone seeing as it's late at night. The joint we're hitting should be empty," Trey replied. "But like I said, that's why I want you watching my back, just in case."

"What joint?"

"A small mom and pop business that's been doing rather well in these troubling times," Trey answered. "With a lot of the businesses struggling to stay open in this crap economy, they've been doing good business. A buddy of mine heard they have a large amount of cash on-site that is set to be picked up in the morning. It's ripe for the picking."

"Security alarm?" Alex asked with one eye on the road and the other on Trey.

Trey dismissed the question with a flick of his hand. "Won't be an issue. I'll handle it."

Alex scoffed. "When did you learn to bypass security systems? That sort of thing is out of your wheelhouse last I remember."

"I've come a long way since we spoke last," Trey answered, bending over and retrieving the duffle bag from the floorboard. "The guy who backed out tonight was going to handle the system, but I can manage. It won't be an issue."

"It better not be. You sold this job as easy money. Just driving. Now, I'm getting out of the car. Any complications or shit goes sideways, I'm gone in a blink, and I'll still expect a portion of the funds for my time," Alex said, peering at Trey, unsure if he believed him or not.

Trey unzipped the bag, then forced his gloved hand into the dark depths. "Let's not forget, first and foremost, that you're also settling a debt between us. The rest is a bonus, so I'd watch the tone and thinking you have me over the barrel, because you don't. Remember, you have a lot on the line, old friend."

The two men locked gazes, jockeying for the dominant role.

Trey looked away first, fiddling with the bag.

"How much farther are we going?" Alex asked, fixing his sights back to the road ahead.

"Take the next exit, then a right at the light." Trey pulled a ski mask from the bag and sat it next to Alex. "You packing?"

Alex glanced over his shoulder through the back window, then shifted lanes. “No. Haven’t carried for some time. It wouldn’t be good to get caught with a piece considering my past transgressions.”

“Here.” Trey sat a Glock 17 on top of the mask.

“You sure you’re shooting me straight on this?” Alex glanced at the gun, then back to Trey.

“It’s better to be safe than sorry. You know that.” Trey fished out his mask, then crammed the duffle bag back on the floor between his legs. “Think of it as more of a deterrent than anything else. I don’t know anyone in their right mind who wouldn’t tuck tail and run the other direction if they had that canon pointed in their face. So it’s a little insurance policy in case trouble does spring its ugly head.”

Alex took the exit down to the intersection. He thumbed the blinker and made his way onto the street.

Trey lifted the front of his shirt and retrieved the Browning 1911 tucked in the waistband of his jeans. He ejected the magazine, skimmed the rounds loaded, then slapped it back into place. His hand racked the slide—cycling a round into the chamber. He sat the weapon in his lap and peered out of the windshield.

The streets and sidewalks had no traffic—vehicle or otherwise. Darkness lurked behind the windows of each business they passed, confirming the absence of any people.

A bundle of nerves tormented Alex the closer they got. He fought to control the range of emotions attacking his mind—maintaining a focused look that sought to break him. Guilt, sadness, and a slew of others attacked him without pause.

“At the next street, hang a right, then take the first alley you see.” Trey rubbed his hands together and leaned forward in his seat. “It’s time to get paid.”

Alex followed his directions, skirting the curb and driving down the long stretch of road that had few lights illuminating the street and buildings. They drove a bit farther, then pulled into the alleyway. The back end of the Camry passed the edge of the brick building. Alex killed the lights, stopped, and shifted into park, then turned the car off.

"It's awfully dark around here. Not too many street lamps or anything." Alex peered at the rearview mirror, watching the road behind them.

"That's why this is the perfect job. Dark and not much traffic." Trey secured the phone and 1911 in his jeans, then covered his face with the mask. "Remember, follow my lead and watch our backs. I'll do the heavy lifting on this. I just need you to be the extra set of eyes and ears out there. That fifteen large is close at hand and will be yours soon."

Alex pulled the keys from the ignition and stuffed them into the front pocket of his pants. He eyed the mask and Glock for a second, then grabbed both.

The pistol went into his front waistband. The bottom of the shirt concealed the piece. He pulled the smelly, itchy mask over his sweaty head, then adjusted the two eye holes.

"Just like old times, brother. Let's get paid." Trey tugged on the doorhandle, then shoved the door outward. He stepped out of the vehicle and shut the door behind him.

Alex got out of the Camry, shut the driver side door, and made his way to the front of the vehicle where Trey stood. He peered down the dark alleyway. Dark splotches along both sides of the wall marked items in the murk.

"Where's the entrance?" Alex asked, glancing over the roof of the car to the street.

Trey pointed down the alley ahead of them. "About thirty feet or so. Come on."

Both men worked their way down the alley, skulking in the darkness. Trey took point and Alex covered their backs. He couldn't help but check over his shoulder every couple of seconds.

Time ticked by at what felt like a snail's pace. Alex wanted the job done and over as quickly as possible so he could get back to Wendy and away from Trey.

A horn honked in the distance, low and subtle. Alex flinched and checked for any lights, scanning both ends of the alley. Trey continued on without pausing or showing any concern for the noise.

"You're one hundred percent sure this place is empty, right?" Alex asked, trailing Trey by a few paces.

"As far as I know. It's late at night. I couldn't imagine anyone being here." Trey wormed his way through the trash cans and other odds and ends that hid within the cloak of night. "Keep it together and chill."

Alex followed through the maze as both men approached the single steel door. The bulb in the lamp overhead showed no sparks or signs of life.

Trey grabbed the doorknob and tested it, turning it clockwise. It didn't budge. He shrugged. "Worth a shot. You never know."

"Are you going to pick it?" Alex stood off to the side of the door next to the hinges. He watched both ends of the alley while Trey went to work.

"Yeah. We should be inside in a matter of minutes." Trey pulled a case from his pocket, then unzipped it.

Alex could hear the sound of the zipper but struggled to see the contents inside. "Do you need some light? It's black as shit out here."

"No. I can work in the dark," Trey answered. "The light will only attract unwanted attention. That's the last thing we need. I've picked locks a number of times in the dark. Nothing to worry about."

Trey worked on the doorknob while Alex towered over him. He messed with the lock for a few minutes before gaining access.

"Is that it?" Alex asked, moving around Trey and taking position near the other side of the door.

"Yep. I'll go in first and handle the alarm. It should be close to the door here and handled quickly before the delay ends." Trey stowed his kit and stood. He grabbed the doorknob and twisted.

The door popped open.

No alarm sounded.

Alex listened for a moment with a raised brow and confusion washing over his face.

A red hue loomed in the ether from a doorway before the men.

Trey scanned the entryway, then waved his arm. "Come on. Let's get this money."

CHAPTER THREE

ALEX

Alex drew a sharp breath, exhaled, and shook the nervousness from his body.

Trey advanced through the doorway with the 1911 down at his side. He looked at the walls in search of the alarm panel. "Got it."

"Are we good?" Alex asked, closing the door behind them.

"Yeah. I don't see any cause for concern. It doesn't appear to be activated." Trey studied the display screen of the panel.

Alex craned his neck, peering to the far end of the hallway. A red hue washed the walls and opening at the far end in a crimson red. He didn't detect any movement, but found it strange for the system to be unarmed. "Why wouldn't it be activated? Isn't that strange considering how much loot they have?"

Trey faced the murk of the hallway, brought the 1911 to bear, and advanced. "I don't know, but I'd consider that a good thing for us. One less thing we have to worry about. Just keep your voice low and eyes peeled for any movement."

A bad feeling tormented Alex's stomach. Something didn't feel right, but the lure of a hefty payday, and pulling his family from the brink of financial ruin, kept him from leaving.

Both men lurked down the hallway, skulking in the shadows. Trey swept each room they passed, pausing for a second, then moving on. Alex reached for the Glock nestled in his waistband, keeping his hand close to the grip in case they encountered trouble.

"Where's the safe?" Alex asked in a whisper, keeping a couple of paces off of Trey's heel.

"Not much farther," Trey replied, maintaining a steady pace. His shoulder hugged the wall as they approached the opening where the red hue emitted. Trey toed the blind corner, paused, then peaked around the bend. "Clear."

Alex glanced over his shoulder at the doorway leading to the alley and his vehicle, then followed his partner farther into the business. They kept low and moved fast. The soles of their shoes squeaked off the tile floor. The noise sounded loud in the silence.

A low hum breathed from overhead. Cold air pushed from the vents they passed under, hitting the back of his moist neck. The itchy fabric of the mask blocked most of the chilled air from reaching his sweaty face and head.

Trey worked his way down the passageway and past another blind corner. A bright light shone in the hall, stopping him in his tracks.

"So, there is someone here," Alex said in a raised voice.

"Let's get a closer look and see. I'm not leaving here without that money." Trey advanced on the light with the 1911 trained ahead of him.

Alex pulled the Glock and held it at his side as he followed. Each step toward the light made his heart pound harder and sent his pulse racing at a gallop.

The sound of raised voices seeped through the door from the other side. There was more than just one person beyond the door.

Trey ducked under the window molded inside the swinging plastic door. He took position on the other side, then peered through the scuffed window.

Alex inched closer and stopped shy of the opening on the other side. His fingers wrapped around the grip of the Glock, holding firm. "Well?"

"I've got eyes on one, but can't see anybody else." Trey lowered his head down a half inch, then craned his neck.

"I heard multiple voices, or thought I did."

"Me too. We need—" Trey clammed up. He shoved his free hand against the door, throwing it inward.

"What the hell are you doing?" Alex pursed his lips and clenched his jaw.

Trey ignored him and marched through the doorway with the 1911 trained at a short, pudgy man's back. Alex grumbled under his breath and gave pursuit.

Clothes sealed in plastic bags hung from racks that covered the perimeter of the space. It made it hard to check for any additional movement.

"Don't move and keep those hands where I can see them," Trey said, stern and loud.

The pudgy man flinched, then turned around. Both eyes widened and the fat rolls under his chin doubled. "Who the hell are you?"

"Doesn't matter who we are," Trey shot back.

Alex spotted another figure standing on the far side of the table in front of the frightened fat man. The lone light hanging above the table cast the suit in partial darkness, hiding his face. He stood still and raised both hands skyward.

Trey grabbed Pudgy by the collar of his white-striped button-up shirt, then pressed the 1911 against his wrinkled forehead. He looked past him to the stacks of cash covering the surface. "Is that all of the cash in the building?"

Pudgy whimpered with his hands raised.

The suit lowered his arm toward the interior of the jacket he wore.

"Don't do that," Alex said, pointing the Glock at the suit's chest. "Keep them up."

"Do you two clowns know who you're stealing from?" the suit asked in a calm but agitated tone.

"Shut your mouth and answer my question," Trey said, pressing his finger against the trigger of the 1911. "Is this all of the money?"

"Yes," Pudgy answered, whimpering.

"Shut it, fat man, if you know what's good for you." The suit inched forward.

"Move one more inch and I'll paint this tabletop with a coat of blood and brain. Don't test me." Trey tightened his hold on the man's collar and forced him back against the edge of the table.

Sweat poured from under the fat man's matted, slicked-back hair. Both cheeks flushed. His chest heaved.

"This is getting out of hand," Alex said, keeping the Glock trained at the suit. "We agreed no one would get hurt."

"No one will as long as threads over there, and this smelly fat bastard, don't jerk us around or try anything." Trey glanced to the side of the table at the large, brown duffle. "Grab that bag and load the cash."

Alex lowered his piece and moved behind Trey to the other side of the table. He'd fallen in deep and regretted accepting Trey's offer, but the stacks of cash and weight of debt crushing him compelled Alex forward.

The money moved from the table to the bag in record time.

Trey held the fat man at gunpoint, muttering to Alex to hurry up.

The duffle bag swelled from the money forced inside. The leather sides bulged. Alex shoved what bound bills he could into every nook.

The suit reached inside the flap of his coat.

Trey removed the 1911 from the fat man's skull and pulled the trigger twice.

The report caught Alex by surprise, making him flinch and reach for the Glock.

The bullets hammered the suit's chest, knocking him to the floor.

Pudgy pushed Trey away and rushed around the table. He charged Alex and slammed into him, taking both men down hard. The Glock popped free from Alex's hand.

Trey grabbed the straps of the duffle bag and wrenched it from the table. He fired two more rounds into Pudgy's back, who laid on a portion of Alex's lower half.

"What are you doing?" Alex pushed against Pudgy's bulk, trying to free himself.

Footfalls sounded from the far side of the room.

Trey jerked his chin toward the noise, then backed away. "Sorry, brother. It's every man for himself, now."

"You bastard."

Trey turned and ran for the swinging door.

The footfalls grew louder.

Alex rolled the dead weight off him as another figure emerged from the darkness behind the suit's body. Gunfire sounded off. Muzzle fire flashed in the corner of Alex's eye.

The bullets zipped past Trey, hammering the dense plastic of the door. He ducked and rammed the door, throwing it open.

A single round grazed his shoulder. He stumbled through the doorway and hit the wall, then vanished.

Alex hurried to his feet and moved to the far side of the table. He kept low and waited. His head pounded from the gunshots and hitting the floor. He sucked in a deep breath, then released it. The door leading to the hallway was within reach, but he wasn't sure he'd make it before being shot in the back.

"You and your partner are dead men. You hear me?" the other man said from the other side of the table near Pudgy.

The Glock had vanished, leaving Alex weaponless. He took a deep breath, moved around the corner of the table, and flanked the remaining gunman.

The suit towered over Pudgy's body, then turned about-face with his heater up and at the ready. Alex hammered his forearm, wielding the gun, with his balled fist, then landed a right jab across his square box chin. The suit stumbled backward but didn't go down. He shook his head, then massaged his jaw.

Alex retrieved the Glock, pushed the suit back, then made for the swinging door. He kept his gaze focused ahead and didn't look back.

His shoulder dipped as he crashed through the swinging door. It flew inward, smashing the wall. A mural of blood painted the far wall and streaked toward the exit.

Trey was nowhere in sight and neither was the money. The side entrance sat open. He'd left Alex behind and taken the money.

Alex rushed down the hall in a dead sprint. Each step echoed loudly, but he didn't care. He had to get out of the building and to his car while he could.

The swinging door at his back swung open.

A light shone over his shoulder.

Alex shoved his way through the side entrance as multiple shots fired in his wake. He flinched and cut to the side, almost losing his footing. His hand reached for the ground to brace his fall.

The bullets missed his back.

The footfalls charged after him.

Alex gathered himself, stood up, and bolted for the Camry. His hand plunged into the front pocket of his jeans, fishing for the keys. The sharp edge caught the interior fabric of the pocket, refusing to come out. He tugged and jerked, feeling the stress mount with each hard step.

The footfalls stalking him hit the pavement of the alley.

Alex stopped shy of the front end of the Camry, turned, and popped off two warning shots in the suit's direction. The man ducked, then ran for cover back inside the hallway. Alex freed the keys, skirted the bumper, and rushed the driver's side door.

Red and blue lights flashed from the street behind the sedan, and came to a screeching halt at the entrance of the alley. Both doors flew open. Two Houston PD officers jumped out with pistols drawn and trained his way.

"Freeze. Drop the weapon and put your hands behind your head," one of the cops shouted.

Alex glanced over his shoulder down the alley but didn't spot the suit. He looked back to the officers, tossed the Glock, and did as directed.

Both officers advanced on his position.

Alex stowed any notion of trying to flee or do anything else. The last thing he wanted was to get shot or killed, leaving Wendy all alone.

One of the cops reached for his wrist and wrenched his arm behind his back. He threw Alex forward into the Camry while his partner covered his back.

The officer read him his rights while cuffing his wrists.

Alex dipped his chin and rested his head against the car. He'd messed up yet again, but this time, it seemed much worse.

CHAPTER FOUR

WENDY

Damn you, Dad.

It had been 120 days since she'd last seen her dad, and before her life got flipped upside down, again. A part of her regretted the heated argument they had and the cold, callous demeanor she drowned him in. Her words had cut deep, and she wielded that weapon with deadly accuracy.

Wendy sat on the edge of her bed, staring long and hard at the picture of her once-happy life. All smiles from the Ryder family Christmas two years prior. Mom and Dad looked happy, as did she planted in the middle of two people who protected and guided her. Now, she faced the dangerous perils of the world with the help of her grandparents.

The phone vibrated in her hand, snapping Wendy from the distant memory. A text dropped into the scores of other messages she'd neglected. Clint, a boy who'd pursued her back home in

Houston, messaged her daily, wondering where she was, and if she planned to come back. She read the message and thumbed a few letters in response, but decided against answering. She knew once she did, he'd bombard her with more.

A knock sounded at the door.

Wendy thumbed the power button, then said, "Yes."

Her grandmother, Alice, opened the door and poked her head inside Wendy's small but quaint room. "Are you hungry, dear? I'm making your grandfather some lunch and didn't know if you wanted anything."

"I'm good for now." Wendy stood from the edge of her twin-sized bed and retrieved the black vest from the chair parked in front of the oak desk. "I think I'm going to head outside and get some practice in. I need to release some stress."

Alice grinned and nodded. "If you change your mind, let me know and I'll whip you up something."

"Thanks. I will." Wendy slipped the phone in her back pocket, then put the vest on. She zipped it up to right below her neck.

"I know you miss your father," Alice said, wiping her hands on the red towel that draped over her shoulder. "We do too. It's hard not being able to visit him in prison, but it's the way it needs to be right now. We told him we'd keep you safe from those thugs. It won't always be like this, though. I'm sure of that."

Wendy offered a half smile. "I know. Thanks for being awesome."

Alice winked. "Anything for my granddaughter."

The door remained cracked as Alice retreated to the hall and down the stairs.

Wendy grabbed her ballcap, slipped her red ponytail through the back, and pulled the bill low on her head. She marched across the room and passed through the door. Her boots knocked on the aged wooden planks. She hit the landing a moment later, then walked down the stairs.

Her grandfather talked loudly from the living room. The TV blared. He was hard of hearing, in more ways than one.

"Did you hear that, Alice?" he said from the broken-down leather recliner planted in front of the large, flat-screen TV mounted on the far wall. "The government is still saying that China and North Korea are a threat, and we're on high alert. Not only do we have to worry about more cyberattacks across the nation, but now we have to add possible EMP strikes against the grid. This is nuts."

"Frank, that damn TV is so loud I'm struggling to hear anything you're ranting on about," Alice replied from the kitchen. "Turn it down before we're both deaf, then repeat what you said."

Wendy hit the landing at the bottom of the staircase and walked toward the back of her grandfather's chair. She leaned over the rough leather top and wrapped her arms around his neck. "What's the latest on the news front?"

Frank flinched in the chair, then glanced up at her. His wrinkled, scarred hand patted the top of Wendy's as he smiled. "Christ, girl. You scared the bejesus out of me."

"Well, you do have that TV so loud that it would be hard to hear anyone sneaking up on you," Wendy said, kissing the crown of his head.

"That's what happens when a grenade goes off close to you," Frank said, pointing at his ears. "War is a bitch, kid." He glanced at the TV and pointed his unsteady skeletal finger at the screen. "More threats from Asia. They've been battling cyberattacks for the past few weeks, now they're saying we may have to worry about an EMP strike on our power grid. If you ask me, the entire world is out to get us, and from the looks of it, they may succeed."

Wendy removed her hands from around Frank's neck. She watched the news and the threats of possible missile strikes and cyberattacks that targeted various vital locations across the nation. A small portion of her worried about what could happen, but knew her grandparents would take care of her.

Alice walked up to Wendy carrying a silver tumbler in her hand. She retrieved the remote to the TV from the arm of Frank's leather chair and turned the volume down. "There. Now I can hear myself think."

Frank huffed, then held his hand up. "Christ, woman. Now I can't hear what they're saying."

"Here." Alice went through the menu and added closed captioning. "Put your reading glasses on."

Wendy snickered and shook her head. "You two are too much."

"I poured you some sweet tea and added a lemon," Alice said, handing her the tumbler. "It's going to be warm out there—another hot Texas day."

"Yeah. Like every other day." Wendy took the tumbler and sipped from the opening. The sugary sweetness of the tea hit her mouth. "This tea gets better and better I think."

"Are you heading out to get some range time in?" Frank asked while reading the text scrolling across the bottom of the TV. "I noticed you've got your cap on."

Wendy sucked down another gulp and nodded. "I am. It helps clear my head and de-stress. Plus, I've been wanting to fire that 357 Magnum you've got. Do you mind?"

Frank waved his hand. "Not at all. I've told you many times you can fire any of the guns we've got. You're more than able to handle yourself. To be honest, you're more capable than a lot of the guys I served with."

"Well, between you and Dad teaching me all those years how to shoot, plus other survival tips, I picked it up easy. I enjoy it now," Wendy replied.

Alice touched her arm and smiled. "Are you sure you don't want any lunch before you head out?"

"I'm good. Not real hungry at the moment," Wendy answered. "I'll get something later as long as we have power." She glanced down at her grandfather, waiting for a snappy response.

"What was that, sweetie?" Frank asked.

Wendy patted his shoulder. "Nothing. Enjoy your news."

Frank touched her hand with his. "I will. Enjoy killing the paper targets."

"He gets so wrapped up in the news," Alice said, glancing down at Frank. "But he enjoys it so much."

"That he does." Wendy walked away.

"While you're down there, can you check on the barn and make sure that hole in the wall near the entrance is holding up? I don't want any wildlife getting inside there," Alice called after her.

"Sure thing. If you need anything, call me," Wendy replied.

"We will. Enjoy your alone time, sweetie."

Wendy made her way down the hall toward the back room that housed her grandparent's guns and other various items. Her fingers repositioned over the chilled exterior of the tumbler and took another hearty swig.

The phone vibrated in her back pocket, but Wendy ignored the incoming message. Clint was relentless. She liked it, but also hated it at times.

The condensation from the tumbler dripped from the bottom and splashed across the top of her boot. She sat it down on the table near the weapons room, as her grandfather called it, and walked inside. Darkness filled the space. She felt along the wall past the jamb for the light switch and flicked it up.

The light attached to the ceiling fan sprung to life. The blades on the large fan turned, spinning fast. The whisp of the air grew louder with each second.

Wendy scanned the well-organized space that had racks lining the walls. Each shelf had an array of green ammo cans, duffle bags, and other various survival gear. Two large gun safes sat side by side against the far wall. Both were filled to the brim with various pistols, rifles, and shotguns her grandfather had collected over the years. She pitied the poor soul who dared to break into their house, if they could out in the middle of nowhere.

The volume to the TV in the living room increased. Alice shouted at Frank.

Wendy snickered, shook her head, then moved toward the safes. She punched the security code in on the safe to her left, grabbed the thick, steel handle, and opened the door.

The spread of guns met her gaze. Rifles, shotguns, and a few pistols sat secured in the vault—all in an organized manner. Wendy reached over to the shelf near her and grabbed a small green rucksack. She opened the top, sat it on the floor, then pulled the SIG Sauer P238 her grandparents had bought for her from the safe.

The 357 Magnum went inside next, followed by extra ammo, magazines for the SIG, and paper targets. A pair of headphones hung from a clip on the side of the rack. Wendy grabbed the silver earmuffs and a pair of plastic safety glasses to add to the other items. She contemplated grabbing one of the rifles, but figured she had enough to practice with.

Wendy finished packing what she needed, zipped the bag, and stood. She closed the door to the vault, then made for the door.

Her excitement built as she thumbed the light switch, shut the door behind her, and grabbed the tumbler. She'd been wanting to practice with the Magnum and was glad she had the chance to do so.

The bag of weapons and ammo dangled from Wendy's hand as she made her way down the hall back to the living room.

Alice stood next to Frank's rocking chair with her arm resting on the top cushion. Both watched the news as Wendy walked past them. They didn't venture a word, too engrossed in the segment of growing cyberattacks threatening the country's digital footprint.

Frank jabbed the tip of his boney finger at the screen and balked, raising his voice as he spoke to Alice. They exchanged some words as Wendy opened the front door and pushed her way through the screen door.

The warm, humid air punched her face, but the air was clean and void of any toxins the big city might have. She stood on the porch for a minute and skimmed over the lush land that spanned for what seemed like miles with no other homes in sight. A line of lush, tall trees encompassed the perimeter of the property.

In the beginning, she'd struggled with the isolation and the lack of hanging with her friends, but she'd soon settled and she enjoyed the peaceful and desolate nature of her grandparents' place.

Wendy marched across the porch toward the west side of the house. Her fingers adjusted on the strap of the rucksack. She nursed the sweet beverage her grandmother had given her.

Her boots clattered over each plank of wood. Sweat brimmed under the tight ballcap. She stepped off the porch and walked past her grandfather's four-wheel drive Chevy Silverado.

The tip of her boots kicked at the loose rocks on the drive. The odd-shaped stones bounced over the ground into the grass.

The firing range sat to the east of the barn and was a good walk from the front porch. Wendy had learned to enjoy the stroll, taking her time and soaking in the lack of horns honking and the hustle she grew up in. The past few months had been a wild ride and the one thing that always helped her through it was popping off some rounds and killing some paper targets.

A wall of hay eight feet tall and ten feet wide sat to the side of the barn. It was a makeshift range that had often been hammered by a wide variety of guns.

Wendy walked the trail that sliced through the growing weeds and ran next to the white farm fence that needed attention and boards replaced. She looked to the entrance of the barn, then made her way to the table positioned back from the hay.

The guns clanked against each other and the ammo cans. She longed for a holster for her SIG but hadn't gotten one yet. Soon, though.

She set the tumbler on the weathered wooden top of the table her grandfather had constructed. The rucksack plopped down next to the drink.

The angry sun overhead beat down without a cloud in sight to challenge its intensity. Birds chirped from close by. The wind picked up, then died down just as fast.

Wendy eyed the patch job done to the side of the large red barn. It looked intact from where she stood, but she would need to get a better look and check the interior after her therapy session.

She pulled her phone from the back pocket of her jeans and sat it face up on the table. The tip of her finger tapped the screen. Wendy scrolled through the loaded apps and started her music player.

Her head bobbed with the rhythmic beat that blared from the phone's speaker. She unzipped the rucksack and pulled the contents out, placing each item in a row before her.

The ground beneath her feet shook. A loud thumping noise battered the air and overtook the alternative music playing. Her gaze flitted skyward while she held the SIG in her hand. The bill of the ballcap blocked the sun's vibrant rays.

Three helicopters flew over the barn and continued on across the expanse of her grandparents' property. The rotors thumped loudly. The ammo can and guns vibrated on the table. She hadn't seen the large, gray choppers before and wondered what they were doing and more importantly, where they were heading.

Wendy scanned the clear skies for any more aircraft, then turned her attention to the task at hand. She racked the slide, checking to see if a round resided in the chamber. It sat empty. She sat the SIG down, grabbed one of the empty magazines, then popped the top to one of the ammo cans.

Her fingers plunged into the depths of the rounds that rimmed the top. She scooped out a handful and sat them on the table. One by one, she loaded each round into the magazine until it reached capacity.

The task always hurt her fingers, but she had no other way of loading the rounds. The more she practiced, the faster she got.

The loaded mag went into the SIG.

Wendy cycled a round, then tucked the heater into the waistband of her jeans. She grabbed one of the paper targets, skirted the side of the table, and advanced on the hay.

The wind whipped the paper in her hand. Her fingers curled and tightened over the top. She secured the target to the board by pushing the edges over the nail heads that stuck out.

The back of her hand wiped at the beads of sweat racing down her forehead and the sides of her face. She longed for some shade, but it wouldn't come with the cloudless sky.

Wendy walked back to the other side of the table, put on the protective headphones and plastic glasses, then removed the SIG from her waistband. The blaring music ceased, fading to a faint whisper. Her fingers wrapped around the grip.

She brought the pistol to bear and focused on the paper target. The sites along the top lined up with the chest of the paper target. Just six or so pounds of pressure was all it took to end a person's life.

Her finger tugged on the trigger.

The SIG barked.

The weapon recoiled in her hand, but she held firm.

The bullet hit above the target's chest area, close to center mass. The many hours of practicing had paid off.

Wendy emptied the remainder of the magazine, depleting the six .380 ACP rounds loaded. The SIG clicked empty. She ejected the mag and set it down on the table. She retrieved the tumbler and brought it to her mouth. She took another hearty swig of the tea, then sat the tumbler back down.

For the next hour, Wendy shredded the targets, switching between firing the 357 Magnum and the SIG at random to keep up with her progress.

The recoil of the beefy Smith and Wesson revolver tested her arm and grip strength as she unloaded her frustrations and stress on the paper targets.

The past years' events swarmed her thoughts, as they did most days while firing the weapons. The feelings of loss and anger hit harder that day for some reason that escaped Wendy.

Spent brass casings littered the table top and the dirt around her feet. A hint of sulfur tainted the air. Torn pieces of the paper target fluttered from the slight tepid breeze that whipped it about.

Wendy took a break. Both palms pressed to the dirty table top. The overwhelming flood of emotions over her deceased mother and incarcerated father drowned her in sorrow.

She lowered the headphones around her moist neck, removed the glasses, and tossed them to the table. Both eyes grew shiny with sadness, and her lids clamped shut, squeezing the tears out.

The music from her phone had stopped. Silence engulfed her.

Wendy pressed her fingers into both sockets and wiped away the hurt. She glanced at the phone. The screen was blank.

Her finger tapped the glass twice. The screen lit up, but showed no bars in the upper right corner. The signal at her grandparents had been known to be shotty in spots and storms made it worse. She chalked it up to bad cell reception and removed her hand.

Wendy turned around and leaned against the edge of the table. The palm of her hand rubbed over her face. She took a deep breath, held it for a second, then released it slowly.

The patch job on the side of the barn caught her attention, as did the gap toward the bottom where the skewed boards attached to the exterior. Her grandmother didn't want animals getting inside the barn and messing around.

A long sigh escaped Wendy's mouth. She pushed away from the table and made for the hole. A portion of the ground had been dug out near the opening. She stooped down and peered at the darkness within the barn, but couldn't see anything.

Wendy stood and marched around the corner toward the entrance. She unlatched the lock and swung the double doors outward.

Light flooded the warm interior. She studied the farm equipment, bales of hay, and other odds and ends tucked away in the structure.

The space looked like it always did and smelled much the same. Her nose crinkled some as she moved inside the barn in search of the intruder.

Wendy rummaged through the front part of the barn, checking the shadows and dark nooks for the animal. All seemed as it should with no evidence to hint whatever animal had made the hole was still inside. She'd report her findings and let her grandparents take it from there.

A figure flashed from the other side of the tractor she stood next to. Wendy flinched, then gasped as she faced the man who lurked on the other side. Her hand pressed to her heart. It took a moment to recognize who it was as they moved out into the light. Clint.

CHAPTER FIVE

WENDY

The shock turned to anger.

"What the hell are you doing here?" Wendy asked, throwing both hands in the air. "You scared the crap out of me."

Clint held his hands up. "I know. I'm sorry. I wasn't sure at first if it was you or not. I remember you saying you liked to shoot guns and all and heard the gunfire and took a chance. You hadn't responded to any of my texts. I tried to call ahead of time, but had no signal for some strange reason."

"The reception out here can be bad. I'm not sure why there's no cell service. My phone lost a signal as well." Wendy's heart raced at a gallop. It took a few minutes for the surge of adrenaline to wane. She pointed a stern finger at Clint. "You're lucky I wasn't armed or that you didn't cross my grandparents. They're not keen on people they don't know trespassing on their property."

"I can see that." Clint lowered his hands. "I needed to see you is all."

Wendy strolled past the tractor and Clint, heading for the opening. She didn't like being caught off guard like that. Not after her father had gotten mixed up with the wrong crowd, again. "How did you find me anyway? I don't recall telling you where I moved?"

Clint jogged after her as they left the barn. "I did some digging around and asked a few of your friends. Janice suggested you might be with your dad's folks since they knew you had no other family around."

"That still doesn't answer how you found me, though." Wendy marched out of the barn and headed for the table. "My grandparents aren't easy to find. There's a reason for that and why they live in the middle of nowhere."

"They're not as hard to find as you think if you know your way around the internet." Clint sped up and kept pace at her side. "I didn't mean to frighten you, though. I hope you believe me."

Wendy glanced at him, then retrieved her phone from the table. She thumbed the power button to pen a text to her grandmother informing her of the opening in the barn and of Clint's arrival. Neither would sit well with her. "Crap. I forgot. No signal. Great."

"Maybe that's a good thing, at least for right now." Clint stood at the side of the table with both palms flat on the top.

"How so? When is no signal ever a good thing, especially when in the middle of nowhere?"

Clint smirked. "Well, it gives us some alone time without anyone disturbing us. I mean, it gives us a chance to talk and all."

"Yeah, right. Talk," Wendy shot back, using her fingers as quotes. "I can't say that I've never heard that line before."

Clint's eyes widened and his mouth gaped open. He shook his head and waved his hands. "Not what I meant. Not at all. I mean, I have thought about it, but not right this moment. I think I'm going to shut up now."

Wendy snickered. "I'm just giving you crap. You're not that sort of guy. Even if you were, and tried something without my permission, I'd make you regret it. I can more than handle myself." She picked up the SIG, loaded a fresh magazine into the well, then cycled a round.

Clint watched her handle the pistol, then gulped. "I don't doubt that."

Wendy tucked the piece into the waistband of her jeans. "Anyway, like I said, my grandparents don't like people skulking about their property. I think you should probably leave, now, before either spot you and come unglued. They're a bit protective of me."

"I understand," Clint replied, nodding. "I'd like to meet them at some point if that's possible and you're okay with it."

"Perhaps. We'll see." Wendy smirked, finding Clint to be charming and not a total creep like other guys who'd pursued her in the past.

Clint dipped his chin and stared at the ground. He cleared his throat, then asked, "I did want to see if you might want to grab some lunch with me before I head back to Houston. It's a bit of a drive and I'm hungry. No strings attached or expectations of anything else. Just grab some food from a drive-thru and we can sit in the car and chat. Might be good for you to get out of here for a bit."

Wendy chewed the side of her lip. Indecision racked her. The idea of stepping away from the desolation of her grandparents' place seemed inviting. She hadn't left the property since arriving months earlier and longed for civilization once more, but the men her father had crossed could be looking for her. "As much as I'd like to, I'm not so sure that's a good idea. My grandparents would freak out for sure."

"They don't have to know," Clint replied in a soft tone. "We'd be quick about it, then, and could chat on the way there and back. I spotted a mom-and-pop burger joint on the way here. Like I said, it might do you some good having a bit of different scenery for a change."

Wendy loaded the ammo cans and 357 Magnum in the duffle bag while pondering Clint's offer. She zipped the top and rested her forearm on the bag. She adjusted the bill of her hat while Clint looked at her with large, hopeful eyes. "All right. We drive to that burger joint, grab some food, and we head right back. No messing around or anything like that, am I understood?"

A wide smile broke across Clint's face. He clapped his hands together. "Yes, of course. You have my word."

"I better." Wendy lifted her arm, grabbed the straps, then jerked the bag from the table. "Don't forget, I know how to use a gun, among other things."

CHAPTER SIX

ALEX

The power remained off, and chaos engulfed the prison.

Alex worked his way through the halls, moving at a good clip. He kept low and out of sight, using the lighter he'd stolen from Davidson sparingly to guide him.

The prison guards raced up and down the halls, tracking down convicts who searched for a way out or harmed other staff within the complex. Alex bypassed the guards, slipping into any nook or open space that would conceal his presence.

Gunshots echoed in the low light. Screams of torment and jubilee melded with the upheaval. A hint of smoke tainted the air.

His nose crinkled. He tilted his head back and sniffed. Had fires been started? Alex wasn't sure and didn't care to find out. Escaping the prison and avoiding contact with everyone inside was the objective. He had no desire to harm or see anyone suffer, convict or otherwise, as long as they didn't get in his way and try to stop him.

The outside world and his daughter called to him and he wanted to get there with the least amount of resistance possible. He'd managed to elude the gaze of his fellow inmates and the guards so far, but for how much longer remained to be seen.

A painful groan sounded from the hallway Alex approached. A flash of light shone his way, then dimmed. He slowed and blew the flame on top of the lighter out. His shoulder hugged the cinderblock wall as he approached the blind corner.

"Let's pound this pig into the ground real good, then maybe, he'll cooperate," an angered baritone voice said.

"Screw that," a high-pitched, country-sounding man replied. "Let's just kill the piggy and be on our way. Other guards could be inbound, and we don't want to let a good disaster go to waste. We may not get another shot at escaping if we do."

Alex toed the corner and poked his head out. He watched the two large inmates tower over the beaten guard who laid on his back on the floor in a pool of blood.

A flashlight rested against the far wall. The beam trained at the two men and the guard. A collapsible baton sat in the middle of the floor away from the group of men.

The guard turned his head and peered down the hall. Alex studied the man's busted face, recognizing him as a familiar guard who had always been kind and helpful to him. Jimmy or John was his name. Alex struggled to remember the correct one.

"Did you grab his keys?" the taller, muscular, dark-skinned man asked, pointing at the guard. "We'll probably need those at some point."

His bald, chubby, country counterpart adjusted his pants around his waist, removed his soiled, white, button-up shirt, then wiped the blood speckling his face and arms. "Yeah. I grabbed them. They're in my pocket."

"Don't lose those keys. We'll need them."

The keys could come in handy in escaping the prison. Another reason for Alex to intercede is to save the guard's life.

Alex stayed low and stalked the two men who continued kicking the guard and shouting at him. He didn't like to see the guard being dealt such punishment, but it did act as a distraction for the two goons who didn't notice him advancing toward them.

The baton grew closer.

The tumult from the riot and chaos funneling down the other halls built. More trouble could be on the way.

Big Country took a knee, grabbed the guard by the scruff of his uniform, then jerked him from the floor with ease. "Where's the nearest exit? This power outage has me turned around. Tell us now and perhaps we'll stop smashing your face into pulp."

The guard's head turned to the side. His shaking arm lifted, trembling fingers pointed past his partner.

Big Country looked in Alex's direction. "Hey." He dropped the guard to the floor. "What are you doing down there?"

His buddy spun around with both fists clenched and up.

Alex sprinted for the baton.

Both convicts rushed toward him.

Footfalls pounded the tile floor.

The two behemoths covered the distance in a blink.

Alex dropped to his knees and slid across the tile. He scooped up the baton, then stood to face the inmates.

The baton smashed the dark-skinned man's kneecaps first. The man wailed in pain, then crumbled to the floor.

Big Country grabbed Alex by the shoulders and rammed him against the far wall. He drove his thick, muscular forearm under Alex's throat and bared down on him.

Alex struggled to breathe while trying to push away from the wall. The stronger convict overpowered him, looking to crush his windpipe.

"That asshole messed up my bad knee," the dark-skinned man said, writhing on the floor and clutching his left knee.

Big Country glanced at his partner on the floor, taking his attention away from Alex. The pressure remained taut—unyielding. His nostrils flared and his jaw tightened.

Alex punished Big Country's side with the steel baton, bashing against his ribs over and over again. The large brute's hold on his neck lessened. He favored his side and winced from each blow. His forearm dropped from Alex's neck and he took a step back. The palm of his hand pressed to his ribs as he doubled over.

The growing clamor of violence built, drawing closer to their position. Alex gasped for air and massaged his throat. He struck Big Country on the side of his right knee, hobbling him.

The big goon's legs gave, sending him crashing to the tile. He wailed in pain, like his partner, as both inmates writhed on the floor.

"You're a dead man, pal," Big Country said, through gritted teeth, spit spewing from his mouth. "You better hope we don't see you again."

Alex held his tongue, retrieved the flashlight, and checked on the injured guard. The guard flinched and put his hands up as Alex took a knee next to him. Alex peered at the guard's badge and squinted at his name. "I'm not going to hurt you, John, but I need to get you someplace safe before more convicts arrive. They sound close."

"The closest guard station... is back... the way you came," John replied, weakened.

"That's a no-go." Alex shook his head. He pointed the baton past the guard. "Is there an office or someplace else I can take you down the other way?"

John thought a moment, grinding his teeth and trying to sit up from the floor. "Yeah. The medical ward isn't too far away. That'll be the safest place to hole up."

A howl loomed from the ether behind Alex. Footfalls echoed down the corridor.

"Come on." Alex stood, grabbed John's arm, and pulled him from the floor.

John huffed. His brow furrowed and teeth gnashed. Pain riddled his battered and bloody face. He moved in ponderous slow motion, making it challenging for Alex to help him get away.

"Give me the light." John held out his hand, wiggling his bloody fingers.

Alex shouldered John's bulk, draping his arm across the back of his neck. He handed John the flashlight but kept the baton.

Both men hurried down the long stretch of hallway as fast as they could. John struggled to keep his legs under him. His knees buckled, sending him rushing toward the floor.

Alex suffered the brunt of the guard's bulk, holding tight and dragging John's weight at a snail's pace.

The shouting and discord from the other inmates behind them built with each laborious step. Alex peered over his shoulder, looking for any prisoners.

John huffed and panted. He lifted his arm and pointed at the junction ahead of them. "Hang a… right at the… hallway."

Alex knew where the infirmary was, but the darkness and commotion frayed his nerves and got him turned around. It felt like a maze and the exit to the prison was the cheese.

They skirted the corner of the wall without stopping and kept on down the hall. Shouldering the wounded guard's bulk wreaked havoc on Alex's body. He'd been put through the wringer for days on end and every muscle fiber and bone felt the onslaught. The surge of adrenaline and staying on the move helped in dulling the discomfort.

"Go left… at the next hallway," John said, dragging his feet.

"Hang in there. We're close." Alex struggled to maintain a decent pace.

"There's someone down this way," a voice shouted. "I can see their light. Could be a guard with keys. Come on."

Damn it.

John's legs gave out, sending both men to the floor. He hit on his side, then rolled over. The flashlight smacked the tile, rolled, then clattered against the wall.

Alex panted, breathing hard while on his hands and knees. His lungs burned with each breath. His legs throbbed with exhaustion. To save John's life, he'd have to do the heavy lifting from this point forward, or leave him to the wolves.

"You better be glad I like you." Alex collapsed the baton and stowed the weapon in the pocket of his pants. He stood, grabbed John by the wrists, and dragged his body across the floor.

The guard's body slid over the tile with relative ease. The flashlight stayed behind, lighting the hallway.

A wave of shadowy figures emerged from the other end of the hall. The cluster of men stood close to one another. They paused for a moment, then rushed after them.

Alex shuffled his feet faster. The soles of his shoes squeaked off the floor. He peered over his shoulder, finding the next passage within reach.

The mob of convicts raced after them.

John had gone limp.

Alex grunted and strained to keep them going. He didn't pause at the next corner and continued on down the hallway. "You're not making this any easier, bud."

The flashlight they'd left behind moved. The beam trained in their direction. Footfalls stormed their way.

John groaned—low and subtle.

Alex glanced at the walls, hunting for the door leading to the infirmary. He squinted, trying to pierce the low light. "Got it."

They moved closer to the wall, then stopped in front of the door. Alex grabbed the silver handle and wrenched it down, but the door didn't budge. He hammered the outside with his balled fist, then jerked at the handle.

"If anyone is in there, I've got an injured guard who needs medical attention," Alex said while watching the light's brilliance come closer.

The lock clicked on the door, then cracked open. A light blasted Alex in the face. He squinted, then looked away.

"You're an inmate," a stressed feminine voice said. "You can—"

Alex held his hand up, lowered his shoulder, and pushed the door open. The woman on the other side resisted but bent to his strength. He dragged John's body inside the room, released his wrists, then lunged for the door.

The gleam from the woman's light washed over the streaks of blood on the floor that led inside the room. The door slammed against the jamb. He secured the lock, then turned around.

"You're rather observant." Alex's chest heaved. He bent over with the heel from both palms pressed into the soft parts right above both knees.

The blonde-haired woman stepped away and pointed at Alex. The loose strands of hair not secured by the ponytail hung on either side of her face. Her white coat had splotches of red on it. She wielded what looked to be a scalpel or something similar in her clenched fist. "If you even think of trying something, I'll slice you open good."

"Lady, I'm the last person you need to be concerned with." Alex stood up and deflated against the door. He pointed toward the hall. "The lowlifes out there are the ones you should be concerned with. Not me. I'm not that kind of guy."

The woman held her defensive posture with the flashlight trained at his face. "Yeah, well, you're still a convict and in prison for a reason."

Alex pushed away from the door.

The woman scooted back and pursed her full, thick lips.

"Listen, this guard needs some medical attention. He was attacked by two other inmates before I intervened." Alex pointed at John. "They beat him up pretty good. Is there a bed I can put him on?"

She hesitated for a moment, then peered down at the groaning guard. "Yeah. I've got an open bed toward the back corner where you can put him."

The handle to the door wrenched up and down.

Alex flinched, then spun around.

Fists hammered the outside of the door, followed by shouting.

"Looks like you brought trouble with you," the woman said, lowering her arm.

"It's never far behind."

CHAPTER SEVEN

ALEX

No good deed went unpunished.

Alex backed away from the shuddering door with his hands up and ready to fight. The hammering fists pounded the barrier that separated them from the other inmates. The door rattled but held firm. "They can't get in here, right?"

The woman shrugged. "That door is solid and should hold, but I can't be certain. I've never been in this sort of predicament before."

"That makes two of us," Alex replied, lowering his arms. "They'll probably lose interest and move on."

John laid on the floor, keeping his movements to a minimum. The subtle groans seeping from his bloody lips faded in and out.

The woman eyed Alex and approached the guard. She bent down and pressed her fingers to the side of his neck. The gleam from her flashlight shone at the side of his head, revealing lacerations and swollen, puffy, closed eyes. "Let's get him back to the bed." She stood and moved away.

Alex dragged John to the far corner of the infirmary. He manhandled the guard's dead weight up on the wafer-thin mattress, then exhaled.

"Are you some sort of do-gooder or something?" the woman asked, hovering above the guard's head. Her fingers pried open his shut lids. "Since the power crashed, most of the inmates have done the opposite of what you're doing here."

"Just because we're in prison, doesn't mean that we're horrible humans." Alex leaned against the wall. "Sometimes, people make bad decisions for the right reasons."

She checked John's other eye. "If I had a dollar for every time a convict said something similar, I wouldn't be trapped in this hell hole with a mob of murderers and rapists walking the halls. Not a safe environment for a woman."

Alex rolled his eyes. "Believe what you want. I don't really care. If I had any intention of hurting you, it would've already happened. I just wanted to help him out."

"He'll be okay." She glanced up at Alex, then stepped away from the bed. "In either case, stay away. I'm a doctor and know how to make you bleed out with the smallest incision."

He lifted his hands up. "Sure thing. Won't be a problem. I'm Alex, by the way. In case you care to know."

"Megan."

"Nice to meet you."

"Yeah. Likewise."

Alex looked to the entrance they'd come through moments earlier. "Is there another way out of this place other than that door they're pounding on?"

Megan shook her head. "Nope. That's the only way in and out of here. It's one of the more secure rooms in the prison seeing as we house a variety of drugs and such in the storage closet."

Perfect.

"From the looks of your coat, I'd say you had a run-in with someone out there," Alex said.

"Yeah." Megan tilted her head forward and glanced at the red dots on the white fabric. Her fingers brushed over the stains. "I had an encounter with one of the inmates on my way here. A real dirtbag who is in here for raping and beating multiple women to death. He tried to drag me to an office. I managed to get away before he could get too far."

Alex nodded. "I'm glad you did. Those sorts of guys are trash. Lower than scum. Bottom feeders that deserve a good beat down, or worse."

"So, what's your story? Why did you help John?" Megan asked. "I haven't seen any of the inmates helping. Well, if you don't count not joining in on the rioting and everything else going on that is."

"He's a good guy, and I didn't want to see him killed is all." Alex peered down at him. "I don't have anything against the guards or other prison staff. I'm not looking to hurt anyone. Truth be told, I'm not a violent person unless I'm forced to be."

"I imagine John appreciates you helping him," Megan replied. "He is a good guy. I've always gotten along well with him. It's nice to see that not everyone in here is a psychopath."

A soft groan sounded from the darkness—faint and weak. It didn't come from John but was close. Alex looked for the source, but couldn't spot it in the darkness of the infirmary. "What was that?"

Megan looked away and stepped back from the side of the guard's bed. She trained the light past the curtain that separated the beds. "It's one of the inmates that came in before the power crashed. I need to check on him. Excuse me."

The groans turned to a muffled voice that spoke softly.

Alex walked around the edge of the bed as Megan slipped behind the curtain. He'd been too distracted to notice anyone else inside the infirmary.

The light stopped moving. He stood at the corner of the curtain and watched her attend to the wounded inmate.

The small, meager inmate looked worse for wear. He was a young kid in his early twenties, from what Alex could tell. His face had bruises covering every inch. Both eyes were swollen shut, and his lip had been split open.

Megan bent over the side of the bed and trained an ear to him. She listened closely, then replied to the battered kid. Her hand patted his arm as she stood and walked away.

"It looks like he crossed the wrong folks," Alex said. "Not hard to do in here. You glance at someone the wrong way and find yourself either getting a beat down or worse."

"Yeah. He's new to the prison and one of the gangs got a hold of him pretty quick," Megan answered. "Sad, really."

The hammering at the door lessened, as did the jiggling of the handle. It soon ebbed all together and silence filled the infirmary.

Alex studied the door that lurked in the shadows.

Megan shone her light at the entrance. "Do you think they're gone for good?"

"Not sure. Maybe. They could be wanting us to think that. We'll give it a bit longer and see." Alex pointed to the lights overhead. "Do you know what happened to the power, by chance? I was in the laundry section when the lights crashed and all of the machines stopped working. Craziest thing. I thought they'd have generators or something that would kick in as a backup, but nothing's come on."

"I'm not sure either. We've never had a blackout before, and I've only been working here for about a year or so." Megan shrugged. "I just hope it's not part of the cyberattacks and other nonsense the news has been going on about. They said China and North Korea were looking to hit us with EMP bombs."

"Really? Is that a thing now? Cyberattacks and EMP bombs?" Alex's face scrunched in confusion. "I've missed a lot since being in prison it seems."

Megan left the young kid's bed and moved across the infirmary to the storage closet. Her hand fished a set of keys from her coat pocket. She shone the light at the doorknob and unlocked the secured door. "The cyberattacks, yes. Businesses and other utility companies across the country have been battling the attacks for months. It's been messing with the power grid and the financial districts as well, among other important areas. Texas has its own power grid, and I guess, up until now, we've been able to steer clear of the attacks."

"That's crazy," Alex replied, standing behind her. "I knew the world was shitty before I got put in here, but I didn't know things had devolved so much."

"Yeah, well, I wouldn't hold what I'm saying as gospel by any means." Megan opened the door and walked inside. She scanned over the racks of medicine and other first aid supplies. "I haven't kept up with the news for the last week or so. This could just be a rolling blackout from the grid being taxed because of the heat. That happens at times. I guess we'll find out soon enough, though."

Alex leaned against the jamb of the storage room entrance with his arms folded across his chest. He ran his hand up and down his face, trying to make sense of what she said. "Do you happen to have a cell phone on you or anything like that?"

Megan gathered a variety of medical supplies and hauled them out of the storage closet. The end of the flashlight sat clutched between her teeth. Her foot kicked the door closed behind her. She walked toward a silver rolling tray and dumped the supplies on the top. "Um, no. They don't allow the staff to carry personal phones on them for safety reasons. Why?"

"It's not what you might be thinking," Alex replied, moving away from the storage area. "I wanted to see if I could reach my daughter. See how she's doing."

"You've got a kid, huh?" Megan rolled the tray past the young kid to John.

Alex trailed her. "I do. She's eighteen. I haven't spoken to her since being put in here. I need to make sure she's okay."

Megan pulled the tray next to John's bed. She grabbed some cotton balls, doused them with antiseptic, then worked on addressing the cuts on his face. "Well, I'm afraid I can't help with that."

Alex paced the floor with his hands behind his head, fingers intertwined. He huffed and sighed, thinking of Wendy being out in the world with Lance Vargas's goons possibly hunting her down. He didn't know if Davidson was messing with him or not, but the thought wouldn't let him be. He needed to find Trey and get the money he stole back. Perhaps, then, Wendy wouldn't be in danger.

"You wouldn't happen to have another flashlight in here, would you?" Alex asked, stopping and glancing about the dark space. "All I have is a zippo lighter that doesn't give off much light."

"Yeah. There's a backup flashlight on the wall on the other side of the door." Megan tossed the bloody cotton balls to the tray. "Are you leaving or something?"

Alex dropped his arms to either side and marched toward the door. He ripped the flashlight from the socket and thumbed the switch, but nothing happened. His palm slapped against the side of the light, then shook it, but nothing happened. "It does work, right?"

"It should be charged," Wendy replied, wiping the sleeve of her coat across her brow. "It stays in that socket and charges that way."

"Well, it's not working at all." Alex sighed in frustration, then tossed the light to the floor. It clattered off the tile and vanished into the murk of the infirmary. He dug his hand into the pocket of his prison-issued threads and pulled out the lighter. His thumb struck the wheel, sparking a flame. "I guess this will have to work."

"Where are you going?" Megan asked, facing him.

"I need to get out of here. It's a matter of life and death for my daughter," Alex replied, glancing at John.

Megan shook her head. "Even with all of the commotion going on out there, you won't be able to escape. You're still dressed like a convict and will stick out like a sore thumb. They'll have this place locked down tight."

An idea gelled. Alex killed the flame and stood at the foot of John's bed. He studied the guard's height, then grabbed the tip of his boot. "I've got a way around that, I think."

CHAPTER EIGHT

ALEX

The best chance Alex had at escaping was the unconscious guard.

Megan looked at John, then back up to Alex. Her eyes narrowed and his nose scrunched. "How is he going to be of any use to you? He can't even—" The lightbulb went off above her head. Her mouth gaped open as shock filled her face. "You're going to pass as one of the guards?"

Alex got to work removing John's shoes. "I admit, it's not the best plan, but it's all I've got."

"You can't do that?" Megan said in a raised voice. "You're a prisoner of the state of Texas. You do realize what they'll do when, not if, they catch you?"

"I know what the risks are, but I don't care. Are you going to try and stop me?" Alex asked, slipping off his shoes and trying

John's on. The fit was a bit tight and his toes scrunched at the front, but he'd make do with them.

"Well, no. I'm not stupid and I value my life," Megan replied, watching Alex slip off the shoe. "They pay me to tend to the patients, not stop inmates from escaping. Besides, I doubt you'll make it out of here, even dressed like a guard. You look nothing like John and that ID will certainly give you away."

"I'm not going to use the ID. With everything going on and the inmates on the loose, I don't think they'll look twice at me." Alex skirted the side of the bed and towered over John. He looked at the haggard guard who stared up at him with his face swollen and beaten. "I'm sorry, but I'm going to need your clothes. I'd rather you not resist. I like you, but I will do whatever is needed to take them off of you."

John gulped and complied, unable to fend Alex off in his current state.

"This is crazy." Megan glanced at the pair of scissors on the tray, then back up to Alex. She remained silent, watching as he stripped down to his boxers and dressed in John's uniform.

"Not as crazy as the power crashing and the inmates running wild through the halls." His gaze never left her while maneuvering John's shirt and pants off his body with care. He kept a watchful eye on her every move, wondering if she'd be brave enough to go for the pointed medical utensils or not.

John grunted from being moved over onto his side and having the uniform peeled from his body.

Alex put on the garb and straightened it out as best he could. The uniform was a bit baggy and hung from his broad shoulders. Blood-stained spots on the uniform in the front and back. John didn't have a hat or anything else Alex could use to help disguise his face.

"It looks better than I thought it would," Megan said, looking him up and down. "Just to let you know, I will report you once I'm able to."

Alex adjusted the button-up shirt a bit more. He bent down, retrieved the baton and lighter from the pocket of his prison garb, then stood back up. "I figured you might. You do what you feel you need to do."

"I still think you're making a huge mistake," Megan shot back. "You'll be tacking on extra time to your sentence once you're back in custody. That isn't going to do your daughter any good."

"It'll be worth it as long as she is safe and sound," Alex replied, securing the baton on the duty belt. "I can't fix any problems stuck in here. I know what I need to do to right my wrongs."

John laid on the bed, stripped down to the white tank and red boxers. Megan covered his lower body.

Alex felt around the duty belt for keys, but couldn't locate them. He ventured a question to John, but then remembered that Big Country had relieved him of the keys in the hallway.

Damn it.

He'd have to improvise, like everything else at the moment.

"Where's the nearest exit from the infirmary?" Alex asked. "I'd like to avoid as many guards as I can."

Megan remained tight-lipped. "Just because I'm not trying to physically stop you doesn't mean I'm going to help you escape. You'll need to figure that out on your own."

Alex pursed his lips and confronted her, standing near the tray that separated them. She reached for the scissors, then drew her hand back. "Smart move. I'll ask again, tell me where the nearest exit is, or my previous statement of not harming you could be revoked. I like you, doc, but I need for you to give me what I want.

There is a lot at stake here. Hell, tell them I forced you to tell me. Probably won't be that much of a stretch for the prison to believe."

"The east… section of the… prison will be the… closest and least guarded," John muttered through strained breath. "Just don't… hurt her."

Megan glanced at John.

"Thanks." Alex grabbed the sharp medical tool from the tray and took a step back from her.

The silence beyond the infirmary remained, and the door was still.

Alex advanced on the door. He grabbed the handle, then placed the side of his head against the surface as an added precaution. No noise sounded.

"Have they left?" Megan asked, walking away from John's bedside.

"Sounds like it. I don't hear anything out there," Alex replied, glancing back to her. He grabbed the silver lock and twisted it. Still, nothing. Alex drew a sharp breath, then pulled the handle down.

The door opened. Alex peered through the narrow gap to the darkness that lurked beyond. A scant bit of light could be seen down the hall. No shadowy figures moved or hastened footfalls charged the entrance to the infirmary.

Megan approached Alex from behind. The squeaking of her shoes gave the prison doctor away.

Alex ducked back into the infirmary, then glanced her way.

"I'm just going to lock the door behind you," Megan said, stopping and holding her hands up. "I wasn't going to try anything."

"Stay quiet and wait for help," Alex said, eyeing her. "I'll send some guards this way if I can."

Megan grabbed the handle. "Good luck to you."

"You too." Alex pushed the door open a bit wider, then threaded his body through. He handed her the scissors, then nodded.

Megan took the surgical tool and shut the door behind him. The lock engaged.

The east side of the compound wasn't too far away. A few guard stations and steel bars separated him from freedom. He had been there once since arriving and somewhat knew the way from the infirmary.

Alex made his way down the dark hall toward the flashlight. His head stayed on a swivel, turning and listening for any footfalls and watching for shadowy figures moving within the low light. He bent over and grabbed the light, then shone it in the direction he'd traveled.

The beam cast its gleam on the wall, then swept down to the linoleum floor. The hallway appeared to be clear for the moment.

He double-timed it to the next junction, sprinting with the light tilted toward the floor. The squeaking of his shoes sounded louder than he liked within the silence. The baton slapped his upper thigh.

Alex paused for a second at the next hall. He inched toward the bend and peeked out into the adjoining passageway. The light swept the area.

The hint of smoke lingering in the air hadn't ebbed. He sniffed. His nose scrunched from the unsettling smell.

A body laid on the floor. It didn't move or make any sounds. It appeared to be a guard from the type of shoes and what little part of the pants that could be seen.

Alex advanced on the motionless body, pointing the light at any rooms or open spaces he passed.

He got back on the move, rushing to the body.

The guard laid prone on his stomach. Both arms reached out in front of him with the side of his head pressed to the floor. He didn't stir as Alex approached.

The light shone at his duty belt. Alex hunted for a set of keys but came up short. The guard's baton was missing, as was his flashlight.

A hat sat on the floor to the side of his body.

Alex stepped over the guard's legs and retrieved it. He placed the ballcap on his head and pulled the bill down to conceal his face.

The guard faced his way. Both lids were shut. Blood seeped from his nose and mouth. He had a gash on the side of his head that wet his hair.

A loud shout sounded from the direction Alex had come. It drew closer.

Alex peered at the darkness, then back down to the motionless guard. He backed away, and sprinted in the opposite direction, fearing that he could be attacked for wearing the uniform.

Wendy filled his thoughts, as did the insurmountable task he faced in escaping the prison and solving the mountain of a problem he'd stumbled into. If anything were to happen to his only child, he'd never forgive himself.

The next hall was taken at full tilt. He kept moving toward the exit on the east side of the facility.

"Stop right there or we'll—" a strained voice shouted.

Two lights flashed his way, hitting his face.

Alex lifted his hand to block the light and came to a grinding halt. His heart raced. He kept his head pitched forward, letting the bill of the hat hide a portion of his face.

"Shit. Lower the piece, Bill," another voice said, reaching over and pushing down his arm.

The lights lowered to the floor. Bill exhaled and kept his finger pressed to the side of the trigger guard. "Christ. You're lucky you didn't get shot."

Alex blinked, then shone his light at the two security guards standing in the middle of the hall. They blocked his way leading through the sectioned-off, gated checkpoint. The keys attached to their duty belts caught his attention. "Yeah. Sorry about that. I was checking on a guard in the hall when a handful of inmates came after me from the infirmary. We've got people in there that need help. I've been searching for backup and haven't been able to locate anyone until now."

Both guards glanced at each other, then back to Alex.

"We're scattered all over trying to get everything back under control," Bill said with his sidearm down at his side. "Communications are toast at the moment, among everything else. Dan and I have been guarding this exit since everything went to shit."

"How many are in the infirmary?" Dan asked. "Was Mrs. Walters in there?"

Alex hesitated for a moment, then said, "Yes. She has a few injured inmates in there with her and didn't want to leave them behind."

Dan nudged Bill's shoulder with his elbow. "I thought she was in her office or had left for the day already."

Bill shrugged. "I don't know. I'm not her keeper or her boss."

"Well, we're going to need to find a way to get down there to her," Dan shot back, jabbing his finger down the hall.

Alex advanced toward the guards with his head pointed toward the floor. He moved slowly and cautiously, watching both men from under the bill of his hat as they argued.

"If she's in the infirmary, then she'll be safe," Bill replied. "That door is pretty solid and if they remain quiet, they should be fine until we get things back under control. We can't leave our post."

Dan trained his light at me. "You can hang here and I'll take…" He paused, then looked my way. "What's your name again and where is your badge?"

"John and it must've come loose." Alex stood a few feet from them. He turned. "I took out a couple of inmates before getting to the infirmary. Damn thugs stole my keys and gave me a beating before I took them out."

Dan studied Alex's face, or tried to. He tilted the light and moved it around to get a better look. "You don't look familiar."

Bill adjusted his hold on the grip of his piece but didn't bring it to bear yet. "Yeah. I don't recall seeing you around before either."

Alex shook his head, trying to think his way out of the predicament. He didn't want to hurt the guards, but they had left him no choice.

"Remove your—" Dan said.

Alex lunged forward and grabbed Bill's arm before he could lift the pistol. He turned and hammered Dan's face with an elbow to the bridge of his nose.

Dan howled, then stumbled backward, palming his face.

Bill maintained a taut hold on the pistol as Alex tried to pry it from his hand.

Gunfire sounded. Muzzle fire flashed from the barrel. The bullet hit the floor next to their feet, missing by mere inches.

Alex lowered his shoulder and rammed the guard into the steel bars. They continued wrestling for control of the firearm. Bill stomped Alex's foot and pushed against his body.

"Get this guy off me, will ya?" Bill said through his clenched teeth.

Dan shook off the blow and advanced toward the two men.

Alex hammered the top of Bill's hand with the bottom of the flashlight, knocking it to the floor. He kicked it away, then punched Bill in the face.

Bill slid down the bars and caught himself before falling to the floor. Dan grabbed Alex from behind, then slipped his forearm around his neck. He panted into his ear and jerked him back.

Alex felt around the duty belt for the collapsible baton. He removed the weapon, extended it to full length, then smashed the side of Dan's knee.

His leg buckled, sending him crashing to the ground. He cried out, writhing on his back.

Bill bent over and searched the floor for his sidearm.

Alex placed the end of the baton under Bill's chin and lifted his head up. "I need you to open that gate."

"Not going to happen," Bill replied, standing up straight. "You're not getting out of here anytime soon."

"We'll see about that." Alex slapped Bill in the side of the skull with the baton.

"Ah," Bill fell back against the steel bars, then palmed his face.

Alex jabbed the tip of the baton into Bill's shoulder and pushed. "I don't want to hurt either of you any further, but will if you don't open this damn gate now."

Dan groaned on the floor, feeling around his waist. Alex hadn't spotted a sidearm or holster on his hip when he first encountered them.

"All right." Bill lowered his hand from the welt on the side of his face. "I'm going to reach for my keys."

"Make it snappy," Alex said, glancing back to the darkness that had sounds of distress lingering about.

Bill grabbed the keys dangling from his belt loop, turned, and staggered toward the gate. His fingers sifted through the keys. He glanced at Alex and sneered.

The tumult drew closer.

Alex peered over his shoulder, watching for shadowy figures to emerge. He looked to Bill, then Dan who scooted across the floor and leaned against the far wall.

The gate unlocked.

Bill slid the section of steel to the side.

"Grab your partner and bring him through," Alex said, nodding at Dan. "I'd hurry up unless you want to be on this side of the gate when they get here. Your call."

Dan pushed himself up against the wall, then looked to the murk beyond what the light could reach. The wall acted as a crutch, keeping him upright. He favored the leg Alex had smashed with the baton.

Bill walked over to Dan who limped toward him.

Alex rushed through the opening, turned around, and grabbed the steel bars of the gate. He stared at the two guards, then down the passageway.

Light shone from the adjoining hall, growing brighter. The stampede of footfalls pounded the floor.

"I'd hurry the hell up," Alex said as the handful of convicts rushed out from the hallway and sprinted up the hall in their direction.

"There's our way out. Come on," one of the inmates said, breathless.

Dan and Bill passed the threshold.

Alex yanked on the gate, but it didn't budge.

The influx of convicts stormed up the hall, cutting the distance to freedom in a blink.

Come on.

Bill shoved Alex out of the way and slammed the gate closed.

The lights left behind on the floor shone at the small group of burly and bald white men. They stopped at the gate, grabbed the bars, and jerked.

"Let us out of here now," Davidson said, reaching through the bars for Alex's shirt. "I can make it worth your while. You won't have to work again. I can promise you that."

Alex locked eyes with him, then grinned. "I think I'll pass."

Davidson's face lit up. Both eyes enlarged and his mouth gaped open. His hand swatted at Alex's chest, fingers reaching for any part of his uniform he could snag. "You son of a bitch."

"Shit. My sidearm," Bill said, lost in confusion and staring at Davidson.

Alex looked away and pointed at the next gate. "Get that open now before they find it."

Davidson stepped back from the gate, dipped his chin, and checked the floor. "The guard doesn't have his heater. Look around and see if you can find it. Hurry."

Bill fumbled the keys in his trembling hands.

Dan leaned against the bars, pressing his hand to his leg.

"Come on and open the gate," Alex said, looking back to the members of the Brotherhood who scoured the floor for the pistol.

"Got it." Bill unlocked the next gate and slid it open. He grabbed Dan by the collar of his shirt and pulled him through.

Alex shoved Dan in the back and passed through the opening behind him.

"Here." One of the members of the Brotherhood stood with the black pistol in his hand.

"Give it to me," Davidson said with his hand extended and fingers wiggling.

Bill and Dan made for the wall on the far side.

Alex jerked on the gate, slamming it closed.

Davidson turned, trained the piece at Alex, then squeezed the trigger.

The report hammered Alex's ears as he ran for the corner of the cinderblock wall. He ducked and raised his arm to shield his head. The bullet punched the corner of the wall as Alex vanished.

"Damn it," Davidson said, his voice infused with rage. "You're a dead man either way, Ryder. Whether it's in here or the outside. You're on borrowed time."

Dan and Bill panted, hunched over.

Alex shone the flashlight around the narrow hallway they stood in and noticed a closed door. He shone the light at the entrance, then peered at the two spent guards. "What's in there?"

"Supply room," Bill replied, standing up straight.

"Come on." Alex waved the baton and advanced on the door. He opened it and shined the light around the small, cramped space. Two racks sat flush against either side of the walls. Both had various office supplies and other items stacked neatly on the shelves. "Get in there."

Bill sighed, and his shoulders sagged. He grabbed Dan and helped him inside the storage room. "You're not going to get away with this, convict," Bill said, facing him.

Alex grabbed the edge of the door. "So I've been told. Twice. You'll be fine in here until backup arrives. Don't forget about the doc."

Both Bill and Dan stared at Alex malevolently. He shut the door, severing their heated gazes.

Davidson shouted and pounded on the gate a bit longer before quietening down.

Alex ventured the remainder of the way through the hallway toward the exit. The darkness lessened and strident light emerged, illuminating the hallway in its radiance. He switched off the light and secured it through the loop on the duty belt. The baton remained fixed in his grasp as he marched toward freedom.

The remaining offices showed no signs of movement beyond the open doors. No footfalls or voices tickled his ears. For now, it seemed as though everyone had fled or stayed in hiding during the crisis.

A single door blocked Alex's path to freedom and redemption. He pressed his hand to the push bar mounted to the center, unsure if it would open. With the power being out, he hoped it would.

Alex applied pressure. The latch on the door retracted and popped open. A sigh of relief escaped Alex's mouth. He shoved it outward and left the building.

The hint of smoke wouldn't leave his nose. It stuck to him no matter where he went. He scanned the grounds of the prison, spotting a scant few guards rushing across the grass with shotguns pressed to their chests.

The security gate that allowed people to leave the prison had a single guard standing watch at the moment. Two others ran off in a mad dash, leaving it vulnerable. The lone guard stood next to the small shack-like building with his shotgun fixed in both hands, watching the grounds before him.

Alex pulled the bill of the ballcap down on his head and secured the baton on the duty belt. He walked down the sidewalk to the open drive. His head turned from side to side, skimming over the yard for any guards inbound to his position.

He had escaped the inner workings of the prison by the skin of his teeth. The last remaining barrier between him and the outside hinged on the guard ahead of him, and whether or not he valued his life more than his duty.

CHAPTER NINE

WENDY

A bad feeling tormented Wendy's stomach, but she didn't say a word.

Clint's older two-door red hatchback sped down the desolate road at full tilt. Wind tore through the open windows, blasting Wendy with the tepid air. She removed her hat and tossed it to the top of the dash. The loose strands hanging from the sides of her face whipped about as sweat populated her glistening flesh.

"I'm sorry about the air conditioning. It's been on the fritz for the past few months." Clint adjusted the controls on the dash, but the unit wouldn't respond. "I'm not sure if it's low on Freon or something more substantial. Once I have the money saved, I'll get it fixed."

Wendy brushed the stands of red hair away from her face and tucked them behind her ears. “It’s all right. If you aren’t sweating to death, are you really in Texas?”

Clint snickered, then smirked. “True. As strange as it sounds, I’ve grown accustomed to my back being wet and my shirt sticking to it. I know that probably sounds gross.”

“It’s true, though.” Wendy held her phone in her hand, checking the screen every few seconds for a signal.

“Anything yet?” Clint asked, staring at the bright screen.

Wendy shook her head. “No. Same as before. No signal. I’d like to call my grandmother and just let her know I’ll be back shortly. I’m feeling a bit guilty about leaving like we did. Perhaps I shouldn’t have. I don’t know.”

Clint adjusted his backside in the seat, then pinched the front of his shirt. He fanned his body with one hand while the other remained on the steering wheel. “I’m sure they won’t be that upset, that is, if they even know. It’s not too much longer before—”

The screen went blank as if the phone had shut down. “What the—” Wendy slapped her palm against the device, grumbling under her breath. “My phone died.”

“You mean like—” The engine clattered, then ceased to operate. The music softly playing from the speakers stopped.

“Did the car just die?” Wendy asked, looking to the dash, then to Clint.

“I-I’m not sure.” Clint held firm to the wheel. A lost look filled his scrunched face. His eyes left the road ahead. He studied the gauges on the dash as his foot pumped the gas. The red needle worked back toward zero. He panted.

“Perhaps you should stop and—Watch out.” Wendy pointed out of the windshield at the small black truck parked in the middle of the road.

Clint jerked the wheel, missing the back bumper by mere inches. The hatchback swerved, then plowed through the weeds and down the slight embankment at an angle. The car tipped over and rolled.

The crunching of tortured metal filled the interior. The world spun. Branches snapped as the car slammed into trees.

Wendy's head thrashed from side to side. A frightened scream escaped her mouth. Something dense punched her face, adding to the disorientation.

The hatchback came to a stop with all four wheels skyward. Wendy hung upside down in the seat, fingers touching the roof. The seatbelt kept Wendy's body secured in place.

Smoke vented from the crumpled front end. The fumes invaded her nose. Both lids opened.

A haze coated her vision. Blood rushed through her head, causing it to throb. The back of her neck felt stiff. It hurt to move her head.

"Clint. Are you—" Wendy peered to the driver's seat but didn't spot her friend. She blinked and opened her eyes wide.

The white airbag protruded from the steering wheel. A hint of blood covered the material. The driver's side window was missing.

Had Clint been thrown from the wreckage? She couldn't remember right then if he had worn his seatbelt or not.

Wendy felt around the belt buckle. Her hand trembled. The ends of her fingers brushed against the release mechanism.

She pressed it in. The latch gave, sending her crashing to the roof of the car. Wendy's head hit first, increasing the discomfort on her neck. She rolled over to her back and laid still for a second.

A flat, solid object poked the back of her ribs. She leaned to the side and reached under her, retrieving the object.

The phone's screen was cracked and busted. She tossed the device and peered through the jagged remains of the passenger side window.

Grass and trees met her gaze. The blurred vision waned. She tilted her head back and looked through the driver's side window, finding it to be less dangerous to crawl through than the passenger side.

Wendy turned over to her stomach and crawled through the opening. The sharpened edge rimming the missing window stabbed her skin. She gritted her teeth and moved both hands to the dirt outside.

Her battered body emerged from the wreckage. Every bone and muscle ached with the smallest movement, but the adrenaline kept her going.

The blistering sun baked the grounds. The dirt, weeds, and loose branches felt heated. The sparse crown overhead did little to provide any shade.

Wendy pulled her legs from the car, then sat up. The side of her head stung. She stood.

The world spun. Both legs shook. The ground rushed up.

She grabbed the bottom of the flipped-over car and braced herself. The end of her fingers touched the sore spot on her head. Blood covered the tips.

"Clint. Where are you?" Wendy lowered her hand and searched for his body.

The sun beamed through the opening above and hit her face. She squinted and raised her hand to block the sun.

Wendy noticed something in the weeds up the embankment. She couldn't tell if it was Clint or something else. Her hand released the safety of the vehicle. Her legs wobbled, but she didn't fall.

She trudged through the grass, one laborious step at a time toward the object hidden among the weeds. Wendy swayed from side to side. Her stomach churned with what she might discover.

A body laid prone on his stomach with both arms stretched out to either side. It was Clint. He didn't stir.

"Clint." Wendy dropped to her knees, weeping and sniffling. Tears left her shiny eyes and rolled down her cheeks. She pressed two fingers to his neck for a hint of life and found a weak pulse. "Thank God."

Both hands grabbed his side. She flipped Clint over as softly as she could to his back. His body moved without life—head bobbling about from side to side.

A deep gash ran across his forehead. Cuts and other contusions populated his young, busted-up face. Blood seeped from his nose and mouth.

Wendy shook him by the shoulders with the hopes he'd open his eyes or give some other response. "Clint, please answer me."

None came.

A flood of anguish, fear, and sadness seeped from her. She placed both hands on his chest and wept, unsure of how to help or what to do next.

Wendy struggled to comprehend the horrid change of events that had happened within a span of less than a minute. Clint's car losing power and the truck left in the middle of the road sealed their fate. It all felt surreal.

A noise grew louder from the road, snapping Wendy from her mournful trance. She listened closely. It sounded like a vehicle approaching.

"Help!" Wendy stood and stepped around Clint's body. She marched up the embankment through the weeds and busted limbs, shouting and waving her arms. "Somebody, please help!"

The sight of the older model brown truck filled her with joy. It stopped on the side of the road near where they'd crashed. Two men sat inside the idling vehicle, watching her.

The engine ceased. Both doors flew open. A burly, bearded man stepped out on the passenger side and made his way toward her.

A meager tall man rushed around the front end. He glanced at Wendy, then to the wreckage that flanked her.

"Are you all right, miss?" the overweight bearded man asked with his fat hand touching her shoulder. "What happened?"

Wendy continued to sob. Forming words or thinking felt like a monumental task. "I don't know. One minute, my friend and I are driving along, then everything lost power and we ran off the road before smashing into the back of that truck. My friend wasn't wearing his seatbelt and was tossed from the car, I think. I'm not real sure. He's hurt bad, but still alive. Please help me. We need to get him to a hospital."

"Okay, miss. Calm down. The Duke boys are here to help," the bearded man said with his hand fixed to her shoulder. "Jimmy, go check on her friend, will ya?"

"Sure thing, Roy." Jimmy shot by Wendy and traversed the embankment to Clint.

Roy turned and stood next to Wendy, draping his arm over the back of her neck. "Come up and sit down for a moment."

The pungent scent of chopped onions escaped from under the chubby man's armpits. It assaulted her senses, but coping with the wreckage and worrying about Clint distracted her enough to not care.

Wendy trembled as tears poured from both eyes. She had no way of reaching her grandparents and knew they'd be worried sick about her. The guilt of leaving, if only for a short bit, racked Wendy through and through.

"Do you have a phone I can use to call my grandparents by chance?" She ran her hand under her leaky nose.

Roy helped her into the cab of the truck. "We don't. Never had much use for one."

Wendy sat down on the edge of the passenger side bench seat. She tucked her arms against her chest. Her head tilted toward the ground.

Jimmy raced up the embankment, then headed for the truck. He pointed over his shoulder at the wreckage. "I think your friend is dead."

"Dead." Wendy leapt from the seat and pushed past Roy. She stomped her way through the grass, then fell to the ground. Her hand palmed her aching ankle that throbbed more and more.

Roy rushed to her aide, bent down, and retrieved Wendy from the depths of the weeds. "You need to take it easy and rest, sweetheart. I imagine you're going to feel the effects of being in that crash more and more."

Wendy sobbed and stood. She used the smelly, plump man's body as a crutch. The tears wouldn't stop and poured without pause.

"We can always take her back to our place and call the police," Jimmy suggested. "It's not far from here. They'll send an ambulance and everything to help her and should send the fire department here to check everything out."

"That's a great idea, Jimmy," Roy replied, escorting Wendy back to the cab of the truck. "You can rest there until help arrives. We've got some first aid supplies we can use to clean up some of those cuts you've got as well."

Jimmy retreated to the driver's side of the truck, sprinting around the front bumper. He hopped into the cab and slammed his door.

Wendy climbed inside the cab and scooted across the seat. Roy quickly followed, blocking her in the middle between the two surly-looking men.

The engine grumbled, then started.

Jimmy pumped the gas. The dash and leather bench seat she rested on had rips and tears. Dirt and dust covered the interior.

Roy rapped his hand against the dash, peered through the back window, then waved his hand. "Go on. Let's get moving so we can get this young lady some help."

"You got it." Jimmy drove along the road and past the small truck.

They got back onto the pavement and gained speed, leaving the wreckage behind them.

Wendy sat with her arms folded across her chest, sad about the death of Clint. Her gut feeling of something bad looming on the horizon had come to fruition. She hoped the worst was behind her and looked forward to seeing her grandparents.

CHAPTER TEN

WENDY

A string of bad luck with no end in sight. Had she been cursed or doomed?

The truck left the smoothness of the paved two-lane road for a dirt drive that snaked through dense verdure. The tires of the aged vehicle dropped into the ruts and other depressions populating the uneven terrain.

Wendy braced her hand against the dash to keep her body from shifting and slamming into the two unkempt men. She peered over her shoulder to the road that soon vanished within the meld of bushes and trees. That bad feeling bloomed in her gut.

Roy offered her a wry grin. His elbow rested on top of the door.

Jimmy worked the wheel, leaning over and sniffing her.

"Um, could you stop the truck for a moment?" Wendy asked, looking at Jimmy. "I'm not feeling so great. I think all of the shifting back and forth is making me nauseated."

"We're almost there," Roy replied, nodding at the windshield. "Another few minutes or so."

The shock of the crash had dulled her decision-making. Wendy would've never normally agreed to hop into a truck with the likes of the two men who now trapped her between them.

"I'd appreciate it if you would stop anyway," Wendy shot back, her voice rising an octave. "I feel like I'm going to throw up and would rather not do it in here."

Roy pointed at a ramshackle house that came into view past the slight bend in the road. "Almost there. Less than a minute."

The SIG. She still had the piece tucked in the waistband of her pants. The top of her shirt concealed the weapon and the two backwoods' hillbillies hadn't checked for it. Why would they?

Jimmy smirked and stared at her, flashing his stained yellow teeth. "You're damn lucky the Duke boys were driving by Miss—"

"Wendy."

"Well, Wendy. My brother and I will help you in any way we can," Roy said, brushing against her arm.

The truck emerged from the thick vegetation to open land. A battery of broken-down vehicles and other various junk littered the property. The house's exterior showed significant rot and wear within the wood facade.

The covered porch leaned to one side. The roof had numerous shingles missing. Weeds grew unchallenged all over. She struggled to believe that anyone lived there.

Help wasn't coming. Wendy doubted the Duke boys had a functioning phone or the intent on helping her. She had made a grave mistake in trusting the two men.

Jimmy brought the truck to a stop next to a rusted car that had no wheels. He shifted into park and killed the engine.

Roy opened his door and stepped out. He turned and faced Wendy with his dirty, fat hand stretched toward her. "Come on, doll. Let's head inside and we'll call the authorities and tend to those wounds."

Wendy didn't budge. Her hands rested on the tops of her thighs as she glanced at Roy, then over to Jimmy who remained seated.

"Well, come on. Don't you want to call your grandparents and let them know you're all right?" Jimmy asked over her shoulder.

Her skin crawled from the rail-thin hillbilly lurking next to her. The smirk on his smudged face wouldn't leave and grew more sinister.

"Now, don't be rude," Roy said, pressing both hands against the side of the truck. "This isn't any way to treat the folks who helped you in your time of need. Let's get out of the truck, now."

"I could think of a few ways to help her move," Jimmy said, running his tongue over his lips.

Wendy frowned at the thought and scooted across the bench seat. "Okay."

Roy stepped back, giving her room to get out of the truck.

The driver side door slammed shut.

Wendy flinched, then dropped down to the dirt.

Jimmy rushed around the front end. Both he and Roy eyed one another.

"Why don't you head inside and gather up what medical supplies we have so Miss Wendy can tend to her wounds," Roy said, reaching for her arm.

Wendy lifted her shirt and pulled the SIG from her waistband.

Roy threw his hands up. "Whoa. No need to do that."

"Back up off me, now." The SIG trembled in her hand. The barrel trained at Roy's forehead. Her finger rested on the trigger.

"All right. Just take it easy." Roy backed away, giving her some space. "I'm not sure why you need that heater. We're only meaning to help."

Jimmy stalked her from the front of the truck. The crown of his head poked over the rusted hood. "Be careful, Roy. She's shaking. I doubt she even knows how to use that thunder maker."

Wendy moved the SIG a hair past Roy's head, then pulled the trigger. The blast made the fat man flinch. "I know how to use it well, and unless you two hillbillies want a hole in each of your heads, I suggest you give me the keys to your ride and leave me be."

"Looks like we got us a live one, doesn't it?" Jimmy asked, holding his position at the front of the truck. "You okay?"

Roy shook his head, then fixed his gaze back to Wendy. "Yeah. I'm fine. I have a bit of ringing in my ear now is all."

"Keys. Now." Wendy held her hand out, palm facing up. "Tell that dipshit of a brother to bring them here and put them in my hand. No funny business or you two are going to have a bad day."

"Go ahead and do as she says," Roy said, maintaining eye contact with Wendy.

"But—"

"Just do it, Jimmy, and don't give me any lip about it," Roy shot back, cutting his brother off. "She means business."

"Damn right I do." Wendy peered through the open window of the passenger side door. Her ankle throbbed, making it radiate pain the more pressure she put on it.

Jimmy moved around the front end of the truck with his hands held high. The keys dangled from his fingers.

Wendy kept the SIG trained at Roy while shifting her gaze between both men. Her heart hammered. She breathed heavily through her nose.

Roy took a small step forward.

"Back. Up. Now." Wendy adjusted her hold on the grip. "Don't think I won't blow your head off. You have no clue who you're dealing with."

Jimmy rushed the door and reached through the open window.

Wendy turned and backed away. She held the SIG up at Jimmy.

Roy rushed her from behind before she could pull the trigger. He wrapped his arms around her chest and squeezed, trapping her limbs at either side. "Oh, sweetie. You done messed up now."

Jimmy taunted Wendy with the keys, smiling and shaking them in front of her face.

"Get your hands off of me, you fat, smelly pig." Wendy thrashed her body and head.

Roy shook her frame from side to side in a fit of anger. The SIG fell from her hand and hit the dirt. He kicked the pistol under the door and moved back while holding Wendy with a taut grip. "Grab her piece, will ya?"

Jimmy pocketed the keys, then bent down.

Wendy lifted her legs up, then slammed her boots against the door. It flung back, smashing Jimmy's head.

"What the hell." He dropped to the ground.

Roy snarled in her ear.

Wendy tossed her head back and busted Roy's nose.

"Ah. Damn bitch." His hold lessened, giving Wendy some space to wiggle her body free.

Her boots met the ground. She stomped Roy's feet, then landed an elbow into his face.

Roy fell back into the side of the truck, cupping his bloody nose. He hunched over, howling.

Wendy limped away, favoring her ankle.

Jimmy emerged from behind the door and tackled her to the ground. He flipped Wendy over to her back, then mounted her waist.

"Get off me." She punched at his face and chest, then lifted her hips up, trying to rid her body of the scrawny man.

"I got her pinned, Roy," Jimmy said, holding onto her flailing arms. "What do you want me to do?"

"Subdue her or something," Roy shot back, shaking his head.

Jimmy punched her in the face. The back of Wendy's head bounced off the ground. She scrunched her face up and stopped moving.

Roy stomped toward them. Both nostrils flared. He grabbed Jimmy's shoulder and shoved him off her. His hands bunched into Wendy's shirt, and he yanked her from the ground. "Grab her pistol and shut the doors to the truck. I'm going inside to get her settled."

Jimmy gave a thumbs up.

Wendy punched and slapped at Roy's broad chest. Her head throbbed even more from the blow to the face.

Roy jerked her from the ground, then said, "If you don't stop that shit right now, I'm going to show you real pain, among other things. You hear me?"

Wendy muttered incoherent gibberish at first, scrunching her bleeding nose toward her upper lip.

"You don't think she'll be any more of a problem, do you, Roy?" Jimmy asked, slamming the passenger side door to the truck closed. "She looks like she could be more trouble than it's worth. Might have a hard time selling her."

"It's too late for that now. We're committed." Roy tossed Wendy over his shoulder with ease, then faced the entrance to the foreboding home. Her body draped over him. "We've already come this far and can't go back. She'll come around. This isn't the first time we've had an unruly guest. We've broken spirits before. Made those gals submissive and obedient. We can and will do it again. If she won't submit, we'll discard her after having our way with her, of course."

Wendy lifted her weary head away from Roy's sweaty and moist back. The blood rushing to her skull added to the pounding.

Jimmy dabbed at the trails of blood running from his nostrils. He shoved the SIG in the waistband of his smirched pants.

Roy stomped off, marching toward the porch. Wendy bounced on his shoulder.

Jimmy moved around the front of the truck and waved at her.

Roy's hand adjusted, palming her butt. He climbed the short stack of rickety wooden steps to the aged porch. Each plank gave under the big man's bulk. Wendy wondered if his giant-sized boot would break through.

He slung the frayed screen door open, then shoved his way through the wooden one. It flew inward, slamming against the wall.

A pungent, unsettling odor assaulted Wendy's nostrils. It smelled like something rotting, mixed with sliced onions, and fecal matter all mashed together. Her sore nose scrunched, and her stomach churned from the vile stench.

"I got you a nice little spot in the back of the house." Roy clomped through the low light of the dusty living room.

They passed the kitchen and headed down a dark hallway. The buzzing of flies tickled her ears. She blinked and spotted a corded cream-colored phone resting on the counter in the kitchen before losing sight of it.

"Please. Just let me go," Wendy said, her tone weak.

Roy ignored her plea and continued on. He passed closed doors on both sides of the wood-paneled walls before stopping. "Here we are."

A clicking noise sounded.

Wendy looked around, trying to see what he was up to.

The hinges squeaked loudly in the silence. The floor creaked under their weight. The gut-wrenching smell wouldn't leave her be, adding to the torment she found herself in.

Roy tossed Wendy from his shoulder to a stained thin mattress in the corner of the space. She hit hard and groaned. The springs stabbed her side.

"I'll bring you some supplies so you can treat those cuts. We can't have our new toy looking in such horrible shape."

Wendy blinked and stared at the bastard.

Roy retreated out into the hall. "See you shortly." He grabbed the handle to the door, smirked, then slammed it shut, sealing her inside.

CHAPTER ELEVEN

ALEX

Alex regretted fighting with the guard, but the sentry left him no choice. He spared the man's life, knocking him out and leaving him face down on the pavement.

The guard's pistol sat tucked in the waistband of his trousers as Alex trudged down the street away from the prison. He scoured the streets for a vehicle hidden from the main road. A lengthy list of to-dos bombarded his mind, adding to the frazzled state he battled.

Trey and Wendy both took up residence inside his head. Davidson's threat toward Wendy rattled him. Alex knew his parents' place was secluded and well away from the dangers Houston offered, but the suggestion of her being targeted warranted a call to make sure.

A few cars were parked in the middle of the street, away from any stop signs or intersections. One of the vehicles had been abandoned while a man stood on the outside of his four-door sedan holding his phone in the air.

Alex watched the man and studied the vehicles, then any surrounding buildings. A handful of folks walked about the buildings on the sidewalks, conversing and pointing at the structures. Something felt off, but Alex couldn't pinpoint what it was.

The man marched around his vehicle, holding the phone up, and tapping the screen. He appeared perturbed from his thin, pursed lips and furrowed brow.

Alex walked past the abandoned car and peered inside the driver window. He grabbed at the door handle and tugged. Locked.

"Excuse me, officer," the man said, shouting.

Alex flinched, ducked, and scanned the streets and surrounding area for the authorities.

"Sir. Hello." The man waved his arms in Alex's direction and raised his voice. "Over here."

Alex stared at the bald, slightly overweight man. He spotted no police in the area and figured he must've been speaking to him.

The man raised his brow and lowered his arms.

Alex stood and tilted his head forward so the bill of the ballcap would hide his face. He marched toward the man, checking over his shoulder for any persons lingering close by.

"Are you all right, officer?" the man asked, studying his body. He tried to get a peek at Alex's face. "You seem a little... off I guess."

"Yeah. I'm fine." Alex avoided direct eye contact and wanted to further the conversation along to something other than his haggard appearance. He locked onto the phone the man stuffed into the back pocket of his blue jeans. "Is there an issue with your vehicle?"

The bald man looked away and pointed at the sedan. "I've always had issues with this damn car, but the weirdest thing happened."

"What's that?" Alex asked.

"I was driving down the street and it just… stopped. Like it lost power or something. I'm not sure how to explain it, really." He scratched at the top of his bald head, then shrugged. "Same thing happened to the guy behind me. He up and left his car in search of a phone to use. Neither of our cell phones are working. Won't even power on. It's the strangest thing, really. I just hope this has nothing to do with the possible EMP threats those commie bastards have been talking about unleashing on us. You haven't heard if that's what it is by chance, have you?"

"I haven't." Alex brushed past him, heading for the opened driver's door. His knowledge of EMPs, and cyberattacks for that matter, was limited, but he knew it could affect the grid and other electronics. He peered inside the vehicle with one hand resting on top of the door and the other on the roof. "So it won't even turn over or anything like that?"

Bald Man shook his head. "Nope. Dead as a damn doornail. Believe me, I tried multiple times with no luck."

The inside of the man's vehicle had copious amounts of empty wrappers and bottles in the passenger side seat and across the floorboard. It was a cluttered mess. He didn't notice anything of use and forwent asking to look at the man's cell phone since it wouldn't even power up.

"That's a real shame about the vehicle," Alex replied, disappointed by the news.

"Um, if I may ask, do you know if the prison back there still has power?" Bald Man stood a few feet from Alex's back. Each word that left his lips dripped with worry and uneasiness. "I'd hate to think any of those vile men might escape during this outage and whatever else is happening. I thought I heard gunshots."

Alex cleared his throat and turned around to face him. He offered a warm smile while keeping his head slightly tilted. "The prison is well secured and locked down. Nothing for you to worry about, sir."

Drop it and leave well enough alone.

"Well, another reason I asked is because you've got some blood on your uniform and some on your face." Bald Man continued pressing the issue. "I'm not trying to beat a dead horse here, but I'm just concerned that some might escape."

Alex took a step closer, then placed his hand on the man's shoulder. He lifted his chin up a bit, making eye contact with the bald man. "Like I said, sir, everything is under control and nothing for you to worry about. My suggestion to you would be to leave the area now just in case a breach does happen. You never know where those vile thugs will show up."

Bald Man gulped. His eyes widened. A look of fear covered his pale skin in a blink. "That… that sounds like a smart idea. I think I'll do just that."

"Good man." Alex patted him on the shoulder.

Bald Man scurried away, running from his vehicle and not looking back.

Alex peered back inside the vehicle, then sat in the seat. The keys dangled from the ignition. He turned the key and listened, but nothing happened.

The gauges within the dash showed no illumination. The needles didn't budge from their resting place. He twisted the radio knob. Still nothing.

Both hands slammed the steering wheel. He got out of the vehicle and continued on down the road, steering clear of any more populated areas until he could change out of the uniform and blend in better.

Alex had to find a vehicle that worked, but that proved to be easier said than done. Each car he happened across had no visible keys he could spot through the windows. He didn't know how to hotwire a car and trying to start each one would take time he didn't have and draw attention to himself.

An eerie silence lingered in the air as he skulked his way through the residential area. The lack of noise from cars running and honking felt… strange. He expected to hear the loud hum of air conditioning units running to combat the intense heat but heard nothing.

The roads had no running traffic, either. More cars sat idle with a portion of the owners staying with their vehicles while others were left behind. A confused gaze lingered on their faces as they peered at phones, then to the surrounding area. Alex kept hidden among trees, bushes, and other blockades as he continued on.

Huntsville to Houston was only about an hour or so away, barring any heavy traffic on Highway 45. On foot, and on the lam, that would stretch the timetable more.

The sound of a grumbling engine called out from close by. Alex stopped behind a tree and listened. He couldn't see the vehicle among the trees, homes, and businesses along the roadway.

The noise subsided. He peered out from behind the tree and looked across the road, scanning for the source. The pitiful whine of the engine started again, followed by an engine backfiring that echoed in the silence. The vehicle didn't sound in great shape, but he had little to choose from.

Alex skimmed the buildings on the far side of the street and stopped at the powerless intersection. A vehicle was parked under the light—immobilized. The working car was in that direction, though.

He checked the road in either direction, then bolted across the street to the alley on the other side. The chain-link fence and tall weeds in the empty lot next to it provided cover.

The clamor of the vehicle's engine built, signaling he was close. His legs moved faster, pulse racing at the thought of finding a working vehicle. He drew near the back of the buildings and slowed as he reached the corner.

Alex checked over his shoulder and stopped shy of the brick bend. He leaned out and surveyed the area.

A black older model Bronco was parked across the street at a gas station in front of the pumps. The driver threw open the door and slammed his hand against the wheel. He jumped out of the SUV and marched toward the front end.

The area around the gas station showed no signs of other folks. Alex spotted two other vehicles parked out front. The building's interior had no visible lights on.

Alex rushed from the alley and made his way across the street, heading for the gas station. He checked both directions of the road, then watched the driver of the Bronco mess with things under the hood.

Lights shone from the interior of the building. The two cars parked near the entrance showed no movement within. Alex lowered and hid behind the back end of the Bronco. He kept close to the edge, then looked around the side.

The gray-haired driver stomped away from the front end toward the driver's side. A scowl resided on his face. His lips moved, but Alex struggled to hear any words coming from the agitated man. He climbed back inside the Bronco and turned the engine over once more.

The SUV grumbled, then died. The driver shouted a slew of colorful words, then tried again.

The engine backfired.

Alex jumped, caught by surprise.

The rough idling smoothed out. The Bronco rattled and sputtered, but didn't die.

The driver hopped down to the pavement and marched back to the front end.

Alex advanced on the open door, staying low and next to the Bronco. He climbed into the driver's seat and closed the door carefully to minimize any noise.

The hood slammed shut.

The older, disgruntled, gray-haired gentleman at the front spotted Alex behind the wheel. His chin dropped and his eyes widened. He pounded his fists on the hood, then shouted and pointed at Alex.

Alex shifted into reverse and punched the gas.

The Bronco stuttered and backed away from the angered man. He reached toward his hip while jabbing his long, skeletal finger at the SUV.

Alex slammed the brake, then shifted into drive.

The gray-haired man pulled a pistol from the waistband of his jeans. He trained it at the windshield and opened fire.

The bullets punched the glass near the driver's side, zipping past him.

Alex ducked, spun the wheel, and hit the gas.

The Bronco lurched forward.

A horrid rattling loomed from the engine.

Bullets pinged off the body and broke through the passenger side windows as the SUV fled to the road.

Alex sat up straight and checked the rearview mirror.

The gray-haired man raced after him, emptying the remainder of his gun at the Bronco. He stopped, then threw his hands skyward.

The Bronco swerved on the road. The tires squealed.

Alex wrestled the steering wheel, bringing the SUV under submission. He checked the passenger side-view mirror.

The gun-toting man ran past the pumps to the gas station entrance. He tossed the door open and disappeared inside.

A sigh of relief left Alex's parted lips. He adjusted his bulk in the seat and continued down the road, leaving the gas station, and prison, behind him.

CHAPTER TWELVE

WENDY

The room closed in around her.

Wendy sat with her back wedged in the corner of the small, smelly bedroom. The springs in the mattress stabbed her backside. She watched the door leading in from the hallway for Roy or Jimmy to enter while thinking of Clint and how they left him to die.

Bastards.

The two men spoke in loud voices, shouting at one another from beyond the walls. Wendy wondered what they spoke about, and more so, what their intentions with her were.

The heated conflict ebbed. A loud bang made her jump. Silence loomed.

Her legs pressed to her chest. The bottom of her chin rested on the tops of her knees. Both arms hugged her legs.

The first aid kit Roy had brought earlier rested on the far end of the mattress. He dumped a water bottle next to the yellow-tinted box.

Wendy studied the scant few supplies loaded inside the opened container. A wad of cotton balls, band-aids, a half empty bottle of peroxide, and a small roll of gauze rounded out the contents.

The rays of sunshine coming through the boarded-up window next to her dimmed. Her frayed nerves and mind created shapes moving within the shadows. She squinted, waited a moment, then opened her eyes. The shadowy figures faded away.

The bottle of water made Wendy lick her lips. Her mouth felt dry—gums tacky to the touch. She didn't want anything from her captors other than freedom, but the dryness of her mouth wouldn't allow her to disregard the water.

Wendy removed her arms and crawled across the mattress toward the water. Any subtle sound made her flinch and stop. She reached her trembling hand out and grabbed the bottle, then scurried back to the corner.

Her mouth watered at the thought of the liquid. She unscrewed the cap and took a hearty gulp. The tepid water splashed her mouth and raced down her throat. She didn't care much for warm water, but she didn't have a choice.

A thin stream dribbled from the corners of her mouth to her chin. She lowered the bottle, took a breath, then drank some more.

The sides of her cheeks bulged. She swallowed, then wiped the back of her hand across her mouth.

Sweat poured from every part of her body. The stagnant air made it unbearable. The salt within each drop irritated any cuts she had.

The overwhelming fear and stress of the situation made it hard to think. She didn't want to wait around and see what devious and deplorable acts the vile men had in store. Escaping was her only recourse, but how?

The panic she wrestled latched to the back of her mind like a leech.

Take a deep breath. You have to calm down and think clearly. That's the only way you'll have any chance of getting out of here alive.

Wendy sat the bottle on the stained, matted carpet next to the mattress. She closed both eye lids and took controlled, deep breaths. The past and present collided in a mashup of memories that had shaped her life, and made her the strong, resilient young woman she'd grown into. She had to be strong once more and fight with every ounce of her being.

The fear and panic subsided after a couple of minutes. Her racing pulse lessened. The cloud inside her head dissipated.

She stood from the mattress. Her ankle throbbed from the rush of blood. She favored the injury, trying not to put much pressure on her foot.

The heel of her hand pressed to the wall. She studied the empty room, then faced the window. The ends of her fingers slipped between the planks of wood nailed to either side. She squinted and moved her head about.

The thick grime coating the glass made it hard to see the outside. She checked other areas for a better view but came up short.

Wendy tugged on the boards, testing if they'd give or not. The wood creaked but didn't budge much.

She turned away from the window and scanned the floor for anything that could be used as a weapon, but found nothing. There had to be something.

The first aid kit. She had only glanced at the contents and might've missed a pair of scissors or other surgical tool in the bottom of the plastic box. It was a long shot, but one she needed to check to be sure.

Wendy limped alongside the mattress, bent down, then grabbed the kit. She turned toward what sunlight shone through the boards and tilted the container at an angle. Her fingers shuffled through the supplies, but there was nothing more she could use.

She dropped the kit to the mattress in a huff and searched the rest of the room. The closet door was locked. Her hand jerked at the doorknob. What did they have in there? Wendy wanted to know but how?

An idea gelled. Her hand pushed into the front pocket of her jeans, fishing for a bobby pin she'd used to put her hair up.

The floor outside the room creaked a warning.

Wendy froze and listened. She looked to the mattress then back to the door, wondering if the doorknob would turn. It never did.

The footfalls trailed away.

A door slammed.

Wendy breathed a sigh of relief, pulled the bobby pin out, then bent it at a ninety-degree angle. She paused for a moment, thinking back to what her grandfather showed her years prior—another lesson he'd felt she needed to know in a worst-case scenario. Her father had agreed.

Her fingers held firm on the pin. She placed the tip in her mouth and pried the rubber from the end with her teeth. Wendy spat it to the floor and focused on the lock.

The exposed end slipped inside the lock. She bent it again, then folded the rest of the bobby pin until it was flush against the face of the doorknob.

Wendy listened for footfalls while trying to concentrate and remember everything she had been told. Heavy breaths left her flared nostrils. The sweat building on her brow ran into each eye. The slight sting caused her to blink and dig knuckles into her sockets.

Crap. What's next?

She racked her brain, struggling to remember the next step. Her chin dipped and her head rested against the surface of the door. She hadn't taken the useless skill too seriously at the time, but now it had become a viable, and potential way to possibly save her life.

The seconds ticked by like tortuous hours. The more time she sat idle meant one step closer to never getting free. That notion added to the pressure.

Hold on.

A moment of clarity hit her. She needed another bobby pin to use in conjunction with the other.

Wendy left the bobby pin inside the lock, stood, and searched her pockets for another. Her hands couldn't move fast enough.

Footfalls sounded from outside the room.

She froze and stared at the door.

The doorknob jiggled. The sound of keys working inside the lock ramped up her nerves.

Wendy limped to the corner of the room and dropped down on the mattress.

The door opened, then swung inside.

Jimmy stood in the dark hallway. His cadaverous appearance showed through the white tank top he had on. A sinister grin cut across his face as he stared long and hard at her.

A plate rested in one hand while the keys dangled from the other. He stepped through the doorway. "I brought you some food. It's not much, but I figured you might be hungry."

Wendy craned her neck and looked at what he'd brought. A can sat in the middle with some other items she couldn't make out. She wasn't in the mood for any food, especially from the likes of them.

Jimmy walked toward the mattress, then peered at the open first aid kit.

Wendy backed away. She glanced at the bobby pin she'd forgotten in the closet door lock—worried he'd discover it.

"Have you not cleaned up those cuts yet?" Jimmy asked, setting the plate that had what looked to be a can of tuna and crackers on it down on the edge of the bed. He picked up the kit and rummaged through the contents. "I know Roy wanted those cuts you have taken care of before they become infected. There should be enough in here to take care of that I think."

Every muscle in her body tensed, ready to act upon the slightest hint of him coming toward her.

Jimmy locked eyes with her. His tongue rimmed his lips. He leaned to the side and squinted through the black eye she'd given him. "That gash on the side of your head isn't looking too great. If you want, I can tend to your wounds. I wouldn't mind doing that for you."

The thought made Wendy ill. Her stomach twisted. The stench of the warm fish didn't help any either.

Wendy reached for the first aid kit. "That won't be necessary. I can manage on my own. I haven't felt too good due to the wreck, but I'll do it shortly."

Jimmy handed the kit to Wendy. His fingers caressed hers. His devious, coy smile only grew larger. "Well, if you change your mind or need any other assistance, please, let me know. I'm happy to help with… whatever."

“I’ll keep that in mind.” Wendy clutched the kit with a firm hold. She peered inside the container, then ventured a risky question, thinking the hillbilly was too dumb to connect the dots. “Um, before you go, you wouldn’t happen to have any scissors I could use, would you? It’d be a lot easier to cut the gauze and such. I didn’t see any in the box here.”

Jimmy cut his gaze down to the medical supplies, then back to her. The warm smile he’d given evaporated in a blink. “Scissors, huh? You think I’m retarded or something? Shit, you must if you’re asking some ignorant questions such as that.”

Wendy tensed and took a step back. She cleared her throat. “Not at all. That’s not what I meant. I just—”

“Yeah. I know what you meant.” Jimmy pursed his lips, then took a step forward.

Wendy gulped and took a step back.

“Perhaps you need to be taught a lesson.” Jimmy raised his hand and reached for the loose strands of hair that hung from the side of her head.

“That won’t be—”

“What the hell are you doing, Jimmy?” Roy stood at the doorway. His voice boomed like angry thunder. Both hands rested on the sides of his wide hips. “I thought I told you not to come in here without me. You know how you get.”

Jimmy cowered. He straightened up and backed away. “I’m sorry, Roy. I thought she might be hungry, so I brought her some tuna and crackers. I was just trying to be hospitable is all.”

Roy walked inside the room. His fat fingers touched the bandage over his busted nose and black and blue eyes. He grabbed Jimmy’s shoulder and yanked him back. “I’m not stupid, so don’t act like I am. I know exactly what you were looking to do. That’ll come, but not right now, so get.”

Wendy clutched the sides of the kit harder. The hint of them doing terrible things to her coalesced in her mind, causing her to breathe heavier.

"Damn, Roy. Why do you always have to do that in front of other people? You know I hate it." Jimmy made fists with both hands, turned, and punched the wall.

His fists busted the sheetrock. Bits and pieces rained down to the carpet. He gave his brother the side-eye, then stormed out of the bedroom and down the hall.

Roy sighed, then ran his fingers through his greasy hair.

Wendy looked to the closet door, then back to Roy as he turned and faced her. He grumbled under his breath, then set his sights on Wendy.

"That damn son of a bitch doesn't listen for crap. Sometimes, I think he's more trouble than anything else." Roy tilted his head, staring at the matted blood from the gash on the side of her head. "You should probably take care of that, along with the other cuts you've got. I believe I brought enough supplies for you to do so. We've also got some other clothes you can change into."

"Why am I here?" Wendy asked, figuring Roy had to be the leader from the way he bossed his brother around. "Please, just let me go. I swear on my life I won't tell anyone."

Roy chuckled, rolled his eyes, then scrunched his face. His hand touched his battered nose. "Yeah. Right. I imagine you wouldn't tell anyone."

"I wouldn't. I swear it." Wendy took a step forward. "I just want to get home. I beg you."

"Does that work?" Roy asked, studying her distraught face. "You're not the first to give the puppy dog eyes and try to appeal to my soft nature. It ain't there. You're wasting your time with that, doll face."

Wendy's shoulders deflated and hung forward. She shot a quick glance to the open door, contemplating making a break for it.

Roy noticed the look and smirked. "Honey, I'd advise not even trying. That would only land you in extra hot water. My nose is still hurting from where you laid into me. What I will do, though, is go grab you some water from the well we've got out back. With the power being out, that's the only way we'll get some. Then you can clean up a bit. My brother and I don't care for dirty women."

That was rich, coming from the overweight, smelly man who took no pride in his appearance, or personal hygiene for that matter.

"Is this some sort of sex trafficking ring or something?" Wendy asked. "Are you trying to sell me off? Is that what this is?"

Roy belted a hearty laugh. "Lord no. I mean, we have tried that in the past with other young women, but haven't in some time. It's more hassle than it's worth. No, no. We just enjoy the company of the fairer sex. We're not the most attractive men in the world."

"So, you just kidnap women, then?" Wendy shot back.

Roy opened his mouth to respond, then paused. His hands balled into fists. He looked over his shoulder to the open door, then shouted. "Damn it, Jimmy. Will you stop your bellyaching?"

Wendy scrunched her brow in confusion. She didn't hear Jimmy speak, or anything else for that matter. It was quiet. She wondered what Roy heard and if he maybe had some mental problems to go along with everything else that was wrong with him.

"Get those cuts cleaned up," Roy said, peering at her. His voice was thick with anger. "I'm going to grab you some water from the well. I'll be back shortly so you can wash up a bit."

He turned to leave the room and stopped, staring in the direction of the closet door.

Wendy's heart skipped a beat, afraid he'd spotted the bobby pin. Panic engulfed her, scared of what the unstable man would do next.

"You wouldn't happen to have any aspirin or anything similar?" Wendy asked, trying to snare his attention away from the closet. "I have a rather bad headache and my body hurts from the wreck. It would help with the pain."

Roy studied the door a second longer before looking back at her. "Let me check. To be honest, I'm not sure if we do or not. Just worry about getting cleaned up. Am I clear?"

Wendy gulped. "Yes."

"Good." He stomped out of the room and slammed the door behind him.

The loud thud made Wendy jump and clutch the first aid kit a bit harder. She held a bated breath. Her mind reeled from the odd encounter and deepened her fright of the two men. Both men seemed unstable at best and hinted at possible mental issues that would only complicate matters and threaten her survival that much more.

CHAPTER THIRTEEN

ALEX

The Bronco rumbled down the road, sounding worse with each passing second. The grumbling engine did little to stay Alex's nerves and worry that it would last much longer.

Come on. Don't die on me.

Alex patted his palm on the dash. His gaze shifted from the highway to the gauges, hunting for any flashing warnings.

The speedometer and other rounded instruments showed no issues even though the rough idling and occasional backfire begged to differ. The gas tank had close to a full tank—one of the few saving graces.

Cars were parked along Highway 45 as far as he could see. He drove on the service road, studying the array of dead vehicles, pondering if he could maneuver the Bronco through. A scant few vehicles were operational, making their way to the nearest off ramps or driving through the medians.

People milled about on the highway, looking lost and confused. Some kept close to their rides while others ventured toward the service road.

Alex wondered why many of the automobiles had stopped working when others, like the Bronco, continued operating. He couldn't piece it together and it made him chew on the conundrum that much more. It had to be part of the EMP attack he was told about.

The parking lots of the shopping centers he passed were full of vehicles. The large retail signs and stop lights showed no power. The intersection ahead had a cluster of large semis and other various cars blocking his way.

Motorists stared at the Bronco with sweaty faces and waved their arms. Alex had no intention of stopping, fearing that someone might try to steal the SUV. He drove into the grass and kept his foot mashed to the floor.

A number of the stranded people shouted and continued waving their arms at him to snare his attention. They navigated the maze of powerless steel toward the grass. Some got close to blocking his path, shouting and pointing at him.

"Move out of the damn way," Alex said, waving them out of the way while his other hand jerked the steering wheel.

The Bronco cut farther into the grass and away from the road to miss the pole holding the road signs. He drove up the slight hill to the street.

A narrow gap presented itself through the cars to the other side. Alex slowed and worked his way through. He craned his neck while turning the wheel to avoid hitting any of the cars.

A portion of the motorists closed in on Alex from all sides. Others kept out of the way, watching as he passed by. He had no intentions of running anyone over, but would if push came to shove.

The Bronco jerked.

The engine rattled and coughed. Alex checked the gauges for any warnings. The check engine light flashed.

A loud thud sounded against the driver's side window like something hit it. Alex jumped in the seat, then glanced out the cracked window. His hand jerked at the wheel.

The Bronco rammed a parked car. He moved toward the steering wheel some. The engine stalled. He wasn't going fast enough to do any real damage, or so he hoped.

"I need this car, please," a man said, dressed in a dark navy-blue business suit. "I have money. I'll pay you for it."

Alex ignored the suit and checked the gauges. He turned the key and pumped the gas to get it started. It grumbled but refused to obey.

Fists hammered the compromised driver side window. The suit's voice raised to a shout. He wasn't leaving Alex be. Each hard strike split the glass more.

Christ. Start, damn you.

Motorists closed in around the Bronco. They mashed their faces against the passenger side windows, knocking on the glass and speaking to him.

The driver side door opened.

Alex yanked his hands from the wheel, grabbed the interior door handle, and slammed it shut. He punched the lock down on the door and eyed the agitated suit.

The pounding fists remained and only grew louder and more intense the longer he sat idle. He needed to get the vehicle started and leave while he could.

"Come on, pal," the suit said. "I'll give you three hundred bucks for this junk heap. It's all I've got on me. Easy money."

"Do you know what happened?" A Latina woman asked from the passenger side window, banging her small hand against the glass. "Is your cell phone working? Can I use it?"

A number of other voices spoke at once, growing more heated and louder by the second. The banging on the windows matched the tumult. The glass rattled. Each strike made Alex's body tense and twisted his nerves.

Alex kept his sights trained on the dash, focused on trying to get the Bronco started. His foot pinned the gas pedal to the floorboard and turned the engine over.

The SUV whined a pitiful groan, spit and sputtered, then grumbled to life. He fed the vehicle gas, revving the engine.

The small group of people around the Bronco hammered the windows more, rattling the glass within the frame of the door. They refused to yield. He had the guard's gun to use against the confused mob as a last resort if he couldn't get away.

Alex shifted in reverse, then tossed his arm over the back of the passenger side seat. He waved his hand at the two bodies he could see through the back window.

The Bronco pulled away from the car he'd run into. The people flanking the SUV leapt out of the way.

The suit followed right along, hammering the glass with his balled fist. "Open the damn door now and get out."

Alex looked through him, stopped, then shifted into drive.

The suit bolted around to the front of the Bronco and blocked his way through the opening to the other side of the access road. He jabbed his finger at the windshield and yelled.

Have it your way, pal. Alex hit the gas.

The SUV lunged forward at the angry suit. His eyes enlarged, and his mouth gaped open with shock. He jumped out of the way.

Alex wrenched the wheel and kept the pressure on the gas, driving through the remainder of the cars to the access road. He checked the rearview mirror, spotting the suit and other stranded people pumping their fists and flashing obscene gestures his way.

The curving road leading toward the highway hit an open gap with few cars blocking the way. More people milled about aimlessly, lost and unsure of what to do. They flashed inquisitive stares in his direction, pointing and flagging him down.

Brake lights up ahead flashed from an older model tan Dodge truck parked in the drive leading into a gas station. Two men stood in front of the vehicle, blocking its path. Its horn bellowed. The truck lunged forward and stopped shy of slamming into the men who pumped angry fists and pointed at the driver.

Alex slowed, watching the heated encounter unfold. He gripped the top of the wheel tighter, anxious to see what happened next.

One of the men jumped out of the way, barking at the truck while the other angry man stayed planted in place. The pickup inched forward again and laid on the horn.

The man blocking his path reached to his hip and pulled a pistol from the black holster attached to his belt. He brought the weapon to bear on the windshield of the truck.

Oh, shit.

Alex laid on the gas and sped up. He made a wide arch around the backend of the truck.

The angered man popped off two rounds into the windshield.

Alex flinched.

The truck flew backward at an angle onto the access road, missing the Bronco by a foot or so. Another couple of rounds hammered the windshield, bringing the truck to a dead stop.

Alex craned his neck and peered through the passenger side windows at the truck. The gunman skirted the front end with his pistol trained at the driver's seat. He charged the door and stopped, then wrenched it open.

Jesus Christ.

The Bronco continued on down the access road. Alex faced forward and peered to the rearview mirror before fixing his sights straight ahead. Making it back to Houston on 45 seemed to be a tall order with the number of vehicles and stranded people milling around. He didn't know where danger would rear its ugly head.

The only safe way he could think to go would be to hit the back roads, away from the abundance of people and cars that cluttered the highway and service roads. Alex figured going around the mess would work out better. Time would soon tell if his plan would work, or if he'd made a grave mistake.

CHAPTER FOURTEEN

WENDY

A way out. That's all she needed to make a break for it.

The silence inside the stuffy bedroom grated on Wendy's nerves. She paced the floor with her arms tucked against her chest and teeth biting the ends of her grungy fingernails. Her mind worked, plotting a way out of the bedroom and to freedom.

The Dukes' heated words and shouting ebbed, causing her to wonder if they might've killed each other. She didn't think it happened, but hoped it might. At least she'd gotten the metal bucket of water and aspirin from Roy before the argument flared again.

The brothers had issues that she worried could manifest into bigger dangers for her. Her future was unknown and she feared what the two unhinged backwoods rejects wanted to do with her. They kept dropping subtle hints of being intimate with her. The mere thought of it made her ill.

Wendy peered at the closed closet door. The bobby pin had been removed and stuck back into her pocket. She didn't have an extra one like she'd hoped, thwarting her attempts at gaining access to the contents inside the closet.

The light shining through the slats nailed over the window beamed in her face. She turned and faced the gleam. The lack of options in escaping made her desperate and bold. To survive the horrors in the near future, Wendy would have to press her luck.

She glanced at the entrance to the room, then listened for any footfalls approaching. No hints of creaking floors or raised voices met her ears.

Wendy approached the wood boards, then glanced at the edges secured to the walls. Her fingers tugged on the ends, testing how well they were secured.

The wood resisted and creaked. The nails gave some, but not much. She paused and listened for movement beyond the walls, but heard none. Wendy tried again, tugging a bit harder. The wood popped and gave some more.

A fleeting bit of hope surged through her body. Perhaps her plan of escaping through the window would work. She'd have to work fast because of the noise.

One by one, Wendy pried the boards off from the bottom up, then sat them on the stained mattress. The window sill had spiderwebs covering the lip.

A small brown spider clung to the silk webbing, and remains of eaten insects tainted the dingy wood.

Her face scrunched in disgust as her palm pressed to her mouth. She detested the eight-legged creatures. They made her skin crawl, but her salvation rested beyond the web and her own fear.

Wendy took a deep breath and forced her fingers through the sticky webbing away from the spider. The creature stirred, crawling across the web toward her hand.

She jerked her fingers away.

The spider stopped.

Wendy shook her hands. *Come on, girl. Suck it up and just do it.*

Two quick breaths and her hands plunged back into the webbing. She grabbed the lip of the window and pushed up, but it didn't budge.

The spider advanced, growing closer to her fingers.

Why is it not budging? Open, damn it.

She sighed, then growled. Frustration built inside her. The back of her hand swatted at the creepy crawler, knocking it to the floor.

Wendy ducked and studied further up the window that the boards still covered. It appeared to have a latch in the center she couldn't reach. She forced her hand up through the tiny opening anyway to see if she could make it fit.

A splinter snagged the skin near her thumb. She flinched. Her hand slammed the glass as she pulled her arm down.

The small piece of wood protruded from her hand. She bit at the tip to remove it.

The spider crawled across the floor, heading toward the base of the wall where she stood. It moved quickly, fading in and out of the shadows.

Wendy stepped on the critter, then spat the sliver of wood from her mouth. She gripped the plank of wood covering the latch and worked it free from the wall.

The mounting pressure and anxiety of the day's events made her hands unsteady. The board slipped from her fingers and slammed against the floor. She gasped, staring at the ground.

Oh, no.

Heavy footfalls rushed down the hall toward the room. Panic consumed her. She battled with what her next move should be.

"What the hell is going on in there?" Roy asked, his tone rising from the other side of the door. "What are you doing?"

Wendy didn't think. She acted on pure instinct. Survive or die was what it boiled down to in that dire moment.

The doorknob turned.

The door rattled inside the jamb.

She bent down, grabbed the piece of wood from the floor, and rushed toward the door. Her back pressed to the wall, hands tightening over the board.

The keys jingled in the knob.

Adrenaline surged through Wendy's body, causing her to be slightly lightheaded.

Roy huffed and puffed. The door unlocked, then swung inward.

Wendy watched the opening, waiting for her chance to strike.

"Damn it to hell," Roy said in a shout. He charged inside the room.

Wendy swung the plank of wood—nails facing outward.

The board smashed into Roy's chest, stopping him dead in his tracks. The rusted-looking ends of the nails bit into his flesh, digging in deep. The keys dropped from his hands and clattered off the wood floor.

"Ah." He wailed in agony, stumbling through the doorway and out into the hall.

The nails pulled away from his chest. His back slammed against the wall, hitting with a dense thud. A grimace formed on his face—brow scrunched as he gnashed his teeth.

Wendy retrieved the keys from the floor and darted out of the room. She stepped over Roy's legs, keeping the nailed board in her grasp.

"You're not going anywhere." Roy grabbed at her pant leg, trying to stop her. The ends of his fingers clawed at the denim fabric. His fingernails took hold.

"Let go of me." Wendy kicked her leg, freeing it from his hold.

The throbbing in her ankle swelled, but the heated moment stayed the pain and kept her moving down the murk of the hallway with only a slight limp. She looked for Jimmy, wondering where he was since she'd heard no other footfalls or voices carrying through the house.

She peered over her shoulder, spotting Roy standing from the floor while pushing up against the wall. His voice boomed. A slew of threats left his taut lips, but she ignored him.

The tip of her shoe caught the edge of something protruding from the corner of the wall as she emerged from the hallway. Her feet intertwined. She lost her balance. Both arms swung to keep her upright.

The floor rushed up.

The nailed board dropped from her hands. It clanged off the floor in front of her. The keys remained in her other hand.

Wendy braced for impact. The palms of her hands slammed the wood. The contact sent a jolt of searing pain lancing up both arms. Her wrists ached and throbbed. The sharpened edge of the keys bit her sensitive palms.

Roy stood from the floor in the hallway.

Wendy watched his wide frame stand in the murk. He rubbed his chest where the nailed board had struck and lurched down the hall after her.

She pushed up from the floor. Her jaw clenched, biting back the discomfort in both hands.

The heavy footfalls of the overweight, inbred swine rushed toward her.

Wendy got to her feet and stumbled away. She positioned the keys between her fingers with the tips sticking above each digit.

Roy reached for the back of her shirt. "You've got no place to go, you stubborn girl. You're so going to pay for that." His fat fingers caught a fold in the fabric. He made a fist, stopping her forward movement.

"You're not going to touch me." Wendy spun around and slashed at his head with the keys. The tips raked across the side of his sweaty face, cutting him open.

"Son of a bitch." Roy withdrew his hand from her garb, then palmed his cheek. He snarled under his breath, growing angrier by the second.

Wendy scampered away, navigating the cluttered mess of junk, furniture, and other trash that resided within the hot, ramshackle home. She spotted the corded phone, but couldn't stop and kept moving toward the front door.

Roy gave pursuit, unwilling to let her escape. He crashed into the array of junk and stumbled, but managed to stay upright.

Thoughts of the truck materialized in Wendy's head. She had the keys and could use the working vehicle to escape. She just had to make it out first.

Wendy slammed into the closed door leading to the outside world. Her hand fumbled on the doorknob. Each hard step Roy took made her flinch and pant.

He shortened the distance, charging up behind her. His heavy breathing cut at her nerves.

She turned the knob and swung the door inward. Wendy rushed outside, sprinting through the doorway.

A figure sprung from the side of the porch, grabbing her by the arms. It was Jimmy.

"Don't let go," Roy said, marching toward the open door.

Wendy jerked her body and arms while pushing forward with her legs. She leaned toward the edge of the porch, fighting with every bit of strength in her.

"Man. She's like a wet fish," Jimmy said, struggling to keep his fingers on her arms. His meager limbs failed, allowing Wendy to gain ground.

She turned and kicked at Jimmy as Roy stomped toward her.

Roy's hand balled into a fist. He took a swing at Wendy, smashing her jaw with his knuckles.

Wendy's legs buckled. The world went dark for a second. She stumbled off the edge of the porch and dropped to the dirt. Her body smacked the earth. Pain filled her mouth and head.

The Duke brothers flanked her on either side, stepping from the porch to the ground. They towered over her.

A boot slipped under Wendy's waist, then flipped her over onto her back. Her head rocked from side to side. The sun beamed down on her face, making it harder to see.

Roy bent over. Blood spots soaked his off-colored white tank where the nailed board had hit. His fingers rubbed at the wound. "Playtime is over. It's time to get down to business."

CHAPTER FIFTEEN

ALEX

The grumbling engine of the Bronco filled the cab in the now silent world.

Alex divided his attention between the gauges and the road ahead, watching for any issues with the engine or elsewhere. The number of immobile vehicles littering the streets had lessened by more than half compared to that of the major highway and service roads. What people he spotted gave peculiar stares as they walked alongside the roadway or meandered about any businesses or homes he passed.

A few others pointed his way, waving their arms to flag him down. He kept going, not wanting to stop unless necessary.

The SUV had nothing of use on the floorboards or seat. Alex did a quick search of the glovebox, splitting his attention to the depths of the hold and the road ahead. He wanted a phone, but doubted it would even work considering the state of things around the city.

A black mass lurked under a mound of papers stuffed inside the compartment. His brow lifted in curiosity.

Alex glanced to the road, then reached inside. His fingers shoved the papers out of the way and touched what felt to be a weapon.

What do we have here?

He pulled out a small silver revolver with a black handle, then shut the glovebox. Alex studied the weapon, turning it and studying it for any markings.

Ruger SP 101 was imprinted on the side of the barrel. He pushed out the cylinder and peered at the five rounds loaded inside. The Ruger was a good insurance policy if the need called for it, but he hoped it wouldn't resort to such things.

Alex flicked his wrist, slapping the cylinder back into place. He looked it over a minute more and sat it in his lap.

A woman darted out from the front of a white sedan parked on the side of the road. She waved her arms while standing in the middle of the road.

Christ.

Alex hit the brake and jerked the wheel to miss running her over. The tires squealed as the SUV cut across the road. The Ruger dropped from his lap, vanishing to the depths of the floorboard.

The Bronco came to a skidding halt.

Alex panted in the seat. Both hands white knuckled the top of the wheel. His chest heaved. He took a deep breath, then gulped.

The woman walked toward the SUV. Alex spotted her creeping up on the passenger side. He reached down to the floor and felt for the weapon.

A knock sounded at the window across from him. The young, Hispanic woman pressed her nose to the glass. She spoke, but the window muffled her voice. Her eyes were wide and looked shiny as she stared at him. She turned and pointed at the white sedan, speaking ninety to nothing.

The young woman reminded Alex of Wendy which made him forgo retrieving the revolver. He didn't notice anyone else on the road, and decided to see why she'd risked her life to jump out in front of him.

Alex sat up straight and reached across to the passenger side door. He grabbed the window's handle and cranked it, lowering it down some.

The woman's fingers slipped through the opening and bent down. She pressed her mouth close to the opening and spoke in an unsteady tone. "Can you please help me?"

"Are you crazy?" Alex asked, propping himself up in the passenger seat with his hand. "You're lucky I didn't run you over."

She pointed at her sedan. "Can you help me, please? I'm trying to get back to Houston. My car suddenly died while I was driving. I'm not sure what happened. I managed to pull off to the side of the road before it came to a complete stop. I've checked under the hood to see what the problem is, but I'm horrible with cars. It won't even act like it's trying to start now."

Alex glanced to the back window of the SUV, then out through the windshield. "Yeah. I don't think it's going to start or do much of anything else. Cars dying seems to be widespread as far as I've seen."

"Great. You're the first vehicle I've spotted that's actually working." She looked in the direction he'd come. "A few people walked past here earlier unsure of what happened. They left their vehicles behind because there's no cell service either. I'm hoping you'll help me out. It's important."

"Are you alone?" Alex peered at the white sedan, hunting for a body or any movement. "I've had some people try and take this from me."

"I am alone. It's just me. I swear," she answered, nodding. "I'm not going to try anything if that's what you're worried about."

Alex mulled it over. His chin dipped. A heavy sigh left his mouth. He didn't want to pick anyone up and play shuttle bus, but the desperation in her wide eyes made him reconsider. "All right. I'll give you a ride, but let me reiterate that if you try anything or if you've got some ulterior motive here, it won't work out well for you."

She nodded. "I promise you that I don't. You have my word."

Words meant little to Alex right now. He'd still have to keep his guard up and watch her closely. She didn't appear to be a threat, but perilous times could make good people do dangerous things in the blink of an eye.

"I'm going to grab my purse real quick from my car. I'll be right back, okay?"

"Hurry up," Alex replied, scanning the road and any surrounding buildings and cars for people. "I don't want to be sitting here for too long."

She tilted her head, then rushed back to her white sedan.

Alex bent down and grabbed the Ruger from the floor, then tucked it between the seat and his legs, hiding the weapon. He watched the woman lean inside through the opened driver's side door and retrieve her belongings. She shut the door, then ran from her vehicle to the SUV. He unlocked the passenger side, granting her access to the Bronco.

The woman threw open the door and plopped down into the seat, breathless. Her hand brushed away the loose strands of dark, brown hair that clung to her sweaty forehead, then shut the door. "I really do appreciate you giving me a ride."

"Not a problem." Alex hit the gas, sending the Bronco on its way, and leaving her car behind.

She stuffed her purse onto the floorboard, then pulled the seatbelt across her chest. A heavy sigh left her mouth. The back of her head pressed to the headrest, then turned toward him. "My name is Ava, by the way."

"Alex." He kept his attention trained on the road ahead.

Ava looked Alex over, staring at his prison guard uniform, then back to his face. "So, you work at the Huntsville prison?"

Alex nodded.

"Did the power go out there by chance as well?"

"It did," Alex replied, adjusting his butt in the seat and leaning forward. The back of the shirt was damp and stuck to his skin.

"From the looks of it, seems you had a rough time." Ava pinched the front of her shirt and fanned herself. "Did the prison manage to lock everything down before anyone could escape?"

"Yeah. It got a bit dicey here and there after the power crashed, but all is secured. The animals are back in their cages." Alex kept his head trained in the direction of the road, trying to minimize prolonged eye contact with her for fear she might see through him.

"That's good. I mean, I know just because someone's in jail doesn't make them a horrible person overall," Ava replied, waving her hand in front of her face. "Sometimes, good people make mistakes in the heat of a moment or when their backs are pinned to the wall. I have, well, had, an uncle that was incarcerated years back. He was a good man who made a bad call. He paid for it."

"Yep. That can happen." Alex glanced out of the driver's side window at the cars and people who walked the sides of the road.

Ava pointed at the air conditioning controls. "Do you mind if we turn the AC on? It's hot as Hades."

Alex glanced at the dash. "Doesn't work. You can roll down the window if you want."

"I guess that's better than nothing. It's so hot outside it makes it feel like a sauna in here." Ava cranked the window down. Wind rushed inside the cab. Her hair blew wildly, covering her face. "That's better than nothing."

The Bronco grumbled down the highway. Alex kept his sights fixed on the road and the woman.

Ava shook her head, pulled the fluttering hair away from her face, then put it up into a ponytail using the purple band from her wrist. The palm of her hand cleared the beads of sweat from her brow. She wiped it on the tops of her pants.

"Where in Houston are you needing to go?" Alex asked. "I'm heading to the north side of the city."

"The Villas," Ava answered. "My cousin lives there. My son's been staying with her for the past few days while I've been out traveling for work. She called me earlier saying he was rather sick. My phone went dead before she could fill me in on what all was wrong. He has a crap immune system and when he falls ill, it can be rather bad. That's why I jumped out in front of you back there. I need to get back to him and make sure he's all right."

Alex looked at her. "I hope he's okay."

Ava dug her fingers into the front pocket of her jeans, retrieving her phone. "Yeah. Me too. My cousin sounded rather stressed, so that has amplified my worrying as well." She fiddled with her phone, mashing the buttons on the sides and studying the device. "I wish I knew why this damn thing wasn't working. I mean, I've had problems with it in the past, but nothing like this. It's like the battery is dead or something. I hate to ask, but would you have a phone I could use really quick to call her?"

"Sorry. Mine's, um, not working either," Alex replied, shaking his head. "I was going to see if I could use yours."

"Ugh. It's so frustrating." Ava tossed her phone to the dash, then looked to the open window. "I'm not sure what happened, but it's messing things up. Of all the days for something like this to go down, it had to be today. I think life is trying to tell me something. I don't think I need to tell you that, though. Seems like we're both having it rough."

More than you know, lady.

Ava shook her head, then messed with the radio. Her fingers twisted the controls. Static hissed from the speakers. She scanned through the many stations only to find more white noise.

"You're wasting your time with that," Alex said, slowing down and working his way through the few cars parked in the intersection of the next street. "From what I gathered, everything is down. Not working. Buildings and cars don't have power. Cell phones and radio stations are dark."

"Why is your vehicle working when others aren't?" Ava asked, removing her hand from the radio.

Alex shrugged. "No idea, but I'm glad it is. The only bad thing about having a working vehicle is that you have a target painted on you."

The cars littering the roadway grew thicker, blocking their way and making it harder to navigate in a timely manner. Threading the Bronco through the gaps and open spaces challenged Alex.

"Are you sure going this way is advisable?" Ava placed her hand on the dash, looked to Alex, then back to the road ahead. "Seems like it's only getting worse."

"To be honest, I'm not sure." Alex stopped the Bronco and scanned the area. A side street a few car lengths down looked to be clear of any traffic blocking the roadway. "I'm guessing more than anything. I know highway 45 is a nightmare and so are the service roads. Well, as far as I could see that is. I figured keeping to these streets would be a bit faster and not as congested. Looks like it's hitting in pockets."

Ava glanced through the opened passenger side window at a fast-food joint. Cars filled the small parking lot with two in the middle of the drive parked near the entrance. Two men bickered out front, pushing and shoving each other.

"I wonder what's going on over there?" She looked at Alex.

"Nothing good, I imagine," Alex replied, adjusting his hold on the steering wheel.

The two large men took pop shots at each other, throwing punches and tugging at the other's clothing.

"Christ." Ava watched the spectacle unfold as the two unhinged men slugged it out.

Alex hit the gas and continued on, driving through another intersection and leaving the brawling men to the heated conflict. He sped up, weaving around the cars while checking the area. "That's why I'm trying my best to avoid people. You never know what someone is going to do until it's too late. I've had it happen once already. I'm not giving this ride up to anyone."

The Bronco brushed past a small, black sports car, hooked around the curb, then down the street Alex noticed moments earlier. A subtle jerk in the SUV's forward momentum grabbed

Alex's attention, pulling it to the gauges. He checked each gauge, unsure of what was wrong.

Ava looked away from the windshield to the dash. "Is there something wrong?"

"I'm not sure. It hasn't been running too well. I just need it to get me closer to Houston is all," Alex answered.

"From the way the engine is sounding, that might be a stretch."

Alex kept his foot pressed to the gas and pushed the SUV down the street. "Worst case is it'll die and we'll be on foot at that point."

Ava sighed. "I hope it hangs in long enough to get us closer. I've got so much riding on this tin can."

"Likewise. I guess we'll see."

CHAPTER SIXTEEN

WENDY

The side of Wendy's bruised face ached. She laid on the hard mattress with her nose buried into the stench-ridden fabric, battling to hold the flood of tears at bay.

Roy had dealt her a hard slap with his open palm before leaving her be. Jimmy secured the planks of wood she'd worked off of the window back in place. He added more nails on both sides of the wall, securing it as best he could.

Wendy jerked both arms, fighting to free herself from the rope that bound her wrists. The coarse material bit at her sensitive skin. A searing pain lanced up her forearms. She gnashed her teeth and grunted.

Every inch of her battered frame hurt. Not one molecule was spared. She had given escaping her best shot and failed. All hope seemed lost and well out of reach.

She rocked her body from side to side, then sat up. The sadness lessened. She squinted, then shook her head.

Keep it together. Don't lose it. Figure a way out of here.

The knot in the rope was formidable. Every tug and jerk only made it tighter. Her lips pursed as she concentrated, focusing on the door to the entrance of the room while she tried to slip her hands out of the bind.

Time escaped Wendy. The sunlight waned, growing dimmer and making the room darker by the second. From the dying light, she figured it was getting closer to the evening.

A mixture of noises sounded from the hall and living room. The Dukes spoke loudly. Their booming voices carried with ease through the walls and silence. She couldn't understand what all was being said, but assumed the worst.

The doorknob jiggled.

Wendy froze.

The door swung inward.

Jimmy stood at the entrance holding what looked to be a bottled water. He walked inside, leaving the door open behind him. "I brought you another water in case you're thirsty. I know it's hot as hell in here."

Wendy brought her legs closer to her chest while watching his every move.

"You know, trying to escape and all only made things worse." Jimmy tossed the water to the mattress next to her legs. "Roy and I don't want to hurt you, but you're making it hard to keep you in line. If you'd just follow along with what is said, then things would be much better."

The hallway behind Jimmy wouldn't leave Wendy's gaze. It taunted her from the background, beckoning for her to try again.

A plan formed. She constructed it quickly while she had the dumber brother alone and at her mercy. "Could I possibly use the restroom? I've been holding it for some time."

Jimmy shook his head and scratched at the wiry hairs growing around his chin. He peered at the hallway, unsure of how to answer. "Um. Roy said not to let you out of here."

"Not even to use the bathroom?" Wendy shot back. "Does he want me to piss in the corner or something? I don't think he'd want me to soil myself."

His hand moved to the back of his neck and rubbed. "No. We don't want you doing that. Roy told me before he left to check on you, but not do anything else."

The heavy-handed brute had gone, leaving his dimwitted brother behind and in charge. Perfect. She could work with that.

Wendy nodded at the doorway. "Come on. I'll be quick about it. I'd be in your debt."

Jimmy faced Wendy. The thought of her owing him made his eyes widen. "Well, if I take you to the restroom, you have to promise to not try anything else, all right? I mean it."

"You have my word," Wendy answered. "I've learned my lesson. I'll be a good girl."

A shiver came over Jimmy. He struggled to contain his excitement. He gulped, then diverted his gaze as if embarrassed by what she'd said.

Jimmy walked over, grabbed her arm, then helped Wendy to her feet. He escorted her to the hallway.

She limped, favoring her sore ankle that throbbed from the rush of blood. Soft grunts escaped her mouth. She leaned against Jimmy, using him as a crutch.

The stench radiating from his sweaty body made Wendy's skin crawl. Touching the vile man tormented her stomach and soul to the point of puking, but she held it together.

"It's the second door on the right, there." Jimmy held Wendy with one hand, grabbing the back of her arm while the other cradled her waist. He shuffled Wendy along, aiding her through the darkness of the passageway.

"Where did your brother go?" Wendy asked, scanning the low light from the living room. "Do you know when he'll be back, by chance?"

Jimmy adjusted his hand, moving it up a bit more onto her stomach. "Here in a bit."

The feeling of Jimmy touching Wendy in such a way made her cringe. His warm breath blasted the back of her neck. She could hear him breathing heavily, excited by what could be coming. He didn't hide it well.

Wendy stopped at the closed door.

Jimmy squeezed past her, rubbing against her leg, then opening the door to the bathroom. A scant bit of light shone through the small frosted glass window on the far wall, illuminating the space some.

The smell of mold and other unfavorable scents assaulted Wendy's senses. She crinkled her nose and fought to disguise the disgust.

"Here you go. The power isn't working so no light other than what's coming in through that window," Jimmy said, backing out into the hall and out of her way.

Wendy presented her back to him, then wiggled her fingers. "Is there any way you can remove the rope? I can't use the restroom without my hands. I sort of need them."

She glanced over her shoulder.

Jimmy peered at the rope, then flitted his gaze up to Wendy. "No funny business, right?"

"Right."

He hesitated a moment longer, then worked on undoing the knot. The pressure released from around her wrists. The bones ached.

"If you need some more light, I can bring you a flashlight or something." Jimmy held the wadded-up rope in his hands. He craned his neck and peeked over her shoulder to the restroom. "I don't think we have one in there."

"That would be good. Thank you."

Wendy walked inside the bathroom, turned around, then grabbed the edge of the door. She batted her eyes at him, then said, "You know, you're a lot nicer than your brother. I'd much rather spend time with you than him."

Jimmy's face flushed with embarrassment. He looked away and smiled like a smitten kid. "I think you're just saying that, but it's still nice to hear."

"Not at all," Wendy replied. "When I get finished, maybe we can hang out for a bit before Roy gets back. Would you like that?"

The hesitation lingering on his face evaporated. He didn't seem as concerned with his brother as he did with the notion of spending time with the opposite sex and the possibilities.

"I would. That would be… fun," Jimmy answered. "I'll go grab the flashlight." He turned and headed down the passageway toward the living room.

Wendy looked to the dim interior of the smelly bathroom she stood in. The amount of light inside the space varied, growing darker, then lighter with each passing second. The floor felt spongy under her feet as if rotted out. Wendy wondered if she might fall through.

The vanity looked aged and as if it hadn't ever received a cleaning. The shower was closed halfway. She dared not sneak a peek inside for fear of what she might find.

The window didn't look big enough for her to get through, or as if it even opened in the first place. She'd have to check one of the other bedrooms and fast.

Jimmy appeared in the hallway with the flashlight held in his hand. A warm smile resided on his sweaty face. The end of the rope sat on the floor near the doorway. He presented it to her. "You'll need to leave the door open. Also, when you're done, don't flush. I'll need to gather some water from outside and fill the tank. Just leave it be."

Wendy didn't buck the request. "Sure. I understand." She took the flashlight and flashed a smile back.

"I know you didn't eat the food I brought earlier. I can see if we have something else in the cupboard that I can throw together for us if you'd like?" Jimmy couldn't stop smiling at her. She had him hook, line, and sinker.

"That would be great. Thank you."

Jimmy continued smiling, then backed down the hallway.

The warm, inviting greeting on her face vanished. A look of determination took its place. Her plan was set in motion.

Wendy toed the edge of the bathroom door, staring in the direction of the living room and kitchen. Jimmy whistled and hummed from beyond the wall leading to the brothers' small, cluttered kitchen area.

She peered down the hall at the closed door across from the room she was kept in, wondering if it might have a window she could use to slip out. It would be another gamble, but worth the risk.

Jimmy poked his head out from around the corner in the kitchen, looking to the bathroom.

Wendy hung near the edge, waiting for him to leave her sight.

He ducked back into the low light of the kitchen.

She slipped the loop hanging from the bottom of the flashlight over her wrist, moved out of the bathroom, and tiptoed down the hall. The floor creaked some under her weight, but the noise was minimal. She grabbed the doorknob. She looked to the far end of the hall and twisted.

The door opened.

The clatter from the kitchen signaled Jimmy was occupied for the moment.

Wendy pushed the door in and slipped inside the dark space. The small room had a single mattress on the floor and a dresser against the far wall. Light shone through the window on the far wall that had no boards or other coverings on it.

She glanced to the hallway, then shut the door behind her with a gentle touch. Wendy sidestepped the mattress and covers and headed toward the window.

Her ankle gave. She stumbled. Both arms swung, then reached out in front of her. The flashlight thrashed about.

Wendy braced herself against the windowsill, then stood up. She scanned over the window, panting and afraid. A latch resided in the middle. She grabbed the end and twisted.

The window unlocked. She shoved it up. It resisted.

Wendy pushed harder, forcing it up within the grooves.

"Damn it to hell." A loud thud hammered the wall from the hallway. Jimmy huffed and growled from the other side of the door.

The fear of being caught kept her going. She climbed up and through the open window. Pain plagued both wrists. Her jaw clenched as the upper portion of her dangled from the other side.

The door to the bedroom burst open.

Wendy peered over her shoulder to the hallway.

Jimmy rushed inside like a raging bull, shouting at the top of his lungs. "You played me, bitch." He grabbed her ankles, then moved up to her waist. His fingers curled over the tops of her jeans and pulled back.

Her forward movement ceased. She braced her hands on either side of the wall and pushed forward, not wanting to be dragged back into hell.

The grumbling of an engine sounded from the front of the house. Her heart jumped into her throat. The front end of the pickup materialized past the corner of the home, then stopped.

Jimmy refused to release her pants and pulled with as much strength as his meager arms would muster. The top of her jeans dipped below her waist, revealing her panty line.

Wendy pushed with all her might, then pitched forward. Her legs flew upward, knocking Jimmy back and off-balance. His hands released her. She dropped to the tall weeds growing around the base of the house, landing on the side of her neck and shoulder, then over onto her back.

Her gaze trained to the open window.

Jimmy shouted loudly from the bedroom, cussing.

Roy answered in a raised voice, then poked his head out. His large hand reached for her shirt.

Wendy stayed low and got to her feet. She stumbled away from the house, stood, then presented Roy with the middle finger. "Eat crap, hillbillies."

A scowl formed on his face. His hand balled into a fist. He slammed it against the exterior of the home, then pointed at her. "You're as good as dead. We're going to make sure of that." The brute dipped back into the house.

Wendy ran backward, watching the window a moment longer. She faced forward, then headed for the dense woods that surrounded the periphery of the property, hoping to vanish within the thick brush and put as much distance between her and the Dukes as possible.

CHAPTER SEVENTEEN

ALEX

The Bronco made it to the outskirts of Houston, then sputtered along.

The SUV lurched across the street, grumbling and spitting exhaust from the muffler. Alex slapped his hand against the steering wheel, infused with anger. His foot pinned the gas pedal to the floor, hoping to eke out some more miles from the waning vehicle.

"For Christ's sake, hang in there a bit longer," Alex said, thrusting his body forward as if that would help.

"I think we've gotten everything out of it," Ava said, unlatching her seatbelt. "We're wasting time. Just stop and we'll go at it on foot the rest of the way."

Alex pulled to the side of the street.

The knocking in the engine compartment grew louder before dying. The SUV rolled a bit farther and came to stop. The back end stuck out in the road.

"It did better than I thought it would," Alex said, shifting into gear.

"It at least saved our legs and energy." Ava reached for the floor and retrieved her purse. "This Texas heat can suck you dry in a blink if you're not careful. Staying hydrated is key. There should be some sort of store close by where we can get some water."

Sweat dripped from both of their brows. The cab felt like an oven. Even with the sun low in the sky, the heat refused to leave them be.

Alex released the steering wheel, then ran the sleeve of his uniform across his forehead. His face scrunched as he stared at the wet spot on the fabric. "Yeah. I imagine there is."

Ava opened her door and exited the cab. She stood next to the SUV and surveyed the street and surrounding buildings. Her purse dangled from her balled fist as she turned away from the cab. "I think I see a 7–Eleven down the street."

"All right." Alex lifted his leg some and grabbed the Ruger. He tucked it into the pocket of the trousers, then pulled the uniform shirt out.

"Excuse me, miss." A man approached the passenger side of the Bronco. The cowboy hat he wore was low on his head.

Ava spun around and faced him.

Alex opened his door and got out. He unbuttoned the prison guard's uniform top and took it off. The musty, damp shirt pressed to his face under the bill of his hat. He wiped away the sweat, then tossed the garment to the driver's seat.

The cowboy and Ava spoke on the other side. She pointed to the interior of the SUV. He peered inside the vehicle, then over to Alex.

"Hey there, friend." He waved, then flashed a smile. His voice had a thick country twang to it. "Do you—"

Alex looked away, shut the door, then walked to the front of the Bronco. He licked his lips, then scanned the nearby businesses, parking lots, and roads for another working vehicle.

Ava conversed a bit longer with the man, then advanced to the front of the SUV. Cowboy followed.

"What are you looking at?" she asked, placing the purse over her shoulder. She adjusted the straps, then pulled any loose strands over both ears.

"Just looking around is all," Alex answered, surveying the area around them.

The cowboy moved past Ava, then waved his hand at Alex again. "Hi, again. Um, you wouldn't happen to have a working phone, would you? Mine doesn't seem to be working. Hasn't for the last few hours."

"I already told him that our phones are dead, but I guess he doesn't believe me," Ava said, folding her arms across her chest.

"It's nothing personal, ma'am," the cowboy replied. "I'm just wanting to be sure is all. I've got a business transaction that's hanging in the balance and need a phone to seal the deal."

"Like the lady said, friend, all phones are dead. We can't help you." Alex adjusted the cap on his head, then glanced over at the cowboy. His face was void of any pleasantries. "Now, if you'll excuse me."

The cowboy held up both hands. "Yeah. Sorry to have bothered you both. Thanks anyway." He grabbed the front of his cowboy hat and tilted his head at Ava. "Ma'am."

He ventured up the grass to the parking lot in front of them.

Ava walked after Alex who marched down the street. She got alongside him, then looked over her shoulder at the cowboy. "I guess he thought I didn't know how to use a phone."

"Maybe." Alex glanced to the sky, then the sun that dipped below the horizon. The intense rays lessened with each step.

"I hope you don't mind me continuing to tag along with you," Ava said, glancing at Alex. "I appreciated you giving me a ride as far as you did. I'm not wanting to be a burden or anything. You seem like you're rather… occupied. On edge."

Alex had the weight of the world resting on his shoulders. No doubt about that. It kept him on edge. He didn't handle stress too well and it showed whether he wanted it to or not. Alcohol seemed to help manage things, but he hadn't had any in some time. Given the current state of the city, and the continual attempts on his life while in prison over the past few months, he struggled not to be an ass.

"No, I don't mind. I've got a lot on my plate is all."

Ava nodded. "I can understand that. I'm much the same way at the moment."

The 7–Eleven came into view. A row of cars sat parked in front of the building. People walked in and out of the convenience store. Those who surfaced from the dark depths of the building went about their way with armfuls of water and other items.

"Oh, crap." Ava opened her purse, then glanced inside. "I don't have any cash on me to pay for anything. All I've got is my credit cards. I doubt those will be useful."

Alex pointed at the ragtag bunch of young people who skulked out of the building, arms crammed with an abundance of snacks and drinks. "I don't think folks are paying for anything from the looks of it."

The teenagers looked about, then darted toward the far side of the building, dropping food and other items along the way. They vanished around the bend in a hurry.

"I wonder how they got inside the store?" Ava closed her purse and held it tight against her body. "You would think they'd lock up with the power being down and all. I mean, that's what I would do to minimize any theft like that."

Alex shrugged. "They might have locked it up. Who knows? People could've broken into the building. They obviously don't seem too concerned with that at the moment. It's not like anyone is going to call the police or anything."

Ava peered down both stretches of road. "Yeah. I'm pretty sure the police are stretched thin at the moment."

"You can wait or come with, but I'm going to grab some water and whatnot before we get back on the move. Your decision." Alex advanced up the drive, gaze fixed on the gaping sliding glass door.

Ava trailed behind him, following a few paces back.

His hand wormed inside his trousers' pocket. He grabbed the grip of the Ruger revolver and skimmed over the cars stationed at the pumps.

A portion of the vehicle's occupants had the doors open. Raised, irritated voices bickered inside. Others looked lost, sitting in the seats with the backs of their heads resting against the headrest.

A number of figures loomed from inside the store. The faint hint of light flashed behind the windows. A loud crashing sounded from the interior.

"You sure about wanting to go in there?" Ava asked as they walked between a red sedan and black Jeep parked in front of an ice machine.

"I'm sure that I'm thirsty and need something to drink," Alex answered, moving past the yellow-painted concrete pylon. "Like I said, if you want to wait out here, you're more than welcome to. No one is forcing you inside."

"That's all right. I think it's better to stick close to you."

Alex craned his neck and peered at the opening. Voices loomed from the interior. A crashing noise sounded.

He remained calm but vigilant. His hold on the Ruger tightened, fingers squeezing the grip and pressing to the side of the trigger guard. He had no intention of using it unless necessary.

Ava flanked him, peeking over his shoulder, then moving forward with him. Her head was on a swivel, glancing to the parking lot and the sidewalk behind them, then straight ahead.

Two teen boys emerged from the building with arms overflowing with junk food and a case of beer in each of their hands. Alex paused, then tugged on the Ruger, but stopped before fully pulling it out. They gave Alex and Ava a quick look, then bolted in the opposite direction.

Alex sighed, shook his head, and approached the entrance. He walked through the doorway. Glass crunched under his shoes. The sliding door leaned toward the interior of the building and sat off its tracks.

People rummaged through the shelves, scooping up whatever they could carry. Beams of light traced along the far walls and coolers on the back side of the store. The few windows toward the front of the store facing the parking lot allowed the dying light to illuminate the interior some.

The bedlam didn't surprise him much. It seemed that things hadn't gotten any better in the world since he'd been incarcerated. The crap economy, lack of work, and racial divide among the populous kept the fires stoked and primed. The blackout, cyberattack, or whatever happened, had sent some citizens over the edge.

"This looks like a mess and a half," Alex said. "Watch yourself. We'll be in and out fast."

"I'm going to see if I can find a flashlight," Ava replied, moving past him. "We might need it since we're on foot now and the sun's going down." She searched the front counter and end caps for any flashlights.

Alex made his way to the coolers in the back. He glanced out of the window to the parking lot, spotting more people heading toward the store from the street.

The floor had an array of goods carpeting the surface. His boots kicked through the packages, knocking them out of the way.

A rumble sounded from his stomach. He pulled his hand from the trousers' pocket and palmed his gut. His blood sugar dipped some, causing a headache to flare. The day's strenuous events, and the angry sun, had zapped a good portion of his strength.

Alex snagged a handful of protein bars on the way. He stowed two of the snacks in the empty front pocket of the trousers and devoured the other.

The alcohol in the cooler made his mouth water. He'd missed the taste of the brew. His tongue traced the outer rim of his lips as his eyes soaked in the glass bottles and beer cans from the other side of the cooler.

He lingered for a moment, shook the restless thought away, then moved on to the water. Heat and alcohol didn't mix well with Alex. He needed to stay alert and on his toes.

The tumult inside the store ramped up. A heated conflict broke out in one of the aisles close to Alex. He turned and watched the men with his hand resting on the handle attached to the cooler door.

A small group of men bickered back and forth, raising their voices and arguing about who had dibs on what items. Swear words and racial slurs erupted between the different ethnic men.

They shoved each other around. Arms tangled and fingers bunched into shirts. Bodies collapsed into the shelving. The discord reached a fever pitch and drew closer to him. It was time to leave.

Alex flung open the glass cooler door, pulled two bottles of water from the slanted shelves, and retraced his steps back the way he'd come. He kept his gaze trained at the far wall and not the brawl.

One of the dark-skinned men took a right cross on the chin, then a knee to the gut from the large, bearded bruiser he tangled with. His dreadlocks whipped through the air. His hands twirled. He fell backward and slammed into Alex, pinning him to the glass front of the coolers.

The water bottles dropped from Alex's hand, hit his boots, then rolled away. He grabbed Dreadlocks by the scruff of his red shirt, then shoved him forward.

The angry, dark-skinned man fell to his knees. His arm rested on one of the shelves.

Alex dipped his chin and hunted for the water bottles, taking his eyes from the stocky man. He peered to the front entrance and spotted Ava heading for the missing door.

Dreadlocks stood in a huff, turned around, and faced Alex. He held a switchblade in his hand. His fingers squeezed the black handle tightly. He wiped the trails of blood leaking from his large nostrils with the side of his hand. "Do you want to die today, white boy?"

"You don't want any part of this," Alex replied, taking a step back. "I can promise you that. I'm going to grab my water and bounce so you dipshits can continue pounding the crap out of each other."

The insult did little to temper the volatile situation. Dreadlocks gritted his teeth and snarled. His face contorted in rage, forehead furrowed and brows slanted inward.

Alex reached for the Ruger in his pocket. His fingers caught the side of the fabric, keeping his hand from going in.

Dreadlocks rushed headlong at him. His shoes kicked the items on the ground away. He thrust the blade at Alex's stomach.

The tip of the blade reached his white undershirt. Alex grabbed Dreadlocks's forearm before it could penetrate. He held his forearm with a firm grip, trying to overpower the strong-willed man.

Spit leaked from between the gaps in Dreadlocks's teeth. He lowered his shoulder and pushed forward. His free hand slapped the end of the blade, driving it forward a bit more.

Alex moved back, keeping distance from him. He hammered Dreadlocks's spine with his fist.

The thug buckled under each strike. His body caved and he lowered the blade.

Alex stopped, then rammed his knee into Dreadlocks's face, sending him upright.

Dreadlocks dropped the knife. He stumbled backward, then shook his head.

The other men who were close by continued their fight, duking it out and wrecking the place.

Alex reached inside his pocket, pulled the Ruger, then trained it at Dreadlocks. He fired a single shot at the floor near his feet. The bullet pinged off the ground. The report echoed loudly inside the building.

The clamor inside the store ceased. The discord ebbed.

The dark-skinned man paused, then lifted his hands skyward. His brows raised, eyes enlarged at the sight of the revolver.

"Now, like I said a moment ago, you don't want any of this." Alex glanced to the floor, spotting the two water bottles. "I'm going to grab my water and leave. You and the rest of the dumbasses over there can continue wrecking the place and pounding each other senseless if you want, but you're going to leave me be. Am I understood?"

Dreadlocks nodded with a scowl. One of his cohorts standing six feet or so from him turned and noticed the Ruger. He stopped fighting and eyed Alex. The other men did the same.

The skirmish ceased. All eyes looked to Alex and the revolver he wielded. Their chests heaved and arms flexed. Each man panted.

Alex cradled the water bottles and backtracked down the far aisle toward the missing front door. Dreadlocks lowered his arms and watched Alex like a hawk, as did the other men. What few people not involved in the uproar cowered at the front, stooped down with arms covering their heads.

A low rap sounded from the window next to Alex.

He looked to the glass and past the free Slurpee window cling.

Ava stood on the other side, waving him on. She flashed two red and blue flashlights in her hands.

Alex lowered the Ruger, then stepped through the entrance. He tilted his head toward the corner of the store and advanced in that direction. "Come on. Let's get out of here while we can."

The Ruger stayed at his side.

Ava bolted down the sidewalk and past the entrance.

Dreadlocks rushed through the convenience store, heading for the busted door. His cohorts followed his lead and charged up the aisles.

Alex and Ava made a wide arch around the blind corner and sprinted for the other building behind the 7–Eleven. He wanted to put as much distance as possible between them and the people hot on their tails.

CHAPTER EIGHTEEN

WENDY

On the run.

Her feet pounded the earth, shoes stomped through the growing weeds and other vegetation. The branches from the trees snagged the fabric of her shirt, tearing tiny holes in the top.

Wendy kept moving, pushing forward through the wooded area. She'd gained some distance from the Dukes, but wanted to widen the gap. The shouting and other noise made from the backwood's rejects trailed off to nothing. Still, she kept her guard up and moved as if they were inches away.

Each branch breaking under her feet made her heart skip a beat. She jerked her chin over her shoulder, searching for any movement within the low light, but spotted none.

The flashlight swung wildly from her wrist. The side of the plastic exterior slammed the tree trunks and bushes she stumbled past.

It hurt to breathe. Her lungs stung with each hard step. The sore ankle caused her to limp some, but she kept going hard, fighting through the discomfort.

Wendy struggled to get her bearings. Her mind drowned in fright and panic, clouding her thoughts and hindering her judgements. Getting back to her grandparent's place was her mission, but with night coming, and the ever-present danger from the Dukes stalking her, that would prove challenging.

The pain in her lungs flourished. A cramp attacked her side. The muscles in both legs burned hot from the stress.

She palmed her side, stopped, then leaned against a tree. Her forearm rested on the rigid surface of the bark. She panted hard—mouth open. Her head dangled toward the dirt as she sought to refill her lungs.

Wendy turned and looked in the direction she'd come from. The sunlight retreated faster, making the interior of the woods darker and harder for her to detect any motion.

The plastic strap around her wrist irritated the rope burn she'd sustained. A layer of sweat coated her body from head to toe. The salt seeped into the damaged flesh and burned. It added to the other trouble spots on her body that flared at various times, tormenting Wendy.

She couldn't keep up the feverish pace she had for too much longer. The lack of water and food drained her to dangerous levels. The high heat and injuries added to the dangers plaguing her. Rest was what she needed, and copious amounts of water, whether she liked it or not.

Wendy stood and stayed close to the tree trunk. She scanned over the area, hunting for any safe space she could take refuge in.

The exhaustion she battled made her vision blurry. Both sockets stung and ached. She shut her lids, squinted hard, then opened them wide. The haze remained.

The tips of her fingers pressed into each socket and rubbed. Anger and frustration built inside her gut. She lowered her hand and blinked, finding a brief moment of pure clarity.

Wendy studied the trees and hills ahead of her. She glanced to either side, finding more of the same. Indecision racked her, making it difficult to commit to a course of action.

A rustling noise sounded at her back. Branches snapped in the eerie silence.

She gasped, then wrenched her head toward the noise.

The Dukes had found her. She searched the woods, but couldn't see the two brothers lurking like the vile, evil creatures they were. It could've been an animal milling about, but she didn't want to take the chance.

Wendy pushed away from the tree and got back on the move. The soreness in her legs increased, a pain she endured and welcomed compared to the ill fate that waited for her if the Dukes managed to catch up.

The snapping branches and rustling at her back faded in and out. She used the long, skeletal limbs of the trees to hold her upright. She turned and checked her flanks, hoping to not see the devious men advancing on her.

The small hill had rocks and trees littering its side. It appeared rather steep from what Wendy could tell. She hit the base and climbed. The soles of her boots slipped on the loose dirt. Both knees dug into the earth. Sharp twigs stabbed her sensitive palms. Wendy cringed and lifted her hand, but kept pushing onward.

The flashlight bounced off the varying-sized stones and other vegetation blanketing the ground. Her fatigued legs gave, reducing any forward momentum.

Wendy grabbed low-lying branches or rocks and used them to help her up the hill. She reached the top, continued on, then slid down the other side on her butt with one leg stretched out and the other bent.

Loose rocks and topsoil gave under her.

The rough terrain poked at her backside.

She hit flat ground and stood. Her tongue rimmed the outer edge of her chapped lips. Sweat poured from every portion of her body. She slapped her palms on her jeans, then marched on.

The canopy overhead made the interior of the woods that much dimmer. She checked the hill and noticed what looked to be a light shining from the other side.

Oh crap.

A slight slope dipped down, catching her by surprise. Her hands lifted and waved.

Wendy fell forward and crashed into a shallow stream. The front of her body splashed into the water, soaking her shirt and pants. The rocks at the bottom hit her forearms and knees. Water dripped from her face and hair.

She clenched her jaw, pushed up, then stood. Wendy remembered a stream that ran through the back portion of her grandparents' property. It was hard to say if this would lead her home or not, but it was the best-laid plan she had.

A whistle sounded from the far side of the hill.

Wendy looked to the top and ducked.

A figure emerged, stood, then surveyed the grounds below. It appeared to be Jimmy from his gaunt frame. What little sun was left shone through the trees at his back. He scanned the area, turning his head from right to left. Roy was nowhere to be seen and that worried her.

Jimmy looked back over his shoulder to the other side of the hill and shouted, but she struggled to make out what he said.

Wendy remained low, then tromped through the water, heading in the direction of what she thought to be her grandparents. Water splashed outward from her boots. The beating of her overworked heart punished her chest.

Another loud whistle sounded, followed by shouting that increased in volume. The frantic, excited voice grew louder. Wendy glanced at Jimmy and discovered him pointing in her direction.

He raced down the hill in a mad dash. His arms stuck out to either side to keep him from falling. He pitched forward, then tumbled the rest of the way, end over end, before vanishing to the base of the hill.

Wendy tromped through the water while glancing back. The trees and bushes that lined the bank concealed her. She heard Jimmy yelling and calling his position to Roy who had yet to reveal himself.

The Dukes no doubt had an advantage over Wendy seeing as the land resided in their backyard and she was unfamiliar with the territory. At some point, she figured she'd have to engage the two oafs to keep them from tracking her home, but she wasn't sure where or how that would play out.

The land running on both sides of the creek gradually grew higher, making it harder for her to scale the exposed dirt face. She darted across the creek bed and climbed her way up and out to the other side.

Her wet fingers clawed at the dirt, making it muddier. The tips of the boots cut into the earth, giving Wendy a foothold. She hauled her spent frame to the top and sat stagnant for a second on her hands and knees.

Wendy studied the area around her. A dense thicket surrounding a large tree showed promise for hiding her.

The splashing of water drifted from the creek. Wendy kept low and scurried to the safety of the thicket.

An opening within the dense brush presented itself. Branches filled with green-colored leaves protruded into the center of the passage, leaving a scant bit of room to maneuver.

"Did you find her, yet?" Roy asked.

"Not yet, but soon will," Jimmy replied.

The splashing stopped.

Silence took hold.

Wendy glanced back to the edge of the short cliff she'd climbed, then faced forward. She lowered to the ground and army crawled through the opening.

The branches poked her shoulders and back, but the rustling of the bushes was minimal.

The splashing resumed and headed her way.

Wendy emerged on the other side in a small clearing between the base of the tree and dense vegetation. It looked like it would fit her, but barely. The noise from Jimmy closing in made her pant. She turned over and sat up, then pulled her legs in. Her hands pressed against the dirt. She shimmied to the far side of the tree, then stopped.

The noisy brother clomped around the area in front of the wall of bushes she hid in. Bits and pieces of the tattered rags he wore bled through the foliage. He milled about, hunting for her.

She ceased any movement and faced forward. Her back rubbed on the bark. Wendy held her breath, trying to reduce any and all markers that could give her away.

Jimmy advanced on the outer edge of the thicket, then paused.

Wendy cringed, fearful he had found her. Her eyes pinched shut. She remained as silent as she could. The rapid thumping of her heart sounded louder in her head.

The bushes rustled.

Jimmy stalked the outside perimeter for a few moments, then moved on without giving the cluster of vegetation a second look.

Wendy breathed a sigh of relief. The taut muscles in her shoulders and back relaxed some. She rested the back of her head on the tree, then peered to the darkening sky overhead.

The sun would be gone for good and night would be upon her fast. It would be more dangerous traveling in the dark as she wouldn't be able to see as well and navigate the woods back to her grandparents' place. The blanket of darkness would help conceal her, though. Either way, she had to hash it out and decide what her next move was going to be. Right or wrong, she had to do something.

CHAPTER NINETEEN

ALEX

The dark of night.

Ava folded her arms across her chest and squeezed. She peered over her shoulder to the desolate city street, watching and listening for Dreadlocks, or any other figures shuffling in the murk. Her hands trembled.

Alex polished off the remainder of the water in the bottom of the bottle. His hand crushed the sides, then discarded it to the pavement. It bounced over the ground. He glanced at Ava every so often, wondering what all was running through her head. "I think we lost them."

She nodded but kept her guarded posture in place. Her folded arms squeezed a hair tighter. Ava adjusted the straps of the purse on her shoulder, then gave him a half smile. "Yeah. Seems that way. I just don't handle conflicts like that too well. It messes with my anxiety and twists my nerves something awful."

"That's understandable," Alex replied, removing the hat from his head and running his fingers through the damp hair. "I don't know too many people, if any, who wouldn't be a bit shaken by what happened back in the convenience store, or just everything in general." He put the hat back on and pulled the bill down.

Ava peered at Alex. "You seem rather unscathed by it."

Alex shrugged. "I've been through many heated encounters over my life. What happened back there isn't anything new to me. I don't look for trouble, but I'm not opposed to defending myself if need be. You're either a wolf or a sheep in this world. The choice is always yours in how you face things."

"I don't think it's always as clear cut or black and white," Ava shot back. "Sometimes, people go through things that make it harder for them to deal with such situations, or they're just not brave enough, in the end, to be a wolf, as you put it."

"True, but I think every person, despite what they've been through, has the power to rise to the occasion if it calls for it." Alex looked around to the powerless buildings and street lights that surrounded them. "The world we live in is filled with horrors, and it only seems to be getting worse. Riots. Wars. Racial division that every person in a seat of power seems to stoke in some fashion or another. Hell, you even have militant factions taking over portions of cities across the country. Those permanent autonomous zones are crazy. I never thought in a million years anything like that would ever happen on American soil, but here we are."

She unfolded her arms and pointed at his trousers. "It's also easy to talk like that when you're carrying a gun."

Alex patted his pocket where the Ruger resided. "In the right hands, this weapon can save more lives than it takes. I'll always believe that."

"If you say so." Ava rolled her eyes, then looked away. "I've had some less than desirable encounters with firearms and I'm not a fan. Although I do agree they have their place, it sets me on edge when I see people carrying one."

"Well, you won't have to worry about me," Alex replied. "I've been around guns for most my life. They don't bother me in the least, and I more than know how to use them safely."

Ava looked to the buildings on either side of the street, then to the sky. It seemed as though she had finished their discussion.

Alex let it be. He'd gotten a bit carried away, much to his surprise, seeing as he wanted to keep any chatter to a minimum and all.

"It's so quiet and creepy," Ava said, pausing, then making a wide arch around the four-door luxury sedan blocking their way. "I'm so used to seeing the city lit up at night from street lamps, pylon signs, and everything else. It's rather eerie."

"That it is. I imagine this is a first for everyone." Alex walked around the passenger side of the red BMW parked in the middle of the street. He peered through the tinted passenger windows and kept moving. "I wonder how widespread it is, or if Houston isn't the only city in the dark, no pun intended."

Ava skirted the front of the bumper, meeting back up with Alex. "No clue. I just hope this is a freak incident that'll be fixed soon. I've seen plenty of movies and read tons of books that have this exact scenario. When something like this happens, people can lose their minds fast and start causing more problems than there already is."

"It'll be all right." Alex dismissed the worried woman's words with a flick of his hand. He was more concerned with setting things right with Mr. Vargas than with any looters or thugs they'd cross in the city. "Just got to keep a level head and be aware of your surroundings. If you do that, the rest will be gravy."

"So says the man carrying the piece," Ava shot back in a snide tone.

"If you want to carry it, you're more than welcome to do so." He already knew her answer.

Ava gave him the side-eye and continued on.

They hit the end of the street and stepped up onto the sidewalk. Alex craned his neck and peered around the bend as they marched down the deserted walkway.

A Houston police cruiser sat among a cluster of cars that appeared to have been in a large fender bender in the street. Each vehicle touched another in some form or fashion.

Alex gulped, then searched the immediate area for any other police or shadowy figures. His head turned and craned as he stopped and checked behind them.

"What's wrong?" Ava asked, stopping and looking at him.

"Nothing. Just keeping an eye out for any movement," Alex answered. "That's all."

Ava scanned over the wreckage, then back to him. She nodded and continued on.

Alex checked behind them one last time, then caught up with her. He didn't see any flashing lights or other signs the authorities were in the area. The last thing he needed was a run-in with a cop.

"You know, even though we're in Houston, it feels like it's taking forever to make much headway on foot." Ava ran the back of her hand across her forehead. "I loathe walking, especially when it's mega hot and humid. Even with the sun gone, it still feels just as hot out here. I'm running on fumes."

Alex dug his hand into the pocket of his trousers that had the protein bars. "Did you want one of these? You probably need some food. Your blood sugar is more than likely zapped."

Ava cringed at the notion. "Thanks, but I don't do protein bars. They mess my stomach up something bad. The last thing I need is to eat one and it screw with my stomach. That would not be good at all."

"No problem. Thought I'd offer it up." Alex studied the buildings around them, noticing they weren't too much farther from his house. His parents had stepped in and decided to maintain the home while he did his stint in prison—a fortunate turn of events that he was thankful for. Alex paused near the intersection, then pointed at the street heading west. "My place is up this way. How much farther is your cousins' home?"

"To be honest, I'm a bit turned around at the moment, so I'm not sure." Ava stared down the street, then to the buildings. "I'll get my bearings soon. Are we close to highway 45 by chance?"

Alex pointed in the direction she'd looked. "Yeah. It's still a ways down the road, there, but you're heading in the right direction at least."

Ava pulled a small flashlight from her purse, then thumbed the button. No light emitted from the lens. She slapped the device against her palm in frustration. "Why isn't this damn thing turning on?"

"Did you get that from the convenience store?"

"Yeah. It looks cheap and feels the same way. Guess that's why they were selling them so cheap." Ava held the flashlight close to her face.

"That five-finger discount is always cheap," Alex smirked. "It might need batteries. They normally don't stock batteries inside of them."

Ava sighed, then smacked her forehead with the heel of her hand. "Boy. That goes to show where my head is at. I didn't think to check if it needed batteries. I guess I assumed they should already be in there or something. Man." She stowed the light back in the purse and mumbled under her breath.

Alex peered at the dark road ahead, spotting two black-clad figures milling about on the other side of the street. He glanced back to Ava who folded her arms over her chest again and looked around aimlessly.

"You got me this far, so I do appreciate your help," Ava said turning to face him. She extended her hand. "Thank you again."

"You're welcome." Alex took her palm and shook it. She pulled back and stared ahead of them. He lowered his head, then peered at the unsettled expression on her face. "You know, if you want, you can come back to my place for a minute to rest while I get changed out of these clothes. We can then see about getting you to where you need to be."

Ava glanced at him with a raised brow, as if he'd said something wrong, or devious.

Alex lifted his hands. "Oh, no. Nothing like that. Just being friendly is all."

"Thanks for the offer, but I'll be good. I need to keep going seeing as I'm on foot." Ava took a step toward the curb, paused, then turned around. "Take care and thanks again."

"You too." Alex gripped the bill of his hat and bowed.

Ava stepped from the curb to the street, then marched to the other side.

Alex watched her for a minute, then jogged to the other side of the road. He peered in the direction of the black-clad figures and found that they had vanished. He jumped up onto the sidewalk and looked over the area, but spotted no signs of them. A good thing, he hoped.

He continued down the walkway and kept close to the brick building next to him. His hands plunged into the pockets of his trousers while his mind ran wild. Everything from what went down at the prison, to Mr. Vargas and the Aaryn Brotherhood, to Wendy and his parents. It all swarmed him in a blink without having something, or someone to distract him.

A dog barked in the distance.

Alex shook his head, blinked away the thoughts, and kept trudging onward.

A gunshot echoed in the silence of the big city. It sounded close. At his back, even, and from the way he'd come.

Ava.

He stopped, then spun around, facing the long walkway. The shadowy figures he'd spotted earlier sent him rushing toward the intersection. He feared the black-clad individuals had stalked Ava and waited for their moment to strike.

Alex hit the blind corner and peered around the bend to the street and sidewalk on the far side. He squinted and surveyed the murk for Ava, or any other movement, but didn't spot any.

A loud scream met his ears that went cold seconds later. It sounded feminine from what little bit he heard.

Damn it.

Alex bolted from the side of the building and darted across the street. His shoes pounded pavement. He panted hard, running at a gallop past the few cars stuck in the road.

A frightful scream, then shout, lured Alex to the sidewalk. It sounded female. His body threaded the narrow opening between two cars parked next to the curb. He leapt to the walkway and charged full steam ahead.

The discord and shouting acted as a beacon. Multiple voices blended with the feminine one. He counted two more men close by.

Alex studied the buildings he ran past while trying to remove the revolver from his pants. He struggled to free the five shooter that was caught on the fabric of the inner pocket.

Another report popped off. A muzzle flash lit up an alley ahead of him.

The shouting trailed off.

Alex worried that Ava had been shot and killed. He prayed that wasn't the case, but couldn't shake the unsettling thought.

The revolver cleared the pocket of his trousers. He brought the piece to bear. Both hands palmed the grip with a firm hold as he slowed and closed in on the entrance to the alleyway.

The hammering of his heart ramped up as he inched toward the corner of the building. A lump formed in his throat. Copious amounts of sweat poured from his body, stinging his eyes and blurring his vision.

Alex swung out from the sidewalk and entered the passageway. At the far end, multiple figures turned his way. He pointed the barrel of the Ruger skyward, then discharged a single round.

"Get away from her you bastards."

The men scattered like rats, fleeing in the opposite direction.

Alex rushed to her aid, scanning the trash cans and other dark splotches within the corridor. The fear of finding her dead body lingered in his brain.

A muttered groan called from the blackness against the building. A figure stirred within the mounded trash bags and tipped over waste containers.

Alex trained the revolver at the pitiful noise. He focused on the movement and advanced with caution. "Ava, is that you?"

The outline of a person emerged from the waste.

His finger pressed the trigger guard a hair tighter. He looked over the immediate area, then at the street for any individuals aiming to get the drop on him.

A soft, feminine voice spoke as she sat up from the city's filth. "Jesus."

Alex lowered the Ruger to his side, then moved toward her. He bent down, then took a knee. He examined the woman's face, finding it to be Ava. "Are you all right? I heard a gunshot and came running back."

Ava nodded, then flicked her hands. "Yeah. I'm—ouch." Her face scrunched, hand palmed the outside of her right arm. She dipped her chin, then turned her head. "Bastards clipped my arm with the pistol they had. I guess they figured I wouldn't fight back. I hate guns, but I'm more afraid of what they would've done to me if I hadn't kicked and punched at them."

"Looks like you handled it well." Alex pocketed the revolver, then stood. "They hauled ass down the alley. You sent them running with their tails between their legs it seems."

"Not after they decked me in the face for hitting them with my purse." Ava glanced at the concrete. "Their gun is somewhere around here. It clicked empty. So is my purse. I knocked the gun from the thug's hand, then he ripped my purse from my grasp. The gun sent them running away like the rat bastards they are."

Alex extended his hand. "I'm just glad you're all right. It seems the predators are coming out after dark."

Ava removed her hand from the side of her arm, then took his palm. "Looks like it. Bastards."

He took a step back and pulled.

She stood and hunched over. Her hand pressed against her stomach. "The other one decked me in the gut. Hurt like a son of a bitch. Pinche pendejo."

Alex hunted for her purse in the dark near the waste she fell in, squinting. He shoved the black trash bags and waste containers out of the way before finding it. "Found your purse. I'm not seeing the gun anywhere, though."

Ava removed her hand from her gut, straightened her back, then extended her arm to Alex. "Thanks."

"Here." Alex handed the purse to her.

"It's going to be a long damn night it seems." Ava grabbed the straps, then placed them over her shoulder. "I didn't even make it that far before someone tried to spoil my plans. I can't imagine how the rest of my trek is going to pan out."

Alex couldn't, in good conscience, allow her to continue on by herself. She handled the thugs, but the encounter proved dangerous just the same and could've gone deadly. "I want you to come back to my place so we can look that wound over and get it cleaned up. After that, I'll help you the rest of the way."

Ava shook her head. "I can't do that to you. You've already helped me out today and have done far more than what was needed. I'll be fine. Really."

"I'm not taking no for an answer," Alex replied, stern and unyielding. She stared at the ground, avoiding eye contact at first. "At least let me tend to that wound. I promise I'm not going to do anything sketchy. I'm not that kind of guy."

"If I thought you were a creepy guy, I wouldn't have hitched a ride with you in the first place." Ava glanced his way, the shadows hiding a portion of her bruised face. "You're not going to stop, are you?"

Alex shook his head. "Nope. It's part of my charm. I can be stubborn at times."

"Like a bull, I'd say," Ava shot back.

“It’s for a good reason.” Alex turned and faced the entrance to the alley. “Come on. Let’s get out of here.”

CHAPTER TWENTY

ALEX

Ava caved and followed Alex.

They left the passageway and navigated the dark streets of Houston back to his house. She didn't move too fast, walking with a slight limp and overall looking worse for wear. Subtle grunts seeped from her pursed lips.

Alex kept a keen eye out for any other threats lurking in the shadows. They arrived at his house about forty minutes later. He scoped out the street for any police or other figures lurking around his property, then helped Ava up the driveway to the back of the dark home. He left her side, approached the back door, and retrieved a key from under a planter next to the small stack of stairs. "Still hanging in there with me?"

She had grown silent for the last fifteen minutes or so before they arrived. He helped her along for the last little bit by shouldering her weight.

"Yeah. Doing great here." Ava glanced at her arm, then palmed the gunshot wound.

"Almost inside." Alex skirted past her up the steps to the door.

Ava gave a thumbs up.

Alex peered through the window, feeling strange to be back at his place after spending months in prison. A wave of sadness and guilt pressed on his shoulders like a weighted blanket as he thought of his daughter and wife. He skimmed over the kitchen for a moment while inserting the key into the deadbolt, looking for any threats scurrying about in his residence.

Mr. Vargas and his goons could spring their heads at any time. No. That was foolish thinking. They didn't know he'd escaped from prison yet, so he had that on his side.

"Is there a problem?" Ava asked.

"Um, no." He glanced down the steps, finding Ava staring at him. "Why do you ask?"

"The way you stopped and stared made me think you were watching for someone. Perhaps for your wife, or a girlfriend even," Ava answered, nodding at the door. "The last thing I need, or want, is to get involved in a domestic dispute."

"You don't have to worry about that." Alex twisted the key, unlocking the door.

Ava stood, then climbed the two steps.

Alex pushed the door open. The hinges squeaked. He listened for any footfalls or other subtle movements within the murk of the house while passing through the doorway.

The tepid air choked him. A musty scent assaulted his senses. His nose crinkled from the environment of the house being locked up and not inhabited since his incarceration.

He owed his parents big time for maintaining the mortgage and not letting it revert to the bank.

"Man, and I thought it was hot and muggy outside," Ava said at his back. "It's like a sauna in here."

Alex scanned over the murky kitchen. Everything was in its place. Just as he'd left it. The only difference he noticed was the blinds had been drawn. His folks must've done it.

He stepped to the side, and out of Ava's way. She advanced inside as he shut the door behind her, then locked it. He sat the key on the counter near the entrance, then opened one of the small cabinet drawers.

"I think I've got a flashlight in this drawer." He rummaged through the contents, sifting through the cluttered space. "Got it."

His thumb flipped the switch as he closed the drawer with his hip. A dull light sprung from the lens, but it was better than nothing.

Alex trained the weak beam at her back.

Ava stood next to a chair at his table. Her bloody hand gripped the rounded steel top. She glanced down, then jerked her arm back. "I'm sorry. I wasn't thinking."

"Don't worry about it," Alex replied, shining the light at the bloody handprint. He stepped around Ava, then pulled the chair out from under the table. "Why don't you have a seat and rest while I grab some first aid supplies to treat that injury?"

The legs of the chair scraped over the linoleum. The noise made him cringe and look toward the swinging door. He did it fast and in a not so obvious way as to avoid any further questions from her.

"Thanks." Ava sat down slowly, acting as if it was a chore to do so. "I'm afraid if I sit down too long, I'm not going to want to get back up."

Her back rested against the seat. Both shoulders pitched toward the table. She ran her hand over her face, then sighed.

"Well, you need to rest a moment." Alex moved on the swinging door. "It's been a long, hot day, plus getting shot and roughed up didn't help any."

"True." Ava removed her purse and sat it on the table.

Alex cracked the door open, then walked into the living room. He swept the space with the light playing off the walls and pictures of his family as the door swung closed behind him.

The blinds throughout the bottom floor had been shut as well, concealing his presence from the outside world. All appeared to be normal with no hint of an intruder. He detected no broken glass on the hardwood floor or any mysterious creaks on the planks of wood.

The rush of memories, good and bad, attacked his mind. It weakened him for a split second as his eyes grew shiny with remorse. He shook his head and continued on to the downstairs bathroom, passing family photos of happier times on the table positioned next to the wall by the staircase.

Alex walked past the banister and trained his light at the landing of the second floor. The gleam crawled up the wall, then swept the black void. He closed in on the bathroom and diverted his gaze to the murk ahead of him.

The door was cracked. Light shone through the narrow opening at the toilet in the corner. His hand pushed against the warm exterior of the door and forced it against the wall.

The reflection of a haggard-looking individual met his gaze in the mirror. The light hitting the glass distorted the image some.

Shadows plagued parts of his face, erasing the tiredness and damage he'd taken.

Alex glanced to the white cabinets under the sink, then stooped down. He opened both sides of the doors and took stock of what he had under the basin.

The vanity had been cleaned up and rearranged since he'd last seen it. The various cleaning and other toiletry items were positioned in an organized manner and not the cluttered mess that he typically did. His mom always complained about how his house felt like a disheveled mess and that it stressed her out. It appeared she'd taken the opportunity to fix things in his absence.

The first aid kit sat against the wall in the corner. He couldn't remember how well it was stocked and hoped he had enough supplies to tend to Ava's wounds.

Alex gathered the kit and stood. He closed both doors with his knee and faced the entrance to the bathroom, avoiding the truth of the mirror.

He trekked across the floor, lost in a battery of thoughts on how he planned to handle the issue with Mr. Vargas and Trey while steering clear of the authorities.

A loud crashing noise loomed from the kitchen. It sounded like glass breaking.

Alex froze, trained the light at the swinging door, then rushed to the kitchen. His shoulder forced the door open. It swung open in a blink, slamming against the edge of the counter.

Ava flinched, then jumped across the space near the sink. She spun around, panting with her hand over her heart. "Christ. Are you trying to give me a heart attack or something?"

"I heard something break." Alex glanced at the window of the back door for any missing glass. "I thought someone was trying to get inside the house."

"No." Ava peered at the floor near her feet. "I wanted something to drink and grabbed a glass. It fell from my hand and broke on the counter here. I feel like I've got two left hands."

Alex released a long breath. The taut muscles in his chest, arms, and shoulders relaxed. He sat the first aid kit on the table, then skirted past the chair tucked under the table near him. "Don't worry about it. How's the water pressure? I imagine it wouldn't be good seeing as the power's out. What's left in the line is all we'll have."

The light shone on the fragments of the busted glass littering the floor. The pieces crunched under his shoes.

Ava moved away from the counter, then pointed at the faucet. "It's weak, but there's some water coming out. Not sure how much more we'll get, though."

"Good. We'll need some water to clean the wound and all." Alex looked to the small nook past the back door. "Let me clean this up real quick. Why don't you have a seat and relax? I'll get you some water in a moment."

"If you have a broom and dustpan, I can help in cleaning up." Ava winced and palmed the side of her arm. "It's the least I can do for making a mess in your home."

Alex retrieved a broom and pan that leaned against the wall, then walked toward the mess on the floor. He sat the flashlight on the table next to the medical supplies, then dropped the pan to the linoleum tile. "You need to sit down and rest. Conserve your strength. This won't take but a moment to clean up."

Ava stepped around the glass, shuffled to the far side of the table, and sat down in one of the chairs. A heavy sigh left her mouth as she plopped down in the seat. Her head slumped back. Exhaustion filled her sweaty, flushed face.

"Do you ever have one of those days where you wish you could have a redo?" Ava asked. "Turn the clock back and start over again with the knowledge you have now."

Every day, Alex thought, sweeping the shards into a pile. "I don't think there's one person alive today that wouldn't do that. We've all got things we wish we could change. That saying is true. Hindsight is 20/20."

Ava nodded. "Tell me about it. I've got a lifetime worth of things I'd like to change if I had the chance. Some more recent than others."

Alex swept the glass into the pan, then hauled it to the opening of the trash can. "Again, I don't think you're alone with that. I know I have many past transgressions that I'd like to go back and change. Dwelling on such things, though, is only foolish in the end. What matters is learning from the past and not repeating it."

The back of the pan slapped the rubber edge of the opening. The glass tumbled into the trash bag.

"True." Ava reached across the table and grabbed the handle to the kit. "You got anything stiff to drink in this house by chance? I don't need it, but I do need it."

"I got you." Alex placed the broom and dustpan back to the corner, then made his way to the sink. "I got a bottle I think still in the cabinet across the kitchen there. Let me scrounge up some water in a bowl and grab a towel, then I'll see."

Ava fiddled with the front of the first aid kit. Her fingers worked the latches, trying to flip them up.

Alex opened the bottom cabinet door and pulled out a medium-sized bowl. He sat it in the sink, under the faucet, then twisted the knob to the left of the spout.

Water poured from the tap, then slowed as it filled the bottom of the bowl. Alex killed the flow a moment later, then hauled the container to the table. He sat it down, faced the sink, and retrieved a towel from one of the drawers.

Ava opened the lid to the kit and sifted through the supplies contained inside. "I don't see any peroxide in here. I guess we can use the alcohol you have to clean this."

"We don't want to use alcohol on an open wound like that," Alex replied, walking past her to the other side. "It can damage the skin and delay any healing. It's best to use water."

"Really? Huh." Ava stared at him as he grabbed one of the chairs and scooted it closer to her side. "I've never heard that before."

Alex sat down, reached across the table, and rolled the flashlight toward him. "We'll clean it off with this towel and water, then bandage it up."

"How does it look? I can't tell. I know it stings like a son of a bitch." Ava turned her arm and studied the wound.

"It nicked the meat pretty good. You should be all right, though." Alex dunked the towel into the water, then rang it out. He patted the damaged flesh with a gentle hand.

Ava recoiled, then drew her arm toward her body.

Alex stopped and moved the towel away. "I'm sorry if that hurt."

"It's okay. I'm a wimp when it comes to injuries." Ava moved her arm closer to him. "Me and pain don't gel too well."

"Yeah, though, you have been shot, so, I think you can cut yourself a bit of slack." He finished cleaning the area, and blood that ran down her arm, then sat the towel in the bowl. Alex stood from the chair, then marched to the cabinet above the fridge. "We'll see if I have some liquid courage in here."

Ava chuckled. "It's been a long time since I've heard anyone say liquid courage."

Alex stretched his arm and reached into the depths of the cabinet. He felt around, then grazed what seemed to be a glass bottle. "I think you're in luck."

He pulled the container out and looked it over. It was the same whiskey bottle he'd nursed the last day he fought with Wendy and made a stupid decision that changed his life for the worst.

"Are you going to bring it over here, or do you plan on teasing me with it?" Ava asked.

"I hope you like whiskey." Alex closed the cabinet door, then carried the bottle to the table.

"I'll like anything that helps calm my nerves and dulls this pain some," Ava replied, reaching for the spirit.

Alex unscrewed the cap. The rich aroma permeated the air around him. He inhaled, savoring the scent he'd longed for from his cell, then handed her the bottle.

Ava sniffed the opening, shrugged, then took a swig. Her face twisted. Both eyes pinched shut. She gnashed her teeth and sat the bottle down. "Good stuff."

"A little dab will do ya, or so they say." Alex sat back in the chair and thumbed through the supplies.

"You want a drink?" Ava scooted the bottle closer to him with her hand. "You look like you could use one."

"I will once I get you fixed up." Alex studied the wound a bit closer, then rummaged more through the kit.

Ava took another hearty sip, shook her head, then dropped the bottle near him. "Just so you know, I don't normally go home with strange men that I just met during a crisis. That's not the sort of lady I am."

"Is that so?" Alex pulled out a few square pieces of gauze and a Coban wrap bandage. "I don't think you'll need any stitches. I don't have anything to do stitches with anyway. I'm just going to place some gauze on it, then wrap it up."

"It's better than nothing." Ava slouched in the chair with her forearm resting on the edge of the table. "And it is so. I'm rather cautious about going home with men that I just met. There are lots of creeps and sick individuals out in the world. No doubt this outage will draw some of the muck from the sewers to the streets."

Alex applied the gauze to the wound, then wrapped the Coban around her bicep. He wondered if she would still feel the same way if she knew he'd escaped from prison. "It's nice to know that I rate above sewage. Come to think of it, that's probably one of the best compliments I've ever gotten."

Ava sneered. "Haha. Funny. I'd put you a hair above toxic waste."

"Good to know." Alex secured the end of the Coban in place, then sat back. "There we go. You're all fixed up."

"Thanks. I appreciate it." Ava removed her arm from the table, then inspected the Coban. "Not bad."

He left the kit lid open, then stood from his chair. "I'm going to head upstairs and change from these clothes real quick. Did you need any—" Alex glanced at the upper cabinet near the sink where he kept the glasses, then pointed. "Water. Let me see if I can squeeze out whatever's left in the line. I imagine there's enough in there to get a decent-sized drink."

Ava looked to the sink, then back to Alex. She waved her hand, stopping him before he walked around the table. "Don't worry about it. I'll grab another glass shortly and get what I want out. I won't break anything this time. Promise."

"I didn't mean to imply that you can't get a simple drink without breaking things," Alex replied. "I'm already up and thought it would be better for you to rest while you can. You're more than welcome to get the water yourself."

"I know you weren't implying that." Ava offered a warm smile through the tiredness and discomfort on her battered face. "Go get what you need done. I'll be in here waiting for you."

Alex glanced at the flashlight on the table. "I'll leave that with you."

"Sure." She pointed at the whiskey. "You can take that with you. I'm good. Just wanted to nip off it some to curb the sting on my arm and face. I don't need to have much more. I need to keep my focus and such."

"Gotcha. Be back shortly."

Ava gave a thumbs up, pressed her hand to the surface of the table, then stood.

Alex grabbed the neck of the liquor bottle and headed for the swinging door leading into the living room. His fingers tightened over the glass neck. He passed the table filled with memories and took a hearty swig from the opening.

His taste buds rejoiced as the spirit splashed across his tongue. He held the stout liquor in his mouth a few seconds while skirting past the banister to the landing, then swallowed.

The steps creaked under him. His free hand held the railing as he climbed to the second floor. He took another swig, pressed the back of his hand to his lips, then gulped it down.

The blackness of the hallway leading to the bedrooms and other bathroom loomed large. His shoes hit the landing. He paused, then fished the lighter from his back pocket.

Alex struck the wheel with his thumb. The flame sprung to life, illuminating the small area around him. He lifted it up and proceeded onward.

The flame danced.

The bottle met his lips again as he advanced down the tight corridor to the last bedroom on the right. He passed Wendy's closed door and the upstairs bathroom.

The creaking wood planks sounded much louder than Alex remembered. Perhaps he didn't pay as close attention back then, or given his time away in prison, maybe he noticed those little things more now.

Alex cradled the bottle between his arm and body. He grabbed the doorknob to his room and turned. The door opened to more stuffy, hot air that further wrangled his throat.

A musty smell filled the dark space. He stood in the doorway and took in everything.

The furnishings Stacy picked out years prior to complete their nest twisted the dagger of loss in his side. A wave of sadness and sorrow crept up his spine. He sniffled, then shooed it away with a flick of his head.

Alex sat the bottle of whiskey on the dresser, then used his lighter to light the lavender candle that had long lost its scent. The wick ignited. Light built in the bedroom, erasing the darkness. He closed the lid to the lighter and set it on top of the dresser.

His hand fished out the revolver and sat it next to the bottle and other items. The wave of emotions crashing into him waned as he pulled the damp, smelly shirt over his head and tossed it on the floor. The shoes went next, followed by the damp socks.

He opened one of the drawers on the dresser, pulled out some clean threads, then tossed the clothes to the made bed. Alex grabbed the base of the candle and carried it to the bathroom with him.

The wick danced with each step as he passed through the doorway.

Alex marched toward the vanity and sat the candle on the counter. He looked to the mirror, examining the filth and bruises he had on his sullen face. His appearance looked haggard and beaten down, almost unrecognizable from the man he used to be.

He turned the cold knob on the faucet.

A weak stream of water sputtered from the tap. His hands cupped, catching it in his palms. He splashed his face, rubbing vigorously to wipe the stench of mistakes away.

The water reduced to a trickle.

Alex got what he could on his hands, then ran his fingers through his hair. The line went dry. He flicked the wetness from his fingers, grabbed a towel from the small closet near the entrance, and dried his face and hair.

The rough texture of the fabric wiped across his chest and under his pits. He discarded the towel on the floor, grabbed the candle, then left the bathroom.

A battery of thoughts attacked him without pause—everything from the calamity happening in the world to Wendy being a possible target of Vargas. The added stress made the knotted muscles in his back and shoulders mound.

Alex stretched his neck, then sat the candle on the nightstand. He peeled the guard's trousers from his unkempt body and tossed them away.

The clean clothes went on one by one. The shirt he remembered fitting a bit snugly hung from his shoulders some. The pants felt loose around his waist. He figured he'd lost some weight while being in the clink, but not that much.

A belt looped around his waist, keeping the jeans in place. He grabbed the candle and carried it to the closet. He opened the door and browsed the cluttered mess that filled the tight space.

A Houston Texas ballcap hung from a hook on the wall. He pulled it off, placed it on his head, then grabbed a pair of boots from the mound of footwear cluttering the floor.

Alex backed out of the closet, then dumped the shoes on the carpet next to the dresser. His feet wormed their way inside the boots as he set the candle down and pocketed the lighter. He grabbed the revolver, then stowed it in the waistband of his jeans.

The faint crackle of gunfire echoed outside of his home. He paused and listened. Alex worked his way around the bed to the far window that overlooked the back of his property and surrounding homes.

He kept low and moved to the wall next to the window. His shoulder pressed against the sheetrock, fingers pulling the closed blinds away from the glass.

The yard below showed no shadowy figures in the darkness creeping around his place. The other houses close to his sat dark and powerless with no lights looming from the murk of the windows or properties.

He thought of Mr. Vargas and the police, wondering if they'd discovered he'd escaped from prison and was on the run. It was a toss-up, seeing how most everything in the city had shut down. The lack of communications and power might buy him some time.

Alex released the blinds and headed for the doorway, wanting to check the rest of the house just to be sure they were alone. He grabbed the candle and stepped out into the hallway. His head turned as he listened.

Silence greeted his ears. No footfalls or creaking wood planks sounded in the blackness. He walked down the hallway with eyes fixed at the other end of the hall that led down the stairs.

The flame swayed from the movement. The light cast its gleam on the walls and other pictures hanging. He glanced at each closed door while closing in on the landing.

Alex looked around the corner to the landing below. All seemed as it should. He made his way down the stairs, scanning the living room from the side of the railing.

His boots tromped down each step, making them creak.

The light from under the swinging door leading into the kitchen dimmed to almost nothing.

A small amount of wax collected in the impression in the center of the candle. A thin line dumped over the edge, from being tilted, and raced down the side. The heated wax met the skin between his thumb and finger as he hit the landing.

Alex cringed, skirted the banister, then sat it down on the table against the wall. His hand flicked and he picked the wax from his skin. He walked to the front entrance of the home and peered through each window to the yard and street, finding it to be clear of any movement.

A sense of relief made his shoulders lift.

He took a deep breath, exhaled, then made his way toward the kitchen to check on Ava. Her head rested on the tabletop. One arm stretched out in front of her with the other tucked at her side.

The flashlight's glow ceased. The battery must've died out. Ava didn't stir.

Alex marched to the back door and peeked through the window, then turned to face her. He approached from the side and placed a cautious hand on her shoulder so as to not startle her. "Hey. Are you all right?"

She shifted her weight in the seat, then grumbled incoherent nonsense. Her head trained in the opposite direction, away from him.

He stood on the tips of his toes and studied her shadowy face to make sure she was okay. Both lids were closed. Strands of hair draped across her wet forehead and face. Long breaths escaped her mouth. She had fallen asleep.

Alex gave Ava a slight nudge to wake her and move her to the couch, but she pulled away from him and continued sleeping. He removed his hand from her shoulder and let Ava rest where she was. She needed the downtime to recoup from the day's events. He did as well.

Running out the door could only slow their journey on foot, and cause more problems than he already had.

CHAPTER TWENTY-ONE

WENDY

The fear of the Dukes roaming the dark woods kept Wendy planted in place, unable to move. The lull soon seduced her, though.

The back of her head rested on the trunk of the tree. Both arms folded across her chest. She had closed her eyelids for a few minutes, waiting for the right time to leave her haven.

A buzzing festered in her ear.

The unsettling feeling of some creepy crawler brushed her cheek, then moved across her face. Her nose twitched, and her head shifted from side to side.

Wendy unfolded her arms, then swatted at the annoying insect. The fly buzzed around her sweaty head a moment longer before flying away. She opened her eyes and looked about in a dazed state.

The knotted muscles in her back and neck were tight from the rigid surface she rested on. Her joints had grown stiff from the inactivity. It hurt to move at first, causing her to grimace.

How long have I been out?

Wendy leaned forward, away from the tree trunk. She stretched her neck and yawned. The knuckles from both hands burrowed into each socket. She slapped the sides of her face to erase the sleepiness, then blinked the haze from both eyes.

Time had all but gotten away from her. She hadn't planned on sleeping.

A rustling in the bushes and trees close by snapped her to attention. She paused and listened.

It sounded like animals scurrying about, foraging for food maybe, but the noise worked her nerves none–the–less. She braced her hand in the dirt, stood, and peered over the top of the bushes to survey the area.

Darkness lurked in every corner, offering snippets of trees and other vegetation. She scanned for any lights or figures but spotted none. The coast seemed clear. The Dukes must have moved on. It was time to get back home.

Wendy moved to the other side of the tree and ducked. Her stomach and chest pressed to the dirt. She crawled on the ground, forcing her way through the limbs that stabbed her sides, back, and head.

The rustling noise stopped.

She heard no snapping of branches or raised voices. For now, it felt as though she had given them the slip.

The back of her shirt snagged on the tips of the branches. Her head emerged from the opening. Her fingers dug into the semi-hard dirt, pulling her forward.

Wendy dragged her legs out, then raised to her hands and knees. She got to her feet and patted the dirt from the front of her clothes.

The never-ending void of night encompassed everything. Her eyes adjusted to the blackness some, allowing Wendy to see a bit more of the world with each passing second. The vague outline of trees, bushes, and other verdure filled her gaze. It would be slow going, moving through the dark woods without any light to guide the way, but she didn't want to wait any longer.

Her grandparents would be beside themselves wondering where she had gone. Leaving had been a bad decision on Wendy's part that she regretted more and more.

The crackle of thunder rumbled in the distance.

Wendy looked to the starless sky, through the canopy overhead, wondering if a storm was inbound. The thought of rain seemed nice, but also bad because of the humidity that would soon follow.

Her head lowered. She got on the move, working through the woods at a slow and cautious pace. Her head stayed on a swivel and her ears perked for any strange noises that lurked close by.

Night wore on and soon gave way to early morning. The scenery of the woods unfolded with each passing second. Light grew brighter, making it easier to see ahead.

The inside of her mouth felt dry, arid even. She hadn't had much to drink in the past day and the unyielding heat sought to drain every bit of moisture in her body.

Wendy kept close to the stream, following along the bank, but staying within the meld of thickets to help hide her. She glanced to the flowing stream that had a good amount of water running through it.

Her mouth opened, and her tongue licked the dried skin of both lips. She craned her neck, looking for an easy path down to the creek bed.

The land leveled off ahead. The ground leading down didn't appear too steep.

She walked along the bank, then worked her way down the dirt-covered slope to the stream. The loose topsoil shifted under both feet. Her shoes crunched the small rocks on the flat ground.

Wendy bent down next to the flowing stream, cupped her hands, then dunked them. The water felt good on her tacky, sweaty skin. She lifted her hands to her mouth and drank.

The water dribbled down the sides of her hands and mouth. She gulped the water, holding her breath, then exhaling. The refreshing liquid did much to refill her well.

She plunged her hands back into the stream a few more times and drank some more. Wendy splashed her face, then rubbed her wet hands on the back of her neck.

The tiredness and soreness clung to her battered body like a leech. She stretched her neck, then back, trying to undo the kinks in both.

Wendy stood and wiped her damp hands on the fronts of her jeans. The back of her hand wiped the moisture away from her bottom lip and chin. She glanced in the direction she'd trekked, studying the flow of the creek bed.

The stream curved to the left, then vanished from sight. The wall of earth, on either side, looked rather steep. Escaping at a moment's notice would prove to be challenging.

Wendy backtracked up the exposed earth to the wooded area above. The ache in her ankle remained, but she powered past the discomfort and pushed on.

The chirping of birds and other rustling noises built as she trudged through the woods. Squirrels raced down tree trunks to the ground, scavenging for food. A rabbit emerged from a thicket ahead of her, eating grass. Despite being hunted, the woods felt rather peaceful.

The animals scattered as she drew closer, disappearing through the verdure and up trees. She followed along a small path that didn't have much grass growing.

The terrain leveled out and remained flat, taking some of the pressure off her ankle. A grumble sounded from her stomach, and a nauseated sensation crept up her spine. She hadn't thrown up in years, but remembered the feeling she got before the gut-wrenching act took hold.

Not what I need right now.

Wendy slowed, then stopped under a tree. She leaned against it, hunched over, and placed her hands above both knees.

The heat of the day built slowly but steadily. It wasn't near as bad as mid-day, but even in the early mornings, it was still hot and the humidity made it worse.

Her eyelids slammed closed. She squinted hard, teeth gnashed. One hand pressed to her mouth, then forehead, while the other remained on her knee.

The world spun, making the nausea worse. Her stance widened to balance her out. The tree kept her upright.

Wendy took a deep breath, held it for a moment, then exhaled through her nose. She repeated the process until the sensation lessened enough to continue on.

A branch snapped.

She dropped her hand from her head, then jerked upright. The sudden motion rocked her balance. She swayed.

Wendy searched the area, hoping it was nothing more than a larger animal moving through. She squinted, turning from left to right, not spotting the source at first.

A figure moved behind the wall of bushes and trees twenty paces to the west of her position. She focused on the area, detecting what looked to be clothing through the small gaps within the vegetation.

Oh crap.

The Dukes.

A wave of panic festered in her already tormented gut. She couldn't tell if it was the loathsome brothers or not, but she didn't want to chance it.

Wendy ducked and looked around in a frantic state for where to go. She moved forward without thought, panting hard.

The front of her shoe caught a thick branch on the ground. She tumbled forward, then dumped face-first into the grass. The sudden movement didn't help the flourishing headache that coalesced in her skull.

More branches snapped, drawing closer to her. Footfalls hammered the earth like a predatory animal charging wounded prey.

"I heard something over here, Roy," Jimmy said, breathless. "I thought I spotted movement a moment ago."

"Do you see her?" Roy shouted.

Wendy pushed up and peered over her shoulder.

Jimmy locked onto her. He leapt over a fallen tree and skirted past bushes. "Yeah. She's dead ahead. I knew she was still around somewhere."

"Don't let her get away this time."

Wendy crawled across the dirt, then got to her feet. She took off in a dead sprint that killed her ankle. The jolt of panic trumped the headache and nausea that still remained.

"Oh, you ain't getting away from me this time." Jimmy ran at full tilt. "You're in my backyard now, honey." He closed the gap.

Her ankle throbbed more the harder she ran. A twinge of pain lanced up her leg, causing her to stumble and slow.

Jimmy's panting tickled her ears. His presence made her skin crawl.

Wendy ducked under a low-lying branch, then cut hard through the wall of bushes. She glanced back, looking for Jimmy while on the move.

The rail-thin man matched her step for step and stayed glued to her six. Regardless of where she ran, he closed in.

His hand stretched out, swatting at the back of her shirt. The tips of his nails grazed the fabric.

The terrain shifted and sloped at a downward angle.

Wendy lost her balance and pitched forward. The trees and sky twisted around. Her body slammed against the ground and rocks as she rolled.

A fallen, rotted log stopped her cold. She hit hard on her back. Air burst from her lungs, and her vision wavered.

Jimmy made his way down to her. He grabbed branches and used tree trunks to help him along. "I told you it was pointless in running, girl. You're gonna pay the piper now."

Wendy blinked and shook her head, trying to clear the dizziness. She rolled away from the log, then tried to stand. Her hands pressed to the ground and pushed up.

He towered over her, looking at her with a devious smirk. Dirt covered his face. Stained yellow teeth materialized from behind his chapped lips. His hand gripped the front of his pants above the crotch.

Jimmy struck Wendy in the side, ripping what little air she had gathered from her lungs. Her arms buckled. Her head fell toward the ground. She gasped, struggling to breathe. He planted his boot into the side of her shoulder, then shoved.

Wendy dumped over against the log. The pain in her ribs tore through her. She fought to sit up and face him, but the pain made it difficult to.

"You know, I do believe you owe me some quality time. I was promised as much back at the house before you tricked me and made me look like a damn idiot." His voice filled with venomous spite. "I think I'll collect what you owe me before we finish you off, once and for all."

She worried what might come next. "Good… luck… with that."

Jimmy grabbed Wendy's shirt, then draped her body over the log. Her backside lifted skyward, presenting him with an opportunity she didn't want to give.

"No." Wendy scrambled to move.

"Oh, you're not going anywhere." Jimmy rammed the sole of his boot into her butt, pinning Wendy to the log.

She thrashed both legs and squirmed, doing everything she could think of to rid herself of the sublevel human.

A large bowie knife stabbed the top of the log near Wendy, puncturing the wood with ease. She flinched, then leaned away. "Settle down now, or I won't be the only thing penetrating you."

Her mind worked in that dire moment on what to do next. Her weakened state and injuries made it harder to overpower him and gain the upper hand. Going for the knife would be difficult given the position she was in.

Jimmy removed his boot, then pressed his groin to her butt. His hand massaged her hips, then smacked the back of her jeans.

Wendy wormed in place, revolted by the man's tiny member rubbing her through his pants. The tips of her shoes dug into the ground. Her arms flailed as she searched for anything she could use.

A small, thick branch caught her sight. It was just out of reach. If she stretched and gave everything she had, she might be able to get it, but at what cost?

A budding wave of excitement gripped the perverted man. A slew of pants and grunts left his lips. The longer he ground against her, the worse it got. He stopped, then stood up straight. A zipping sound increased the worry tenfold.

Wendy lunged forward and grabbed the dense branch. She elbowed his face, wiggled her body over, and swung the branch at his head. The thick, rounded bottom smashed the side of his skull, knocking him off balance.

Jimmy palmed the side of his face. A growl seeped through his gritted teeth. He stumbled back while shouting a slew of obscenities. "Ah. You damn bitch."

She took another swing.

He lifted his arm to shield his skull from another brutal blow. The branch smashed the side of his arm. The wood cracked but held together.

Jimmy yelled. His legs buckled, sending him to the dirt. He dropped to his hands and knees.

A groan leaked from his mouth, followed by a whimper that she ignored. Blood ran from the open wound on the side of his head and down the length of his face to his chin.

"You're not so big and tough now, are you?" Wendy towered over the weeping man who cowered at her feet.

The tables had turned. The hunter was now the hunted. The predator had become the prey.

Jimmy raised his bloody, dirt-covered, trembling hand from the ground. "Please."

Wendy hammered his spine with the branch, snapping it in half. The busted portion bounced off his back to the earth on the other side.

His head snapped back, face contorted in pain. A howl left his mouth. He squinted and furrowed his brow.

She punished his ribs twice with her foot, unleashing a score of stress and anger on the battered and beaten lowlife.

Jimmy wheezed, unable to catch his breath. He tried to speak, but couldn't string together a sentence. His head drooped forward as he crumbled to his side.

Wendy threw the busted branch away, then glanced at the Bowie knife wedged into the log. She shifted her gaze from the large, sharp weapon to the sadistic man who'd tried to do unspeakable things to her.

The anger and bloodlust for revenge took hold. Payback and justice were a couple feet away. None would be the wiser, or care if the deviant left this world, or had the weapon taken from between his legs.

She grabbed the handle to the Bowie, then pulled it from the log.

Jimmy rolled to his stomach, then tried to crawl away. The subtle wheezing noise loomed from his mouth. He wriggled slowly across the ground like an inchworm.

Wendy bent down and grabbed his arm, then flipped him to his back. His head bobbled about as if fixed on a spring. The side of his face was painted red with blood that leaked into his eye.

She towered over him, then lowered at his side. Her free hand made a fist in his damp shirt. The tip of the knife pressed to his manhood. She jerked him upward and stared at him with malevolent eyes.

His whimpering increased. Both eyes enlarged in a blink.

"I'm… sorry. Please… don't." His voice sounded like busted glass, choppy and hard to make out at first.

Wendy applied a bit more pressure against his groin. The begging increased, as did the whimpering.

"Perhaps I should rid you of that tiny thing you've got down there between your legs," Wendy said, sounding beast-like. "Do the rest of the world, and women, a favor by taking your manhood away."

"Shit. Please don't cut it off." Each eye glassed over. Tears formed, then ran from the corners of his eyes.

Wendy panted. Her nostrils flared. She saw red while looking at Jimmy. The utter contempt and rage whispered to her to continue, twist the knife and dig in. Stop the menace from harming anyone else. Despite how much she wanted to, in the end, Wendy wasn't a stone-cold killer, at least, not when she had the upper hand. Perhaps now, he'd leave her alone.

Jimmy sniffled and sobbed like a weeping baby. He didn't try to make a move on her, keeping his hands up where she could see them.

The tip of the knife left his package.

He breathed a sigh of relief.

Wendy clutched the handle of the blade, then pounded his face with her balled fist. "I wouldn't be too relieved if I were you."

The back of Jimmy's skull dropped to the dirt. Blood oozed from his nostrils to his upper lip. His hand pressed to his face, muffling the squeal.

She leaned in close. "You'll be going to jail. I do imagine some of those burly men would love a slender piece of meat such as yourself."

The rustling of leaves and snapping branches sent Wendy to her feet and searching for Roy. He was still out there, loose, but where?

Wendy gazed at Jimmy one last time, stepped back, then moved up the hill to flat land. The knife remained in her clutches. Her legs drove her forward.

The lightheadedness plaguing her remained, as did the pain that radiated from most of her body now. The rush of fighting Jimmy had distracted her.

Roy seemed like a chameleon, hard to spot with the rich vegetation that encompassed the land. The footfalls and disturbance of the woods followed, but she couldn't lay eyes on him.

Jimmy groaned loudly, then shouted for his brother. His voice trailed off as she hit flat land.

Wendy hid behind a thicket, then poked her head up and over.

Where are you, you bastard?

The pressure in her skull mounted. Each pump from Wendy's heart made her head swell.

She dared the fat, smelly ogre to try something, seeing as now she had a weapon that he'd regret encountering. Her hand wiped the beads of sweat from her grungy brow as she crept from behind the bushes. A taut hold remained on the handle, ready to slash and stab at a moment's notice.

The rustling ceased.

Wendy turned and scanned the trees and bushes while staying on the move. She gulped, then licked her lips, unable to detect the remaining Duke.

Footfalls stomped the earth at her back. Twigs snapped.

She gasped, then spun around with the Bowie knife up and ready to do harm if need be. Her body swayed from the sudden movement.

Something blunt slammed against her forehead. Wendy's head snapped back.

Roy flashed in front of her before the world went black. Her legs gave, causing her to hit the dirt. The taut hold on the knife lessened, but it remained in her hand.

"I see you got Jimmy's toy," Roy said, standing at her feet with his rifle trained at her skull. He moved to the hand wielding the knife and stomped on her wrist, pinning it to the ground. "Did you gut the bastard? Slit 'im from neck to nuts?"

Wendy gnashed her teeth and tugged at her arm, trying to pull it free from under his boots.

"Well, we can't have you running around with a big man's blade." Roy bent down, then pried it from her fingers. "I'll take that."

She tried to hold onto the weapon, curling the ends of each finger over the grip. It didn't matter.

Roy stood and peered at the blade, examining it. The barrel of his rifle stayed pointed at her head. "I see no blood. Maybe you didn't have the lady balls to go through with it." He glanced around, then whistled. "Where's that dipshit at, anyway? I heard his feeble cries calling out a bit ago."

Jimmy shouted again in a weak tone.

Wendy laid flat on her back, staring up at Roy with the rising sun behind him. Beams of light pierced the canopy and blinded her. She squinted, then looked away.

"You all right, Jimmy?" Roy asked, shouting. He placed the Bowie knife between his belt and pants. "This girl didn't hurt you too bad, did she?"

No reply came. Only groans and grumbles.

"I take that as yes." Roy peered at Wendy, bearing down on her wrist. The pressure made her cringe and grunt even more. He sniffled, then scrunched his nose from the beating she'd given the previous day. "Let's go check on my brother, then we can settle things."

CHAPTER TWENTY-TWO

ALEX

The sudden jolt of movement snapped Alex out of his slumber. His hand slipped from under his chin. The table rushed toward his face. He caught himself before smacking the top.

A look of confusion filled his sleepy eyes. His hand reached for the Ruger tucked in the waistband of his jeans, but he didn't pull it out. He blinked multiple times, trying to rid the tiredness from his body.

The disorientation waned. A heavy sigh left his mouth. The darkness evaporated, giving way to light that shone through the backdoor window and sides of the closed blinds above the sink and far wall.

Alex jammed his fingers into each eye socket and rubbed. Frustration churned in his gut. He hadn't planned on falling into such a deep sleep and wasting any more time than needed. It seemed as though life had other plans.

He squinted, then yawned. His eyes watered. He shook his head, then glanced to the far end of the table.

Ava had vanished. He looked about the kitchen, searching for her. Had she left in the middle of the night? She could've gone elsewhere in the house, but he didn't know.

Alex removed the Texas ball cap from his head, ran his hand up his face, then through his hair. He tucked it back onto his head, pressed both hands to the table, then stood.

The floor creaked from the living room. His hand stayed near the grip of the Ruger. He advanced on the swinging door, silently.

The footfalls ceased, then started again.

Alex leaned against the edge of the door and pushed.

The squeaking made him cringe. He poked his head around the side. Ava stood in the living room near the table against the staircase. She held a picture frame in her hands, studying it.

Alex pushed the door all the way open and stood in the doorway. "I thought you left in the middle of the night or something."

She jumped a little, then gasped. "Christ, you scared me."

"Sorry. That wasn't my intent. I didn't see you in the kitchen and thought you might've flown the coop," Alex replied, pointing behind him. "I didn't know if someone else was in my house. You can't be too careful."

Ava palmed her chest, then set the picture frame down next to the others. "It's all right. I didn't realize you were awake. You were fast asleep when I got up a bit ago." Her brow scrunched. "Who else would've been in here?"

"Never mind. Doesn't really matter." Alex marched into the living room, removing his hand from the front of his jeans. "It seems like sitting down for a minute caught up with both of us. You fell asleep rather fast as well. I meant to only let you rest for a short stint before we got back on the move. That backfired for sure."

"Yeah." Ava nodded, then lowered her arm. She winced while peering at the wound on the side of her bicep.

Alex craned his neck, trying to look at the wound. "Is the arm hurting bad? Did you want to change the bandage out?"

Ava rotated her arm, then dipped her chin. "It does hurt, but whatever. Not as bad as having a kid. I'll deal with it."

"If you want any pain meds before we head out, I can see if I have any aspirin or anything else. I imagine I do somewhere," Alex said.

"That won't be necessary." Ava glanced at the photos. "Beautiful family. I hope you don't mind me looking and poking around."

Alex walked toward her, then glanced at the pictures of him, Stacy, and Wendy together. "Thanks. They're my world. Well, were my world, that is."

"I'm sorry. I didn't know they were—" Ava looked at the photos. Her head tilted in sadness.

"Oh, no. My daughter isn't dead," Alex said, clarifying. "My wife passed about a year or so ago. Cancer."

Ava stared at the picture a bit longer, then looked to Alex. "You have my condolences."

Alex offered a warm smile, looked to the photos of his smiling wife and daughter, then cleared his throat. "I think it's time we get back on the move. I can imagine how anxious you are to get back to your son."

"I am." Ava glanced at the floor. "In all fairness, I was going to just leave when I came to and not say anything."

"Why didn't you?" Alex folded his arms. "You could've. No one is keeping you here."

"After what happened back at that 7–Eleven, then those thugs who attacked me in the alley, I'm a bit apprehensive on venturing out there on my own. If push came to shove and I had to I would, but I hoped you might stick with me." Ava lifted her head, avoiding eye contact at first. "Mind you, I'm a strong woman and all, but whatever's happened out there has changed things. More so than I can ever remember. It's almost like we're on our own. Hell, we'd be lucky to come across a cop or anyone else, seeing as they are more than likely swamped with a mountain of other problems sweeping across the city, and beyond even."

Alex nodded, understanding her position. He didn't mind the cops being pulled in a billion different directions. That meant good news for him while he tried to straighten out the clustered web he'd weaved that had ripped his daughter from her life and endangered her future. He had the workings of a plan but was still hammering the details of it out inside his head.

"There's no need to explain. I get it." He placed his hand on her shoulder. "The unknown beyond these walls is scary, but we'll get you back to your son this morning."

Ava wiped the wetness forming from both eyes, then smiled. "I do appreciate it, and so does my son."

Alex didn't see her purse hanging from her shoulder. "Where's your bag?"

"In the kitchen, on the counter near the sink," Ava replied. "I took it to the window so I could see better. I was looking through it earlier."

"Okay. I didn't want you to forget anything. Ready to leave?"

"More than ready." Ava walked past him and headed for the kitchen.

Alex looked to the photos of his family one last time before following her lead.

I will make this right.

Ava passed through the swinging door with Alex a few paces behind her. She moved around the table and grabbed her purse from the counter. The straps nicked the bandage on her arm. She grunted and secured it over her shoulder.

"Are you sure you don't want to change that out?" Alex asked, nodding at the wound.

"I am. I feel like I've wasted enough time already." Ava wiped the grimace from her tired and flushed face.

"All right." Alex moved on the backdoor, then peered through the window. He scanned over the backyard, then gripped the doorknob.

"There aren't crazy people lurking about, are there?" Ava asked, flanking him.

Alex looked a moment longer. "Not that I can see. I heard a faint gunshot last night. Not sure where it came from, though. It was hard to see any movement through the windows with it being dark."

Ava craned her neck and peered over his shoulder. "I thought I heard that as well but wasn't sure if I had or if I'd imagined it."

"It should be fine." Alex twisted the knob and pulled the door toward him.

A slight breeze blew through the narrow opening. The air felt humid already and warm—a sign of how the day would go.

Alex moved through the doorway onto the landing, then stepped to the black cast iron railing to let Ava past.

She walked out of the home and past him. A frown formed on her face. She trudged down the steps, then looked about the yard. "It already feels terrible out here, and it's not even the worst part of the day."

"Yeah. Going to be another miserable one for sure. Well, more so than normal." Alex faced the backdoor, locked the knob from the inside, then shut it. He tested the doorknob to ensure it was locked.

"Do you smell that?" Ava tilted her head back and sniffed. She looked around with her nose pointed upward. "Smells like something might be… burning. You don't think it's close, do you?"

Alex trotted down the stairs to the walkway and parroted her action. The air smelled of smoke. Although faint, it was there and made him ponder what had caught fire. "No telling. Houston always has a weird smell. You get used to it." He looked to the morning sky and the haze that clung to the clouds. "The air pollution here is horrible. The six chemical disasters the city had over the last few years filled the skies with dark plumes of smoke for days. It could be something like that."

"Or folks could be burning down buildings and causing all sorts of mayhem." Ava lowered her head and faced the driveway. "I'm not sure if anything would surprise me much now."

"In either case, we'll watch for any trouble and try to steer clear if we happen across it." Alex marched past her toward the driveway, then peered around the corner of the house to the street. All seemed as it did yesterday with no different cars parked next to the curbs.

They moved away from the back of the home and headed for the street. Alex kept his gaze fixed on the road ahead while Ava flanked him.

"What do you think the odds are of us finding a working vehicle?" Ava asked, walking faster to stay alongside him. "I normally wouldn't suggest stealing a car, but circumstances being as they are, we may need to."

Alex shrugged. "Chances of finding a working car are about as good as me winning the lottery."

"So, not likely then, huh?" Ava smirked as they hit the end of the drive. "I'm not that lucky either. Never have been. More of the opposite. I know some people that could walk up to any of these parked cars and find a set of keys dangling from the ignition. Not me, though."

"Well, we'd waste time trying to find a car with keys in them." Alex pointed to the stagnant cars parked on the sides of the street. "That's only half the issue. Even if you do, they may not be operational, so the keys would be a moot point."

Ava nodded. "That is true. I didn't think of that."

Alex looked to the east, down the road. "45 is in that direction. It's not too far."

"Excellent." Ava placed the ridge of her hand above her brow to shield her eyes from the sun's rays that bled through the canopy of trees that lined the sidewalks.

"You lead and I'll follow." Alex tilted his head in the direction of the highway.

Ava marched down the sidewalk with Alex following off to the side. They trekked through the residential neighborhood toward the highway. People stood on their porches or the green lawns, staring around and conversing with those close by.

Alex kept his face trained at Ava's feet with the bill of the ballcap tilted forward. He peered at the various folks who didn't give them a second glance. Alex knew some of the people from the brief conversations they'd had over the years. He wasn't outgoing in the neighborhood and kept to himself.

The people milled about for a bit longer, then retreated to the inside of their homes.

The long walk ahead gave him time to think and plot his day out. He had to track down Trey and get the money back by any means necessary. Alex knew money to Trey was like trying to hold water in your hand, but banked on the fact that he might need it as insurance in case Vargas's men caught up with him.

Last Alex had heard, the police hadn't found Trey yet, meaning he was still on the run or even dead. He didn't mind the latter as long as he could get what he needed from him, then after that, his fate was his own.

A list of possible locations and contacts of where Trey could've gone ran through Alex's head. His main residence would be a crapshoot, seeing as the law and Mr. Vargas's men could be keeping a watchful eye on it. Still, some clues might reside there.

The other locations consisted of skanky women Trey messed with and unscrupulous thugs he did odd jobs for. In the end, Alex would have to pick a place and go from there.

They reached the end of the residential area that morphed into businesses lining both sides of the road. Fast-food restaurants and other shops had a small bit of foot traffic in front of them. The pedestrians stood outside the entrances of the powerless buildings, peering through the windows.

The number of cars left on the street varied. The occupants had left the dead steel. Windows were shattered. Glass littered the pavement. Car doors hung open, revealing the interiors.

Alex watched the people in the area, mindful of any uprising or turmoil that could rear its head. The riots and other upheavals usually steered clear from his neck of the woods, but that didn't mean it couldn't happen, especially now.

Ava glanced at the storefronts and wrapped her arms tighter across her chest. She continued on down the sidewalk toward the access road and highway.

A thrumming car engine revved, then plowed down the street from the way they'd come. Tires squealed loudly, capturing the attention of any people near the road and the businesses they stood in front of.

Alex looked to the street and stopped. Ava did the same.

A light blue vintage Ford Mustang muscle car drove toward them at full tilt while trying to navigate the vehicles stuck in its path. It swerved, missing the cars by mere inches, and drove toward the shoulder, then into the grass.

A small group of people, huddled together on the lawn in front of the fast-food building, scattered, fleeing for safety from the inbound car.

The front end of the Mustang clipped two of the men as its backside went wide. One of the younger-looking gentlemen flew into the air, smashed the hood, then rolled over the top. Another vanished under the carriage. The others dove for cover, trying to avoid the wrath of the metal beast.

"Jesus Christ." Ava watched in horror. Her hand pressed to her open mouth.

Alex drew closer and moved them toward the buildings flanking them.

The Mustang darted into the street and t-boned a pickup truck. Metal crunched, followed by busting glass. The pickup skidded across the ground.

A horn bellowed. Smoke plumed from the engine of the classic ride. A handful of people charged the muscle car.

"Come on. Keep moving." Alex pushed Ava forward.

The doors to the Mustang flung open. Two burly men stepped out. They stumbled about, disoriented, then leaned against the side of the smoking wreckage. Their hands pressed to the side of their heads as they gathered themselves.

The small mob closed in, shouting and hollering.

The two surly-looking brutes faced the threat, then lifted the bottoms of their shirts.

"Shit. Go, go." Alex kept a firm grip on Ava's arm.

They sprinted away.

Gunshots exploded behind them. They flinched and ducked. Another shot followed. Screams sounded, followed by more gunfire.

The people charging the muscle car stopped and took cover. Some were wounded and lying on the pavement.

The gunmen bolted across the street with guns in hand, leaving the wrecked Mustang in their wake. They sprinted through the space between two parked cars near the curb, then charged down the sidewalk in the opposite direction.

Ava dropped to a knee at the rear of a cream-colored sedan. Her back pressed against the bumper. She panted hard, chest heaving.

Alex watched the men flee, waving the scant few people out of the way who crossed their path. He looked over the roof of the sedan to the street for any further trouble. "I think it's safe to move."

CHAPTER TWENTY-THREE

ALEX

The morning had started off with a bang, making Alex wonder what the remainder of the day had in store for them.

"Did you see that guy fly over the hood of that car?" Ava asked, looking in the direction of the wreckage. "His arms and legs swinging in all directions. Just horrific."

"It was, but we should keep moving." Alex tugged on her arm, pulling her back onto the sidewalk.

They left the scene in a rush and hoofed it to the intersection at the edge of the highway. Alex took point with Ava as his shadow. They wormed through the maze of cars to the access road on the far side and continued on.

Silence lingered between them as they kept to the grass and away from the road.

Minutes ticked by like seconds.

The hint of smoke tainting the air grew thicker. The sky overhead had brushstrokes of gray that choked the city. Crackles of gunfire kept them on edge and looking over their shoulders.

A scant few vehicles passed on the streets and roads, driving through stop signs and intersections without braking. Alex pondered why some cars ran while most didn't. It seemed strange.

The morning wore on, bringing forth hotter, stickier weather.

The heat baked the earth without thought or care. Sweat bubbled off Alex's forehead and ran down the sides of his face. The rhythmic hum of Cicadas built, becoming louder the more they walked.

Ava nudged Alex's elbow with hers. She panted, face contorted from the brutal heatwave. "You know, I normally don't mind the hot Texas weather, but I'm well over it."

Alex removed the ballcap and wiped his moist forehead on the sleeve of his shirt. He put it back on and nodded.

"So, tell me more about your daughter." Ava made a wide arch around a steel pole. "She's beautiful."

"Huh?" Alex glanced at her with a furrowed brow and scrunched nose.

"Sorry. I know that came out of nowhere," Ava replied. "The silence is killing me. I need my mind distracted. It's a thing with me."

Alex looked around the buildings, cars, and smoke-filled sky. "I'd say there's plenty of distractions around us at the moment. No shortage of that."

Ava tromped through the growing weeds, drawing closer to him. Her head stayed pointed at the ground as if ashamed or embarrassed. "I'm sorry. It was a stupid question. I'm a ball of stress right now and feel anxious. My mind is working overtime and I'm trying not to crumble under the pressure of everything."

Alex looked at her. He understood what the weight of the world on one's shoulders felt like and having one's mind ripped apart with more thoughts than one could handle. "No need to apologize. I'm not that great with small talk either when my mind is occupied. I've always struggled with such things. It hasn't gotten better with age; I can tell you that much."

"I know escorting me wasn't what you had planned for things to do today," Ava replied, staring at the grass. "Given the dire situation that's befallen us, I can only assume you have more important matters to tend to. Like that daughter of yours."

"I do, but those will be handled once you're dropped off with your son," Alex replied, knowing what it felt like needing to be with your child during a crisis, regardless of their age. "My daughter is, let's say, more than capable of handling herself. She's a strong, confident woman, with an attitude to boot—much like her mother. It's been pressing on me not being able to speak with her. Our last real conversation didn't go so well."

Ava nodded. "I imagine it's weighing on her as well. Is she away at school or something?"

Alex looked away, then stared at the vehicles littering the access road and the highway beyond that. "Something like that. She's spending time with family for a bit."

"Family time is good. I miss being able to do that and having my son, Juan, speak with my parents." A frown formed on Ava's face, followed by a sniffle. "The only family I've got in Houston is my cousin and her kids. The rest of my family is in Mexico. It's… hard being apart, especially when times are tough. I'd give anything to be able to call them, but that's not possible, and not because of the power being toast."

Tough. Alex knew the struggle and battled it daily. It was a slugfest that pounded his soul into submission with each waking moment, whether he wanted it or not.

"That loneliness can weigh heavily on a person. I am sorry to hear that," Alex replied in a sincere tone.

Ava wiped under both lids with the tip of her finger, then cleared her throat. "It's okay. Man. I'm just all over the place. An up and down roller-coaster of emotions. Thanks for not being a typical man and getting frustrated with me. I've had that happen more times than I can count. It never ends prettily. At least for me, it hasn't."

"Don't worry about it." Alex pressed his fingers to his chest. "I've not been the best husband, or father, or human for that matter, and have more than my fair share of doing stupid things, but at the end of the day, I strive to be a good, decent person who does right by my family and those I come into contact with."

"I know I just met you and all, but from what I've seen, you seem to be doing a good job of that." Ava raised her chin, glanced at Alex, then offered a warm smile through the emotional stress on her face and in her shiny eyes.

Alex nodded. "I do appreciate it. It's been some time since I've heard such words of kindness instead of ones filled with hate and contempt."

Ava parroted the gesture. "We all need to hear nice things every now and again. It does wonders for the soul." She looked ahead at the large, green road sign. "We're not too far away. A couple more exits and we'll be at the street the apartments are located on."

They climbed the short incline and reached the top.

The intersection below had a collection of various vehicles and an eighteen-wheeler parked under the non-working traffic lights. The big rig was turned at an angle, heading under the bridge. Both large doors hung open.

A mob of ragtag people gathered at the rear of the trailer. Their faces were covered with bandanas and various types of masks. They dressed in all black. Some had rifles slung over their shoulders while others moved in and out of the trailer.

Alex ducked into the growing grass.

Ava lowered to his side and watched. “Great. More trouble. What are they doing?”

“Robbing whatever’s on that truck, I’d guess,” Alex answered, studying the armed men standing guard around the perimeter of the trailer. “From the three red markings on the fronts of their garb, they appear to be part of the radical Brothers for Justice group.”

“Oh, really? That’s them?” Ava asked, her mouth slightly open. “I’ve heard about them, robbing businesses at random to combat corporate greed and such, and setting fires as well. Doesn’t make sense to me, but whatever.”

Alex tilted his head. “Yeah. They’ve been seen all over Houston looting and burning businesses to the ground, rioting, and mainly causing a slew of problems for everyone and the police. The group has no love lost for the authorities. That’s been evident. They kill cops at random and lure them into ambushes. Nasty stuff.”

An older model gray van with dented side paneling and a cracked windshield rolled up on the scene. It slowed, made a wide arch in the street, then backed toward the rear of the trailer. The doors to the van opened. More men jumped out, dressed in similar garb.

“We’ll need to find another way around,” Alex said, scanning over the terrain next to them. “I’d like to steer clear of that to avoid any trouble. Don’t want to risk an encounter with them.”

Ava agreed, nodding while staring at the men unloading boxes and other goods from the trailer and transferring them to the back of the van. "We can use the next street down to cross. That'll take us to where we need to be."

The armed radicals patrolling the perimeter of the rig, and watching the intersection, looked their way.

Alex lowered farther into the grass, as did Ava. His heart pounded a bit harder. He studied the men, hoping they didn't see him and Ava.

"I don't think they noticed us," Alex said. "It doesn't look like it anyway since their rifles aren't trained in our direction."

Ava lifted her head some and craned her neck. "How are we going to move without them seeing us? They seem to be looking our way every few seconds now."

Alex rubbed his chin, plotting. "I'm not sure. Give me a second here to think." He peered over Ava's shoulder to the buildings across from them, then checked their flank. "If we stay low and move slowly, we could make for that row of buildings. The grass seems rather tall and thick. It should conceal us some. That, or we can backtrack down the hill, then work our way around and over."

"I think we should—"

A single shot snapped the militant group to a ready stance. They brought the rifles to bear, shouldering the weapons, and searching for the shooter.

Ava dropped to her stomach and covered her head.

Alex flinched and kept hidden, watching the Brothers for Justice fan out among the cars and the big rig.

Muzzle fire flashed from under the bridge. The incoming rounds pinged off the side of the trailer and other nearby vehicles.

The sentries returned fire at the shadowy vehicles under the bridge, taking cover behind the graveyard of steel in the road.

Alex spotted multiple flashes of gunfire at different points under the bridge. He couldn't lay eyes on the force of men pushing toward the rig.

The workers standing at the rear of the trailer hurriedly tossed varying-sized boxes from the back to the other grunts on the ground loading them into the van. A man jabbed his hand at the back of the trailer, then pointed at the van. He waved his arm at the other men wielding weapons who surrounded him, directing them on where to go.

"Get up and move toward those buildings while they're distracted," Alex said, emerging from the tall grass. His hand balled in the back of Ava's shirt and pulled her from the ground.

Ava bear crawled across the dirt, fighting to get upright and her legs in working order. She stayed low and gathered her footing, sprinting away from the access road toward the structures.

Alex trailed behind, looking to the intersection, then ahead of them. His head was turned every few seconds, trying to scout out the way ahead while keeping a close eye on the shootout.

A stray round whizzed past them, going over their heads and missing by a good margin.

"Keep going and don't stop," Alex said, panting.

Ava darted through a portion of damaged wood fencing, vanishing from sight.

Alex chanced one last glance while breaching the opening. One of the Brothers for Justice faced his way with a rifle shouldered.

The report made Alex's head sink below his shoulders. His wide frame plowed through the opening. Wood busted, then splintered from the frame.

Alex lost his footing and crashed to the ground. He rolled, then stopped on his back.

Ava reached down and touched his shoulder. "You didn't get hit, did you?"

Alex shook his head and sat up. "No, but it was close. Whoever was using the rifle got close to tagging me. A second slower and he might have."

"Come on." Ava stood and tugged on Alex's upper arm, trying to heave his bulk from the ground. "I'm glad they missed. That intersection turned into a war zone fast. Were the police closing in from the other direction? I didn't look to see."

"Doubtful." Alex gathered himself, then glanced at the damaged portion of fencing he'd charged through. "Police don't normally open fire like that, though, I could be wrong."

Ava glanced about the alley they stood in that ran the length behind the row of shops. "Whoever the hell it was must not like them too much seeing as they didn't bother asking any questions before they started shooting."

Alex stared at the far end of the buildings where the gunfight sounded off, searching for any movement from the armed radicals, but spotted none. The weapons fire kept coming with little pauses every now and again. He remained calm and focused, devising their next move inside his head.

A small opening up the alley toward the direction they needed to go caught his attention. "Right there. Go."

Ava stayed close to the buildings with Alex on her hip. They charged the gap, running full tilt.

Alex stuck his arm out and slowed her pace. He moved ahead of her, craned his neck, and scoped out the passageway. "Looks clear."

A van tore ass past the entrance to the alley from the street down from them. It flew by in a blink.

Ava rushed around the brick bend and advanced through the clutter of pallets leaning against the walls, trash cans, and other miscellaneous junk.

Alex trailed her, skirting the maze of discarded waste. She threaded her slim, but fit hourglass frame through the path toward the other end. Alex wasn't as nimble and acted more like a bull in a china shop, bulldozing his way through and creating a cacophony of noise.

"Let me check it real quick," Alex said, skirting past her.

Ava got out of his way, then said breathlessly, "By all means, be my guest."

Tires squealed, followed by the grumble of an engine headed their way. Alex flicked his hand at Ava, motioning for her to stay back and out of sight.

He toed the blind corner of the passage that dumped them out onto a sidewalk. His hand reached for the Ruger tucked in his waistband. Alex took a deep breath, ready to draw the gun at a moment's notice.

The van barreled down the desolate street going ninety to nothing. The driver swerved past the few cars in the road and kept going at full speed, blazing by them without braking.

The van turned down another street, leaving the area. Alex checked the sidewalks and buildings for any additional threats.

"Well?" Ava asked, kneeling next to a trash can. "Are we good to move?"

"Looks like it." Alex leaned out from the passageway onto the sidewalk a bit more to get a better look at the street in the direction they had to go. "I'm not seeing any of the armed men. We stay low, move fast, and keep close to the buildings until we clear that section of street. Sound good?"

Ava stood, then tilted her head in agreement. “You lead. I follow.”

CHAPTER TWENTY-FOUR

ALEX

The gunshots ebbed.

Alex and Ava worked their way down the sidewalk toward the street. They stayed close to the powerless businesses, moving at a good clip. He kept a vigilant eye on the far corner of the building ahead of them for any movement breaking the blind bend.

Ava matched his stride step for step. She fell in sync with him, stopping, slowing, and moving as if she were his shadow.

Their shoes pounded the walkway. Panted breaths escaped their parted lips.

Alex removed the Ruger and held the revolver down at his side. His finger rested on the trigger guard as they approached the intersection.

They slowed their pace to a slow walk.

Ava brushed against his arm and nipped at the heels of his boots.

Alex stalked the corner, advancing with caution. He lifted the Ruger and stopped at the edge of the building. His hold on the revolver tightened as he peered out to the street and toward the bridge.

Men shuffled within the meld of cars in the road and near the rear of the trailer. It appeared the Brothers of Justice had thwarted the other armed group of men from taking the rig.

“Are they still by that big truck?” Ava asked, leaning against the wall.

“Yeah. Not sure what they’re up to at the moment,” Alex replied, spotting some of the armed men glancing their way. “They’re still congregating next to the trailer. A handful are patrolling the perimeter. I’ve got two staring in this direction.”

Ava moved up alongside Alex and stopped. “Can we make it to those vehicles in the road there? Use them to keep us hidden until we reach the other side of the road.”

Alex shrugged, then licked his tacky lips. “Maybe. We’ll have to move together and fast to avoid detection.” He held his free hand up, palm facing her. “When I say go, you stay on my six and do exactly as I do, all right?”

“You don’t have to worry about that.” Ava stood at a ready position.

The sentries patrolling the street turned and looked back toward the trailer and the other men standing about.

“Come on. Stay low.” Alex ducked, then bolted from the corner of the building across the sidewalk.

Ava hunched over and trailed close behind.

Alex stopped at the rear of a white hatchback and crept to the far side of the vehicle. He worked his way across the bumper with Ava an inch off his backside.

The cars up the street hindered his view of the men. He lowered and stretched his neck, trying to get a better angle of the rear of the rig.

Damn it.

"What's wrong?" Ava asked in a whisper.

"I can't get a good look at them from here," Alex replied, resting his back on the bumper. "The cars in the road are making it hard to watch them."

Ava stood and peeked through the back window of the small car. She stayed low and out of sight. "I see them. Two men with guns pacing around the cars looking this way. The others are occupied. I don't think they know we're here from the way they're holding those rifles."

Alex skimmed the street down from them, then back the other way. The coast appeared clear for the moment. He glanced at the red minivan twenty paces away. A tan Dully was parked on the other side near the curb, giving them enough concealment to stay out of sight. "We've got a bit of open space to make it across, so be ready to haul ass."

"Got it. I'm just waiting for them to… go." Ava tapped his shoulder.

Alex stood and rushed across the open space. She mimicked his hastened pace.

Footfalls hammered the pavement. He gave a quick glance toward the bridge. The men patrolling spoke to the other members of their clan, then turned back around. He ducked behind the rear of the minivan and stopped.

Ava grumbled, then punched the back door of the vehicle. “Damn it.”

“What?” Alex faced her.

“I dropped my purse,” Ava replied, pointing to the bag in the street. “I lost my balance and almost fell. It slipped down my arm. I tried to grab it, but my fingers couldn’t get the straps in enough time.”

Alex stepped away from the minivan and looked around her. “It’s too dangerous to get. They’re on our ass.”

“My life is in that purse,” Ava shot back, panting. “I can’t leave it behind.”

“Shit. All right,” Alex said. “The next time they look away, I’ll grab it.”

Ava hung near the edge of the van, staring at the bag. Her hands rested on both sides of her hips. “Don’t bother. I’ll grab it. It’s—”

A shot sounded.

Alex grabbed her arm and jerked her toward him. She lunged forward, eyes wide.

The lone bullet punched the driver side near the rear of the vehicle.

Ava flinched, then gasped. Her body tensed, and her muscles tightened.

“They must’ve spotted you,” Alex said, pushing her to the far side of the minivan.

“I’m sorry. This is all my fault.” Ava stooped below the two back windows, distraught.

Alex inched toward the corner of the vehicle and checked the road. Another gunshot crackled. He stepped back.

The bullet busted the driver side taillight. Broken pieces of plastic fell to the pavement.

"We need to move, now." Alex lowered beneath the two windows at the rear.

"What about my purse?" Ava asked in a raised voice. "I can't just leave it there. My life is in that bag."

Alex blocked her, placing his wide frame between her and the purse. "Your life will be over with if you try to get it. They know someone's back here and they will put a hole in you if you try to go for it. We've got to go."

Ava resisted a moment longer, then turned around.

"Keep low and head for the building over there." Alex covered their retreat, working along the tailgate of the Dully toward the sidewalk.

The gunfire stopped.

Alex wondered if the armed men were in tow, closing in on their position. He pushed Ava up on the sidewalk toward the corner of the building.

Ava moved fast while keeping her head lowered. She breached the corner of the building, then stood.

"Keep going," Alex said, waving her onward.

Another crackle sounded. The bullet hit the side of the brick wall as Alex ran for safety. He glanced over his shoulder at the street.

A masked man appeared with a rifle shouldered. He trained the barrel at Alex's back.

Alex lifted the revolver and squeezed the trigger.

The Ruger barked.

Fire spat from the shortened muzzle.

The masked man dove for cover behind the minivan.

Ava sprinted down the sidewalk, running full out. She panted, flinching with each shot.

Alex glanced back toward the minivan, looking for the armed, masked man, but didn't see him. He faced forward and caught up to Ava, then pointed at an opening within the wall of shops they were passing.

She slowed, then ducked inside the opening in front of the store. Alex ran past her, turned around, then faced the way they'd come.

"Are you all right?" Ava asked, winded.

"Yeah. I'm fine." Alex gulped, took a deep breath, and watched the sidewalk for the gunman. The revolver pointed at the ground. Sweat poured from under the Texas ballcap and ran down his face.

Ava palmed her side, then walked around. Her face scrunched in pain. Both lids closed for a second, then opened again.

"I'm not spotting him or anyone else." Alex relaxed and fought to control his breathing. "Are you okay?"

"I'm fine, just winded, and my side is cramping some," Ava answered. "So, we're good, then?"

Alex shrugged. "No telling. But from this point forward, we'll need to book it to your cousin's and put as much distance between us and them as we can."

CHAPTER TWENTY-FIVE

WENDY

One step forward, two steps back.

The throbbing in Wendy's head magnified, making it difficult to think straight. The dizziness persisted, not leaving her be. The torment of being on the edge of puking lingered in the back of her throat like a lump and built with each passing second.

Wendy sat on her backside, hands bound together with rope that sliced into the already raw skin around her wrists. She tugged her arms in a futile manner, then stopped.

Her shoulders deflated. Both lids pinched shut to cull the sickening sensation.

Roy had left her alone and headed down the slope to find his brother. He'd been gone for a short bit. The rustling leaves and snapping branches marked their movement. Soon, they'd be back and seal her fate.

A number of bleak futures ran through Wendy's mind like a bad nightmare. It all ended with her grisly death and being left in the woods for the animals to pick clean. That was if she was lucky. The simple thought made her shiver and fear the Dukes that much more.

Wendy wanted her family. She needed them more than ever. A familiar face that would reassure her that everything would be all right. It didn't matter if it was her grandparents or her father. Each would handle the vile backwood's men with the fury of a thousand suns. Help wasn't coming, though, and she had to face that reality and figure out how to save herself.

The Dukes emerged from the bushes and trees close to the hill she'd tumbled down earlier. Roy lugged his brothers' body onto flat land with Jimmy's arm draped over his broad shoulders.

Blood coated the side of Jimmy's head. The greasy hair was matted to his skull. His legs trembled as his arms reached for the dirt.

Jimmy lifted his chin and stared at her. A scowl formed on his bitter, angry face. Both nostrils flared. His hand raised, finger trained in her direction. "Why the hell isn't this bitch dead yet?"

Roy removed his arm from across Jimmy's shoulders, then stood upright. "Don't be sore 'cause she kicked the shit out of you, then took your knife."

"She threatened to cut my wiener off, Roy," Jimmy shot back, raising his scratchy voice an octave. "The damn tip was pressed to my crotch."

"Stop your bellyaching. It's not like you've needed it or anything," Roy replied, dismissing the rant with a wave of his large hand. "Besides, she didn't go through with it. Doesn't have the stomach to do such a thing, I reckon. Bad on her part, I guess. I'd be more concerned with what she actually did—messing up the side of your face."

Jimmy probed the gash on the side of his skull. He recoiled, then pulled his finger away. The skin puffed up and was discolored where the branch had impacted. "You never answered me. What are we going to do with her?"

Wendy felt acid burning her throat. A cold, clammy sensation washed over her.

Roy walked toward her. "I figure we take her to the spot and finish her there. I don't want to leave her here and risk a hunter finding her body. You know as well as I do others walk these woods. We muck this up and it'll be our heads on the chopping block, and I don't plan on that happening."

"I don't know, Roy. She ain't looking too good now," Jimmy said, pointing at Wendy. "I think she's sick or something."

Roy bent down, grabbed Wendy by the arm, then wrenched her from the ground.

The sudden jolt rocked her. The bite of acid scorched the lining of her throat and raced to her mouth.

Wendy bent over and spewed what contents resided in her gut on Roy's pant leg. The vomit splattered his boots and the dirt like wet cement.

"Jesus Christ." Roy jumped back and released her arm. "She threw up on my damn pants and boots."

"I told you she looked green under the gills," Jimmy said, steering clear of her. He looked away. "I can't be around that stuff. Makes me sick just thinking about it."

Wendy dry heaved a few times after, then spat on the ground. The bad taste lingered in her mouth. The expulsion of her gut relieved a bit of the nausea and lessened the pounding headache. She still felt weak, but at least she could think a bit more clearly than before.

Roy kicked his foot, slinging the puke from his boots to the leaves. “Come on. Let’s get moving. The sooner we get to the spot, the faster we can wrap this up.”

Jimmy made a wide arch around the vomit and took point.

Roy snapped his fingers, then shoved her forward.

Wendy dragged her feet through the dirt and stumbled, but didn’t fall. She glanced back at Roy and moved as ordered, holding her tongue and the slew of colorful words she wanted to say.

They pressed on through the woods, steering away from the creek and venturing further into the unknown. Jimmy moved about as sluggishly as Wendy was, navigating the rough terrain at a less than desirable pace for his brother.

Roy brought up the rear, sighing and scolding his brother what felt like every other second.

Wendy spat the remnants of the leftover bile to the ground.

“That’s not too ladylike,” Roy said.

“Does that mean you don’t want a kiss?” Wendy shot back in a snide, scratchy tone. “I’ve smelled and felt your breath. It isn’t much better.”

“Shut that mouth and keep going.” Roy rammed the buttstock of his rifle into her lower back.

Wendy cringed. She stopped, then dropped to the ground.

Roy kicked her boot. “Get on up and keep moving.”

Jimmy paused, then whistled. “Be quiet, will ya?”

“Why?” Roy asked, clutching the barrel and stock of the rifle.

“I thought I heard something up ahead,” Jimmy answered.

Wendy blinked the tears forming away, leaving a slight haze that tinted her vision. She looked to the trees and bushes. The foliage covering the area made it hard to see. She blinked again and stood, wondering what he heard.

"Do you see anything?" Roy turned and scanned the trees, and other verdure with his rifle shouldered. "I've got nothing. It's probably an animal or something."

Jimmy wiped the blood from the side of his face off with the sleeve of his shirt. "Not yet. I can't—"

Branches snapped.

Wendy opened her mouth to venture a scream but felt the muzzle of Roy's rifle nudge her in the spine. "You keep quiet now, you hear? I'd think twice before opening that mouth of yours."

Jimmy pointed to the west at a trail that sliced through more dense vegetation and rocks. He turned about-face. Both brows raised and his eyes enlarged. He held up two fingers, trained at his sockets, then back at the trail before them.

Roy muttered a curse, sighed, then lowered the rifle from her back. He grabbed Wendy's bicep and jerked her toward him.

Wendy hunted for the cause of concern, figuring it had to be people heading their way. The Bowie knife poked her back as Roy kept her close.

Jimmy nodded at them but remained silent.

Roy dragged Wendy behind a dense thicket and settled within the tall greenery. His body rubbed on hers, mouth positioned next to her ear. The tepid breath from the heavy-set man blew against the back of her neck and side of her face.

A small opening in the thicket offered a glimpse at Jimmy who stood like a statue, peering at them. He grabbed the sling attached to the rifle. He paced about, biting at his fingernails and glancing in the direction where Roy and Wendy hid.

"What the hell is that idiot doing?" Roy asked in a soft whisper.

"Giving you away from the looks of it," Wendy replied. "He doesn't look nervous at all. I think it's safe to assume that you two are one hundred percent screwed now."

"Shut it." Roy jerked her arm.

Two men dressed in camo garb appeared past the trees and other vegetation near Jimmy. One had a thick, gray beard and rounded, puffy cheeks. He stood taller than his shorter, skinnier partner who had a young, clean-shaven face. He looked to be in his low to mid-twenties. Each man had a rifle slung over their shoulders and rucksacks strapped to their backs.

Gray Beard carried a black device in his hand, then held it skyward. It looked like a radio or phone from what Wendy could see through the opening. He moved it around, pointing it at various spots in the sky.

His partner slapped Gray Beard's broad chest with the back of his hand to get his attention, then pointed out Jimmy who blocked the path.

Both men stopped. Gray Beard lowered his arm.

Jimmy waved at both men, then gripped the sling attached to his rifle.

They spoke for a moment. Gray Beard pointed at the side of Jimmy's face. The younger man peered around the woods, scanning the trees and other greenery around them.

"Keep calm and send them away," Roy whispered. "He better not mess this up. More bodies equal more problems."

Jimmy shrugged and turned his busted face toward the hunters. Gray Beard looked him over, then showed him the device in his hand.

Wendy adjusted her stance, trying to take pressure off the sore ankle. She moved her feet and nudged the bushes.

"I told you not to move," Roy said, his low voice growing thick with anger.

"My ankle hurts," Wendy shot back, feeling the tip of the Bowie knife dig into her flesh.

The hunters looked toward the thicket Roy and Wendy hid within. The younger hunter kept his hand fixed to the sling, then pointed at the thicket.

Jimmy turned, stood next to Gray Beard, and glanced at the wall of vegetation. He flicked his hand, then reached for the phone in Gray Beard's hand.

"Come on, you idiot. Get them moving already." Roy sighed, then removed the Bowie knife from her back. He wiped his forearm across his forehead while keeping a firm hold of her arm.

Wendy seized the opportunity and sprang into action. The heel of her boot stomped his toes. She threw her head back, busting his bandaged nose.

Roy howled in pain, then released her arm.

The hunters flinched, then went on the defensive. The younger man slipped the rifle from his arm and shouldered the weapon.

Wendy lurched around the thicket, screaming and yelling. "Help me. Please, help me."

Roy slashed at her back. The sharp edge of the Bowie sliced a small piece of her forearm.

"What the hell is going on here?" Gray Beard backed away and scrambled for his rifle. The phone dropped from his hand to the ground as he reached for the sling.

The young man trained his rifle at Wendy as she rushed toward them.

"That weasel standing next to you and his brother back in those bushes kidnapped me. Please, you've got to—"

Jimmy hammered Gray Beard's face with his fist.

The older but stout hunter recoiled, dropping back onto the heels of his boots.

Wendy hid on the far side of the younger man. He turned and trained his rifle at Jimmy and Gray Beard as they wrestled for the rifle, tugging at the stock and jerking one another in all directions.

Roy emerged from the thicket with his rifle shouldered, sight set on Wendy and the young hunter. A cold, callous look washed over his face. He gnashed his teeth and squinted.

The skin in the corners of his eyes folded.

The young hunter panicked, shifting his focus from Gray Beard and Jimmy to Roy.

"Shoot him or he's going to kill you," Wendy said in a strained voice. "Do it. Do it now."

Gray Beard threw Jimmy to the ground hard, then worked to get his rifle shouldered and trained at him.

The young hunter hesitated.

Roy didn't.

Fire spat from the muzzle of his long rifle.

Everyone flinched.

Wendy ducked and moved toward the trees.

The bullet struck the young hunter in the right shoulder, twisting him sideways. The barrel of the rifle lowered, pointed at the ground. He yelped, then fell to the dirt, palming the wound.

"James." Gray Beard spun around and rushed to the young hunter's aid. "No, no." He brought the rifle to bear in Roy's vicinity and fired at the same time as Roy.

Both rifles barked. Muzzle fire flashed from each weapon.

Wendy escaped through the trees as Roy howled in pain.

"Roy." Jimmy's voice rose an octave.

She lost sight of the men through the verdure and thickets. Wendy's heart hammered, beating a mile a minute. Her chin snuck over her shoulder and she looked for either of the Dukes, but spotted no one chasing after her.

Wendy ran as fast as her tired legs and sore ankle would allow. Having puked made her feel a bit better, but the brutal heat scorching the land and lack of water and food had taken its toll, keeping her sluggish and weak.

A cramp twisted her side. It grew more painful the longer she ran. A grimace formed on her sweaty, beet-red face, slowing her down.

She stopped and hid behind a stack of rocks. Silence loomed large at first. Two shots echoed loudly, one right after the other.

Wendy tugged at the rope, trying to slip free. She feared the hunters had met a fatal end at the hands of the two psychopaths who sought to end her life.

CHAPTER TWENTY-SIX

WENDY

The rope loosened some, but not all the way.

The coarse, twisted material ground on the red, damaged skin around her wrists. She needed to rid herself of the binds and fast.

Wendy watched the path that cut through the trees and other greenery for any movement. She listened for footfalls or snapping branches as she felt along the outer surface of the rocks and bushes.

The tips of her fingers touched the rough texture, finding a jagged edge she might be able to use. She turned and stared at the busted portion of stone that had a sharp edge to it.

Both arms lifted up and placed the rope on the exposed, jagged stone. She worked her arms back and forth, sawing at the dense material.

Wendy panted, going as fast as possible. She feared Roy or Jimmy would materialize around the bend at any second and find her. The thought made her panic and kept her arms moving at a fast pace.

The rope gave more and more as Wendy worked it along the jagged edge. She moved her hands outward, stretching the rope. It snapped, freeing her arms.

A crick resided in both shoulders. Rotating her arms caused a bit of pain to flair. She winced and extended her arms, then massaged the inflamed skin around each wrist.

Wendy glanced about, lost and unsure of where to travel next. The creek was her best bet at reaching her grandparents' place, but she had to find the way back to it somehow and also deal with the Dukes who'd shown to be unyielding in letting her go. Between the blazing sun, not feeling great, and being manhandled, she struggled to gather her bearings and make a decision.

The rampant thoughts of the vile men hunting her and the death of Clint assaulted her spent mind, plunging Wendy into a spiral of self-doubt. Her backside rested on the rounded surface of the rock while her dirt-covered hand batted the sweat away from her brow.

She'd been through hard times in the past, like her mother's passing and her father's trouble with the law, but nothing like the Dukes and people being murdered. It was a bad dream that seemed to have no ending.

Her grandfather's voice whispered into her ear to calm down, take a deep breath, and focus. He'd taught Wendy, much like her father, to be strong and fight back if the cause warranted it.

Running from trouble only got one so far before one was forced to stand one's ground and deal with it head-on.

Wendy glanced at the ground, hunting for any sort of makeshift weapon. She wanted to be prepared and end the Duke's path of deviant behavior once and for all. No other female would be a victim to their sick desires if she had anything to do with it.

The search continued around the base of the rocks and trees. She gathered the rope from the ground and held it in her hands.

She could fashion a stone axe using the rope. A weapon of sorts forged from what mother nature had at her disposal. The thought injected a bit of hope into an otherwise bleak situation.

Wendy gathered a piece of stone from the ground that came to a point at one end. She advanced down the path, peering over her shoulder every few minutes, then back ahead of her.

The grass sprouting from the earth made it challenging to see within the foliage. The tip of her boot tested the ground near the path, probing for another stout piece of wood she could attach the rock to.

Come on. Come on. Give me something.

She followed the winding path a bit farther, navigating the changing terrain that tested her footing and body. The chirping birds and other sounds kept her alert and on guard. Any rustling noises sent her searching for the source. The sun beat down with little shade or relief.

Wendy scavenged a bit more until she found a tree lying on the ground near the path. She moved through the knee-high blades of grass.

The timber looked in decent shape, with only a few rotted patches on the trunk. The thick, solid branches protruding from the tree felt stout in her grasp.

The stone and rope were placed on the face of the trunk while she hunted for the right size branch. Wendy walked the perimeter of the tree, studying any limb that might work. A portion of the wood she tested didn't budge when she pushed against it. Others snapped with ease.

She climbed over the trunk to the other side and examined the tree closer. A thick branch hid among the grass. Her hand swatted at the swaying blades.

Wendy grabbed the bark and tugged. It felt solid in her hand and wasn't too big to swing nor too small where it would break easily.

The lightheadedness lingered in the back of her head, rocking her balance as she looked to the stone on the trunk. Her hand pressed the bark to stabilize her. She waited a moment, ventured along the side of the tree, and grabbed both items.

Her thumb tested the pointed edge. It felt sharp enough to maybe hack or saw through the bark. She wanted to minimize the noise made and hoped sawing it would work and the rock wouldn't crumble.

Wendy sat the torn strand of rope on the trunk and marked off where she wanted to cut with the stone. Her hand held the wider end of the rock and started sawing at the far end of the branch.

The jagged edge sliced into the tree. Her arm worked back and forth, eating away at the bark. The tips of her fingers and hand held firm but ached from the unnatural grip.

The muscles in her arms tired quickly. A burning sensation fired through the limb, up to her shoulder, then her back. She pushed on until the stone cut through.

Sweat dripped from every portion of her flushed face. She stood up, took a deep breath, then worked on the other end. Her hand hurt from gripping the hard stone.

Wendy stopped halfway through and set the rock down. She shook her hand, then stretched her fingers.

The sole of her boot pressed against the side of the bark.

She pushed.

The branch snapped off from the tree.

Wendy retrieved the wood and skimmed over it, making sure it was sturdy enough for what she needed. She flipped the bill of the tight hat she wore up, then wiped the wetness from her brow. She grabbed the rock and placed it against the side of the branch.

It's better than nothing.

She sat both items on the trunk and secured the rock to the stick using what rope she had. The tattered strand wound around the rock and stone in an X pattern until she reached the end.

Wendy secured the rope as best she could and looked over her work. She grabbed the rock and wiggled it about, seeing if it would come loose. The stone stayed in place and had little to no give.

The heft of the weapon felt substantial in her grasp. She lifted the stone axe skyward, then brought her arm down as if striking the tree trunk, but didn't. It could do some damage if it didn't fall apart upon impact. That would be the real test.

Wendy left the fallen tree and made her way through the grass to the path she'd traveled along. She stood still, looking both ways and trying to decide the best course of action.

The Dukes wouldn't stop hunting her and would keep coming until the deed was done. That much was certain. The brothers wanted her dead and her body disposed of so no one would ever discover what had happened and they could continue their sick, perverted work. She'd have to stop them once and for all.

A disturbance in the grass across from Wendy caught her attention. She looked to the long blades and took a step back.

A snake slithered out from the weeds toward her. Its tongue flicked from its mouth, testing the air. The back of the reptile had chestnut crossbands with a lighter-colored body between. Its length looked to be around twenty-five inches or so. A copperhead snake.

She remembered her granddad saying the venomous snakes lived near streams and rivers. The scaly creature had ventured away some, but the creek had to be close by.

The copperhead hissed, then coiled.

Wendy took another small step back, watching the reptile.

The thumping of her heart spiked. Fear grabbed hold and made it hard to turn and run. Given her weakened state and the quick-strike ability of the dangerous creature, the odds of getting bit increased in her head.

The copperhead slithered toward her, then lunged forward with fangs drawn.

Wendy hopped back, then lost her balance. The heel of her boot hit a low impression in the dirt and sent her to the ground. Her backside smacked the unforgiving earth.

The reptile advanced, slithering through the loose dirt. Its tongue flicked out. The golden black eyes on either side of the creature's head locked onto Wendy.

She backed away on her butt.

The scaly, deadly animal drew closer, then lunged forward again.

Wendy swung the stone axe at the copperhead. The jagged edge nicked the creature just below its wide head. It dropped to the dirt a foot or less away, injured.

The meaty inside of the snake showed through the wound. Its body continued moving. The hissing persisted as it tried to strike once more.

The stone axe smashed its head, pinning it to the dirt. A portion of the snake's skull vanished under the rock. The back half of its body moved about, trying to get free. Blood ran from the opening in the snake's body and head, staining the end of the rock a crimson color.

Wendy stood with her hand fixed to the end of the stick. The long, scaly body of the cold-blooded creature slithered in the dirt, unwilling to die. The sole of her boot crushed its damaged head, ensuring it couldn't sink its fangs into her.

She removed the stone axe, then hacked at the exposed, damaged portion of the body, just below the head. The blood-stained rock crudely chopped through, severing it.

The copperhead thrashed about a bit longer, then stopped.

Wendy removed her boot from the severed head, studying the venomous snake's crushed skull. She kicked it to the grass, then the body.

The stone axe remained intact. A portion of the end was chipped some, but it had held together. It did a good job handling the snake, but soon, it would be tested against a more dangerous predator.

CHAPTER TWENTY-SEVEN

ALEX

The wave of anarchy spread through Houston like wildfire and showed no signs of letting up.

The smell of smoke grew stronger, tainting the air. Gunfire increased, echoing in the gray sky.

The criminal element of the once-bustling metropolis sank its teeth in and refused to let go. More and more factions fought over neighborhoods and businesses. The deadly conflict claimed lives from both innocent people and those who sought to exploit the turmoil.

"We're almost there," Ava said, breathless. She stopped for a moment and bent over, huffing in the alley they stood in. "It's right up the road. Not much farther."

Alex held his arms above his head, panting. "Good deal. Things are getting worse out here by the second."

Ava pressed her hands against her knees and nodded. "Seems like the thugs and radicals are taking full advantage of the outage and the police being a no show. Not that it would matter. They've been causing enough problems for the authorities before any of this even happened."

"Yeah. It's a bad situation all around." Alex looked to the other end of the alleyway and tilted his head. "Let's keep moving."

They moved down the passage toward the street. Ava flanked him, staying on his heels. She took long, deep breaths, then sighed.

Alex lifted his hand, holding her up at the corner of the building they walked next to. He scanned the streets for any masked men or other armed individuals, then looked around the blind bend.

The road leading to the Villas appeared deserted of any threats. Cars parked in the road congested the street. He waved his hand, then advanced out onto the sidewalk.

They hurried down the walkway, moving at a good clip. A few of the shops on either side of the street had been damaged from looting and other such upheaval. Glass crunched under their feet.

Shadowy figures lurked inside some of the structures. Voices shouted from the men milling about in the low light, looting whatever they could get their hands on.

Alex paid them no mind and kept on.

The pylon sign for the Villas came into view, reaching past the edge of the building next to it. He slowed at the next blind corner at the intersection and surveyed the streets in both directions. All looked clear.

They raced across the intersection to the other side and skirted past the lone pickup parked in the crosswalk.

Ava pulled ahead, leaping onto the walkway and passing Alex. She raced toward the entrance of the complex in a dead sprint.

Alex trailed after her, slowing a bit. The muscles in his legs burned hot from sprinting most of the way.

A black cast iron fence ran the length of the complex next to the walkway. It reached ten or so feet into the air with no other way through.

Ava craned her neck, peering through the black fencing at the tan and red building. Her hand glided over the bars. She slowed her pace, allowing Alex to catch up.

"Where's the apartment located?" Alex asked, winded.

"Near the back. East side of the building," Ava replied.

They reached the end of the fence that led into the entrance. Ava slipped past the dense bar and marched across the pavement. Her head turned from left to right, staring at the cars in the parking spaces.

Ava seemed on edge from the way she studied the vehicles, then the surrounding area. It looked as though she was watching for someone.

Alex may have been reading more into it than he should be, but the thought stuck like glue. He considered letting Ava go the rest of the way since he'd gotten her there, but her odd demeanor and body language kept him engaged.

The entrance to one of the bottom-floor apartments opened. An older, Hispanic woman hobbled out from the blackness. A high—pitched bark escaped the white Chihuahua she cradled in her trembling arms.

The tiny dog bared its fangs and yapped in their direction. The frail woman stared at them as they rushed past. She dropped the barking dog and held firm to the leash attached to the canine's collar.

The Chihuahua lunged forward and raised on its hind legs, pulling the leash taut as they passed the far edge of the building. The yapping from the small dog ebbed, then stopped.

Ava slowed a bit more, out of breath. She kept moving, eyes fixed to the apartments and cars facing them. "It's right up here. 14B. Second floor."

Alex checked behind them, then followed through the gap between the parked cars toward the staircase. He glanced at the exterior of the three-story building, looking it over.

The blinds to the apartments on the first floor were closed. All windows and screen doors were shut. The immediate area had no foot traffic that he could see—no kids outside or people shuffling about.

Ava raced up the steps, taking two at a time. Each footfall echoed loudly as she hit the landing. She skirted past the railing and charged to Apartment 14B.

"Lucy, it's Ava. Open up." Her fist pounded the door. She tested the doorknob, then peered back to the parking lot.

Alex marched up the remaining steps, stopping shy of the landing. His arm rested on the top of the railing. He leaned against it, taking a minute to catch his breath.

Ava hammered the door again with a heavy hand. It shuddered. "Lucy, unlock the door and let me in."

"She might've left and tried to get him to a hospital or something," Alex said.

"Lucy wouldn't leave the apartment. She's probably just afraid it's—" Ava clammed up and jerked the doorknob.

Alex lifted his brow, confused by the frantic words that didn't make much sense. He opened his mouth to respond but spotted movement from below on the walkway.

Two Hispanic men emerged from the side of the building. Each had a bandana around their bald heads. Pistols sat tucked in the waistbands of the sagging pants they wore. Both men stared at Alex, then Ava while reaching for the hardware.

The door to Lucy's apartment unlocked.

Alex stepped away from the railing and eyed the hard-looking men. His hand drifted down toward his waist, ready to pull the revolver.

Ava twisted the knob. The door swung inward.

A young, black-haired woman stood in the entryway. Tears streamed down her flushed light-toned skin. "I'm sorry, but I couldn't—"

"Where's Miguel?" Ava asked, raising her voice.

The men from below pulled their guns.

Alex did the same. He trained the small revolver on them. His finger moved inside the trigger guard. "We've got a problem down here."

A man shouted from the interior of the apartment.

Lucy flinched from the thunderous boom of the deep, rich Hispanic accent.

The familiar voice tingled Alex's memory. He struggled to place a face and name with the accent in the heated moment.

Ava backed away, stopping at the railing. She glanced at Alex, then down at the two-armed men with weapons locked on him.

Lucy disappeared to the interior of the apartment.

A dark-skinned man with slicked back, black hair emerged in the doorway, taking her place. He wielded a silver 1911

Browning pistol in his hand. His arm rested on the jamb. He smiled at Ava who cowered before him.

"Hello, dear. Surprised to see me?"

CHAPTER TWENTY-EIGHT

ALEX

A rock and a hard place.

Alex kept the piece trained at the men on the sidewalk while staring at the doorway. He seemed familiar, but Alex couldn't think of his name. Alex tilted his head down some. The bill of the hat hid his face. The wheels ground inside his head as to the identity of the man. The name clicked after a few seconds, hitting him like a bolt of lightning. Diego Cabal.

Shit.

"Drop the revolver, friend," Diego said, raising his voice. "I'm only going to ask once."

Alex hesitated for a moment, then lowered the Ruger, and dumped it over the side of the railing to the walkway below.

The revolver clattered on the concrete.

One of Diego's goons from below retrieved the weapon.

Ava gripped the top of the railing with trembling hands. She kept her distance at first, then looked past him to the apartment. "Where's Miguel?"

Diego tilted his head back. "He's in his room. Safe and sound. From your haggard appearance and the look of that bloody bandage on your arm, I can't say the same for you. It's a dog-eat-dog world out there, sweetie, especially now. You shouldn't have left me, Ava."

"If you and your thugs are here, then he's not safe." Ava pushed away from the railing in a huff, stomping toward him. Diego blocked her path, denying access to the apartment. "I want to see MY son. You're not supposed to be anywhere near him unsupervised. And you know damn well why I left."

"Thanks to you, I can't see my son unsupervised," Diego shot back. His finger stabbed at her face. "Because of your big mouth and whining to the court, it's been months since I've seen him. I'm a bit irritated by that."

Ava took a step back.

Alex looked to the two men who inched toward the landing of the staircase he stood on. Their pistols were trained at his head and chest.

"I must admit, I'm rather shocked by the way you're acting. You never had a spine when we were together. Is this newfound sense of power because of him?" Diego glanced at Alex. "Did you run out and get a new boyfriend or something?"

"He's not my boyfriend, not that it's any concern of yours," Ava replied. "He's a good man who helped me get here. I can't say the same about you, though."

Diego placed his hand over his heart. "Ouch. That tongue has grown sharp. Seems you've forgotten what happens when you don't remember your place."

The muscles in Ava's arms tightened. Her body tensed.

"Remove the hat, friend," Diego said, turning his attention to Alex.

The two men stood at the base of the staircase, boxing him in.

Alex dipped his chin, then removed the hat from his head.

"Holy shit. It can't be," Diego said, shocked. "I know that's not Alex Ryder because that son of a bitch is supposed to be in Huntsville prison and not out here walking these streets."

Ava wrenched her chin toward Alex. A surprised look washed over her sweaty face. Both eyes widened and her mouth dropped open. "As in prisoner? You're not a security guard?"

Diego belted a hearty laugh. "Is that what he told you? If he's a security guard, then I'm the president."

"So, you broke out of jail, then?" Ava stared at Alex a moment more, then looked away.

"I'd say he did," Diego answered before Alex could. "He's supposed to be doing time for robbing and killing some of Mr. Vargas's men. That was a pretty gutsy move on Trey's and your part to steal from the big boss man. I'm surprised you're not dead, yet."

"Not for lack of trying," Alex replied, placing the hat back on his head. "I've had a target on my back since that night went down. Damn convicts kept trying to shank me and everything else in that hell hole. But here I am, still alive and kicking."

Diego chuckled. "Alive for now. I imagine once word gets around that you're back on the streets, you'll not only have to contend with the police, but Mr. Vargas will be coming for your ass."

Alex shook his head. "Trey robbed that store and pulled the trigger that killed that guy. Not me. I'm wanting to set things right with Mr. Vargas so he'll leave me and mine alone."

"Good luck with that. You're going to need it," Diego replied.

The two armed men standing on the sidewalk whistled at Diego. They nodded toward the street.

Diego tilted his head, stepped back into the apartment, then waved the Browning. "Come on. Get inside. Both of you."

Ava glanced at Alex with an unsure gaze. She cringed, brows slanted inward.

"I'm not asking twice." Diego trained the Browning at Ava. The cocky smirk vanished from his face. "Get inside, now, and we can continue our little discussion."

The two men advanced up the stairs with weapons trained at Alex. He peered at the goons, then to her, hesitant about entering the space.

Ava moved toward the apartment, slipping past Diego.

Alex marched to the open doorway with a gun pressed to his back and his hands raised. His eyes locked with Diego's who looked him up and down.

Lucy sat on the far end of a couch in the low light of the small apartment. Her knees pressed together as she reached for Ava who sat next to her.

"Sit his ass at the table," Diego said to his men who funneled into the apartment and shut the door behind them.

Alex was escorted to a chair at the small, rounded, oak table. A hand gripped his shoulder and shoved him into the seat. He jerked his body away from the goon.

"I want to see Miguel, now, Diego," Ava said, sitting next to Lucy.

"You'll see *our* son once we've had a chance to discuss a few things." Diego looked to the murk of the hallway. "Besides, he's having a good time playing with one of the homies. Juan is keeping him well occupied."

Alex peered at Diego, then the other two men who separated and spread out. One stood guard on the far side of the table with his gun trained at Alex while the other paced the living room, heading toward the sliding glass door.

Ava stowed her tongue and folded her arms across her chest.

The stifling heat inside the closed apartment unit made it hard to breathe. It added to the already uncomfortable tension that circulated within the cramped space.

Diego wiped away the sweat brimming on his forehead, then flicked the wetness from his fingers. He whistled at his man who stood near the long, vertical blinds hanging in front of the sliding glass door, then spoke in Spanish.

The slender, short man nodded, then walked toward Lucy. He reached across her and grabbed Ava by the arm.

"I'm not going anywhere or getting up until you bring Miguel out here," Ava said, jerking her arm away.

The slender henchman grabbed her arm once more and wrenched her from the couch.

"I'd advise you to settle down and watch your tone," Diego said. "I'm not sure what you told Alex to have him tag along with you. If you thought it was going to make a damn bit of difference, it hasn't. Now, get your ass into that bedroom and I'll be in there shortly to… visit with you. We have some matters that need straightening out."

Ava walked away from the couch with the henchman attached to her arm. She glanced at Alex for a brief moment before vanishing into the dim hallway.

"Women. I tell you what, they can be a pain in the ass," Diego said, shaking his head and turning toward Alex.

"Is your son even sick?" Alex asked, feeling played.

"Not at the moment. He's perfectly fine, though, he does suffer from some health issues on occasion." Diego secured the Browning in the front of his pants, then paced the room. "Seems as though both of you lied to each other. Not a good way to start off a relationship."

Alex bypassed the dribble spewing from Diego's lips and got to the point. "Listen. I'm not trying to get in the middle of any family drama or anything. That's between you and Ava. I'm just looking to track down Trey so I can get the money back he stole and get Mr. Vargas's men off me and my family's backs."

Diego chuckled, then pointed at Alex while looking at his man. "You're assuming Trey still has the money. That's wishful thinking. You know that man can't hold onto any paper. It's like water. Slips right through his hands as fast as he gets it. That, or the hookers take it. In either case, you'd be better off skipping the country and falling off the face of the earth. Might be easier now that we've been thrown back to the stone age. You have that going for you."

"I'll worry about Trey and the money. Thanks. Besides, running isn't a long-term plan." Alex rested his elbow on the corner of the table. "Not with Mr. Vargas's reach. I doubt the end of the world would stop that man."

"Neither is staying alive after what you two pulled," Diego shot back. Raised voices loomed from the hall. Diego glanced at the darkness for a moment, then looked away.

Alex sighed, growing tired of Diego's mouth and the runaround. "Whatever. Can you tell me when the last time you saw Trey was? I think you owe me that much."

Diego raised a brow. "Owe you? How do you figure I owe you?"

"From back in the day. The jobs both Trey and I helped you out on," Alex answered without pause. "We've been a helpful hand to you and your crew over the years. Don't forget that."

"Do you hear this asshole?" Diego looked to the goon covering Alex, then to the slender henchman who emerged from the murk of the hallway. "Did you get her settled?"

"She tagged me in the face, boss. Scratched the shit out of me, but she's settled and taken care of." The slender goon stood next to Alex, touching the scratch marks on his cheek.

"Man. This day is just getting better by the second." Diego muttered something in Spanish. The man moved from the entrance to the hall and crossed the living room. Diego rubbed his chin, then wiped more sweat from his angular jawline. "You and Trey have helped me out in the past, but I've also done you favors that make up for that. To be honest, I should deliver you to Mr. Vargas's people. He'd probably reward me real nice like for doing so."

Alex glanced at the two men, then back to Diego. "If that's how you want to play it, you can give it a go. I can promise you it won't pan out well. It didn't for the Aryan Brotherhood in the clink and it won't now. Besides, you value loyalty over money, right, or has that changed?"

Diego snapped his fingers, then nodded at Alex. "Times change, homie. Not everything can stay the same. You of all people should know that. You should've just cut your losses and run, but it's too late for that. Fate has brought us back together and with it, a nice payday for myself and the end of the line for you."

CHAPTER TWENTY-NINE

ALEX

The betrayal didn't surprise Alex, but it stung just the same.

Backstabbing bastard.

The two henchmen closed in on Alex. He stayed planted in the chair, refusing to budge while staring at Diego. A scowl twisted his face. His nostrils flared as his temper rose to a volcanic eruption in his gut.

"You're going to regret doing this," Alex said as he was ripped from the seat of the chair.

"It was nice seeing you again, Ryder," Diego shot back with a smug smirk. "Give my best to Mr. Vargas. Tell him Trey will be joining you soon. I can promise that much."

Alex made it two steps, stopped, then elbowed the slender goon flanking him on the right across his face.

The goon smashed against the shades, breaking them in half. His gun dropped to the carpet at Alex's feet. Both hands covered his face, and he howled through his palms.

Alex took a hard left cross on the chin from the other lackey. His head wrenched to the side, and his knees buckled. He stumbled about.

Diego recoiled from the sudden outburst and reached for the Browning in his waistband. His voice rose, and he shouted Spanish words so fast that it all melted together in Alex's ears.

The slender henchman attacked Alex from behind, wrapping his arms around his broad chest. He squeezed with all his might, trying to wrangle him.

The other minion pummeled the side of Alex's face with a balled fist. His jaw clenched. Spit spewed from between each tooth. He shouted, sounding more beast than man.

Alex took a quick beating. His head flung around. Each heavy hand rocked his world and rung his bell.

Diego charged the trio, grabbed the bruiser supplying the beat down, and shoved him out of the way. The muzzle of the Browning pressed into Alex's wet forehead. Diego squinted, staring at him with fire in both sockets. "Do you want to die right here, homie? It won't take much to make that happen."

Lucy whimpered on the couch, tucked into a ball with her legs against her chest and feet resting on the cushion.

"Shut up," Diego said, glancing her way and shouting at the distraught woman.

Blood dribbled from Alex's nostrils and his busted bottom lip. His head swelled with a throbbing pain, and his jaw ached from the repeated blows. He looked Diego dead in his eyes, then said, "You pull that trigger, you're going to have a ton more problems on your hand."

Diego pursed his lips, then adjusted his hold on the grip. "I guess we'll see if I do or not, vato."

Alex held his ground, feeling the warm steel of the Browning burrow deeper into his flesh. The eye contact with Diego grew more intense with each passing second.

Footfalls pounded the floor, rushing down the hall, then stopped.

"Papa?" a young male voice asked from the shadows. "What's going on?"

"Sorry, boss," a Hispanic man said right after. "He ran out of his room before I could stop him."

Diego shifted his gaze from Alex to the hallway. "Mijo. What did I tell you earlier? You need to stay in your room until I come get you."

Alex glanced at the young boy who ventured out from the shadows and into the low light of the living room. He looked to be about ten or so from what little Alex could see. "Are you going to pull the trigger and traumatize your kid for life? That will mess him up."

The shadowy figure flanking the boy placed his hands on both of his shoulders and kept him close.

Lucy continued whimpering from the couch.

Diego kept the Browning in place a moment longer, then lowered it. "Seems as though your luck continues, my friend." He held the firearm behind his back and approached the kid.

The thug holding Alex kept a tight hold around his chest while the other henchman remained planted at Alex's side.

Miguel glanced at Alex, then his father who stooped before the timid boy.

"Why don't you head back to your room, mijo, and play a bit more with Juan?" Diego patted the side of the kid's arm. "It shouldn't be too much longer."

"Can I see Mom?" Miguel asked in a soft voice. "I heard her earlier. Where is she?"

"Soon, mijo. Soon." Diego cupped the boy's jaw with his hand, then stood. He nodded at Juan, who drifted back into the murk of the hallway with Miguel.

Alex jerked his shoulders from side to side and grumbled under his breath, trying to rid himself of the smelly goon pressed against him. The other henchman decked him in the face. Alex stopped thrashing.

"What do you want done with him, boss?" the minion asked, standing tall in front of Alex.

"Take him to Mr. Vargas's people. Use the Impala, not the caddy," Diego answered, retrieving the slender man's gun from the floor and handing it to him. "We can't reach them with the phones out, so we'll just have to drop in. I doubt they'll mind, though, seeing who it is. His partner will be next."

The slender goon released his arms from Alex, took the weapon, and pressed it into Alex's back.

"You've signed your death warrant, Diego," Alex said while being forced across the apartment. "It didn't have to go down this way."

The front door opened. The strident light from outside blasted Alex's face. He squinted and diverted his gaze.

The two minions wrestled him through the doorway and onto the stoop in front of the apartment.

Diego waved his hand and smiled as the door slammed shut.

The slender goon shoved Alex forward into the railing. He spoke to his partner in Spanish. It sounded heated from the raised tone and how quickly they talked.

"Your boss is making a mistake here," Alex said, pushing away from the railing. "He isn't thinking this through. Perhaps you two might have better heads on your shoulders and can reason with him."

"Shut your mouth and move your ass." The slender goon flanking Alex grabbed his shirt and pushed him toward the stairs. "You're damn lucky that kid was there. Anywhere else, you would've caught a bullet to the head, homie. Best believe that."

Alex was sandwiched between the two thugs who escorted him down the stairs and across the walkway. He glanced at the windows they passed, spotting beady eyes looking through the closed blinds.

"Open the trunk, Hector," the slender goon said.

Hector moved around the two-door gray coupe, then headed toward the rear of the lime green lowered Impala. His hand wormed into the front pocket of his sagging pants, fishing for the keys.

"If you let me go, I'll make it worth your while," Alex said, walking between the Impala and coupe to the rear of the vehicle.

"With what, vato? You don't have a bucket to piss in," the minion escorting Alex to the trunk replied. "Diego would cut our junk off and feed them to his pitties, not to mention what that crazy, loco kingpin, Vargas, would do if he found out we let you skate. Naw, homie."

Hector popped the trunk, then stepped away. "Start the car, Luis. I'll get him situated back here." He tossed the keys to his partner.

Luis caught the keys in mid-air and brushed past Alex. His hand massaged his busted face as he walked around Hector to the driver side of the car.

"Get in, now." Hector motioned with the piece trained at his stomach.

Alex contemplated going for the gun. His eyes dropped down to the weapon less than a foot away, then back up to Hector. He decided against it and faced the trunk. A bullet to the gut would end him quickly and leave Wendy exposed to the dangers that threatened her.

"Now, fool. Get in." Hector slammed his fist on the trunk lid.

"All right. Damn." Alex climbed into the spacious trunk.

Hector pistol-whipped the side of his skull, sending him to the floorboard hard.

Alex groaned, then palmed the side of his face. He rolled to his side, looking up at the mad henchman who towered over him.

The Impala grumbled, then thrummed to life.

"Enjoy the ride." Hector slammed the trunk lid, sealing Alex inside the heated, stuffy interior of the lowrider. A car door slammed shut a moment later.

The rattling of the steel coffin jumbled his throbbing head. It shifted into reverse and backed away from the building.

A tooth felt loose inside Alex's mouth. He probed the molar with the tip of his tongue.

The Impala stopped, then lunged forward.

Alex rolled to the back of the vehicle, hitting the bottom lip of the enclosure. His day had gone from crap to shit, and it only looked like it would get worse from there.

CHAPTER THIRTY

WENDY

The woods and open land around Wendy grew silent. No footfalls or movement lingered in the hot, boiling countryside. She kept moving, pushing through the tall grass and navigating the battery of trees in search of the creek, and home.

Where the hell are they? Wendy thought, scanning the area around her for the troublesome brothers.

The chirping birds she'd grown accustomed to ceased their squawking. She peered to the canopy overhead to the leafy branches.

The wide umbrella of leaves shielded the area from the heat, giving her a moment from the direct sunlight. A light gust of wind blew through the woods. The abundance of sweat coating her beaten frame and soaked shirt fluttered some.

The tepid breeze felt good, better than nothing. It did much in providing some relief from the dreadful, hot day.

Wendy pushed on through the foliage and thickets until she reached the creek. She paused at the edge and peered at the rocky bed below, scouting for the Dukes. They'd trailed her before using the stream that sliced its way through the country. She hoped they'd continue that same pattern.

The interior of the gutted land had a good amount of water flowing through it. Water cascaded over the rocks and fallen trees. The noise sounded peaceful, almost serene. Too bad she couldn't enjoy the splendor of nature.

A branch snapped.

Wendy's fingers gripped the homemade axe with a taut hold. She ducked below the bushes and scanned the area around her.

The slight breeze blew the leafy limbs and dense, green bushes, giving no sign of figures rustling the foliage or lurking between the thick trunks of the trees.

A clatter rose in the wide creek bed.

Wendy craned her neck and looked to the west, hunting for the source.

Jimmy emerged from the slight bend in the earth, slinging a rock at the stones embedded into the wet dirt on the far side.

Bingo.

Roy stood at the edge of the embankment, pointing at his brother. The two conversed for a moment.

Jimmy waved his brother off, then walked toward the water.

In a huff, Roy turned away and vanished within the trees and bushes around him. Her window to act had presented itself.

Wendy waited a moment, then got on the move. She kept low and skulked down the rim of the embankment. Her gaze fixed on Jimmy, watching his every move, then back to the ground in front of her.

Jimmy kneeled next to the water, dunked his hands, then splashed his face. His fingers ran through the damp locks of hair, then down his sunburned neck. He was oblivious to the fact of being stalked and that his life hung in the balance.

The stone axe sat ready and willing to do Wendy's bidding. It hung by her side as she flanked him. Each step was precise and silent.

Wendy took position on the far side of a tree near Jimmy. She glanced over the perimeter for Roy, but didn't spot him.

Jimmy drank from the flowing water, then flung out his hands. He probed the gash on the side of his skull and recoiled. He stood in a huff and ran his mouth aloud, speaking about how Wendy threatened his manhood. Jimmy stabbed at the air with his Bowie knife and scolded anything that would hear him.

This guy is off his rocker, Wendy thought, watching him meltdown.

He paced back and forth on the bank.

Wendy looked for a way to sneak up on him and discovered a path leading to the bottom close by.

Jimmy spouted some colorful words, then faced the water. He unzipped his pants and proceeded to taint the stream with piss.

Wendy rushed from the tree and made her way toward the path. Her body hunched over. She watched the disgusting subhuman relieve himself as she climbed down the rigid slope.

Jimmy stood with his back to her and didn't flinch from the subtle footfalls, or any other noise. He bent and turned. He stretched his neck, gave his privates a good shaking, then stuffed them back into the smirched rags he had on.

The dirt face of the slope gave under Wendy's boots. She slipped and landed flat on her backside, then slid to the bottom.

The stone axe flew from her grip and bounced off the dirt and rocks. Wendy rolled over, coming to a stop prone on her stomach. She clenched her jaw from the pain points pulsating throughout her body.

"Jesus." Jimmy spun around with his pants down some around his waist. Holey tighty-whities flashed her. His hands messed with the two flaps of the denim, rushing to button them up.

Wendy searched for the handle of the axe while getting to her hands and knees. Her fingers felt everything but the weapon she'd dropped.

"Roy, she's here," Jimmy shouted while securing his pants. He fumbled the sling to his rifle, trying to pull it up and over his chest.

Wendy grabbed a stone and stood. She hurled the rock at Jimmy, nailing him in the forehead. Direct hit between the eyes.

His head flung back. Both hands released the sling. He stumbled back into the water, palming his bloody face. A pitiful, muffled howl erupted from under his hands. Blood streamed down his sullen, unkempt face.

Wendy skimmed the ground around her and spotted the stone axe. She bent down, grabbed the weapon, then stood.

Jimmy lowered his hands, revealing the damage done from the rock. Both eyes watered. The skin around each eye socket was bruised. Blood ran from his flared nostrils, discoloring his upper lip and the sides of his mouth.

He reached for the sling once more with bloody, trembling hands. Pain turned to rage. His face twisted to a scowl and his voice deepened to that of a satanic demon summoning her.

Wendy charged Jimmy over the unstable, rocky ground. Each step made her ankle throb, but she continued forward.

The sling lifted above his head. Jimmy brought the rifle down and shouldered the weapon as she closed in.

Wendy swung the stone axe, smashing his fingers and the forestock.

"Ah." Jimmy bellowed another painful cry. The rifle pitched downward, barrel trained at the rocky, dirt surface beneath them.

His arm shot back and his hand released the weapon. He flicked his wrist, then stared at the bloody mess that was his hand and fingers.

Wendy took another swing, aiming for his skull.

Jimmy leaned back.

The stone axe missed his face by mere inches.

He slammed the stock of the rifle into the side of Wendy's gut while favoring his shaking, meat-burger hand.

A sharp grunt left her mouth. She stumbled backward, bending over.

Jimmy tried to shoulder the weapon and bring it to bear, but the damaged hand wouldn't cooperate. It lifted a few degrees, trained at her legs. He pulled the trigger.

She flinched, her ears ringing from the sound. She hopped back, avoiding the stray bullet that missed her thigh by a scant inch.

Wendy spun around and buried the rigid edge of the stone axe into the side of Jimmy's neck.

His head snapped to the side. The rifle fell from his hand and clanged off the rocks. He stomped through the ankle-deep water, then crumbled to his knees. His good hand plunged into the water, keeping him from falling over.

The injured, trembling hand reached for the open gash. Blood pumped out and stained the front of his shirt. He tilted his head upward, peering at her.

Wendy towered over the broken, vile man. Her chest heaved. She held the stick at her side and glared at Jimmy.

He blubbered under his breath, trying to speak, but couldn't form the words. Tears streamed down his cheeks. Drops of blood splashed the water below, changing it to a crimson hue.

Jimmy's eyes moved to the tree line and bushes Wendy had snuck through.

She chanced a glance over her shoulder to the top of the ridge. Wendy had a good idea of who Jimmy was looking at.

Roy emerged from the greenery with his rifle shouldered, sweeping the area. He peered at the both of them. His brows rose in disbelief.

The long barrel dipped toward the ground for a split second. He shouted and pointed at them, but the ringing in her ears made it hard to hear him.

Jimmy's arm buckled. He fell into the water, flat on his back.

Wendy took off in a dead sprint, running past him as quick as her sore ankle would allow. Her hand held onto the stone axe, keeping it close.

A gunshot boomed.

She flinched, but kept going, trying to reach the thick tree trunk that grew from the side of the cliff near the stream in time. Her heart pounded like a jackrabbit. Each breath was more labored than the last.

The bullet punched the stream at Wendy's back, missing her body by inches. Water splashed. She ran harder.

The rocky and uneven terrain tested her balance while moving over the misshapen stones and ground. She tumbled forward, reaching for the blind bend past the tree. Her arms stretched out in front of her, hands pressing to the bark to stop her from eating dirt.

Another shot fired at her back.

Wendy skirted past the tree and the thick roots that crawled toward the water.

The bullet hit the tree's trunk as she passed it. Bark chipped off in her wake.

The ringing in her ears subsided.

Roy screamed and cussed her name. An endless list of unspeakable acts he sought to do to her rang out.

Wendy peered over her shoulder while navigating the dwindling land near the stream. She didn't spot Roy chasing after her, but he wouldn't be far behind.

CHAPTER THIRTY-ONE

ALEX

The darkness made it hard to see and work. He had to find a way out of the trunk fast, but how?

Alex laid on his back with his knees bent and feet pressed against the far side of the cargo hold. His hands felt along the trunk lid, hunting for a latch, or anything else he could use to escape.

The bumpy ride and constant stops made matters worse. He bounced and rolled, unable to focus for any length of time in one area.

Frustration built.

His hands balled into tight fists. He punched the unforgiving steel lid. It only bruised his knuckles.

Diego's minions shouted from the front of the Impala. The road noise and seats muffled their rich Hispanic accents, but he figured they were demanding that he stop.

Alex cursed under his breath. His mind slipped from the task at hand as the anger surged. He slammed his foot against the hinge of the lid, creating more noise, daring the two goons to stop and pop the lid.

Multiple gunshots sounded close to the Impala. The shouting from the interior increased. The engine revved. Tires squealed.

The Impala swerved, tossing him about in the cargo hold. The chassis bottomed out over what felt like a dip in the road, sending Alex into the lid, then back down.

The back of his head hit the floorboard of the trunk. It dazed him, making his skull throb.

Alex cringed, then rolled over, facing the back seat. He reached out as the car came to a skidding stop, throwing him forward. He touched what felt to be a bag of sorts, then the back of the seats.

A loud crashing sounded from outside. His body thrashed about from the impact.

The horn blared.

The Impala idled but didn't die.

What happened?

Diego's men fell silent.

The horn ceased its blaring.

Another shot fired on the passenger side at close range.

Alex feared they'd be gunned down, and soon. His ticket would be punched next. He felt around the bag in front of him, then reached inside. His fingers sifted through what felt to be an array of various tools.

He grabbed the handle of a flathead screwdriver, then turned toward the rear of the vehicle. His sore fingers grasped the handle with a taut grip.

The doors to the Impala squeaked open.

Alex laid there, still and quiet.

"Check the trunk and see if they have any goodies back there," a deep, baritone voice shouted from the cab of the car. "I'll dump these two and we'll bug out."

A second later, keys scraped against the lock of the trunk.

Alex panicked, wondering what waited for him on the outside.

The lock clicked.

He hid the screwdriver under his leg as the lid opened.

Sun blasted into the ether of the trunk, blinding him. Alex spotted a quick glimpse of a dark-skinned man towering over the cargo space, wielding a pistol in his hand.

Both lids pinched shut, then opened. His hand lifted to block the light that framed the man in a golden brilliance.

"Yo, Slim, they've got someone back here," the African-sounding man said in a worried tone, standing next to the back bumper of the Impala. He grabbed at the top of his jeans, then wrenched them farther up on his hips.

"Don't shoot," Alex said, cowering and blinking away the stars that fluttered around him. His vision returned, allowing him to see the scrawny, young black male bearing down on him with his gun.

The young thug peered over the top of the trunk lid, taking his eyes off Alex for a split second. "Slim, what—"

Alex sprung from the cargo hold, grabbed Scrawny's wrist, then jerked him downward.

The young hoodlum recoiled, then fell forward. His face smashed the trunk lid. He yelped in pain, then palmed his face. “Ah, shit.”

The gun barked.

Fire flashed from the muzzle.

The bullet punched the floorboard at Alex’s side, tearing through his shirt, but missing the meat of his stomach. A loud ringing filled both ears.

Son of a bitch.

Alex removed the tool from under his leg and thrust upward.

The tip of the screwdriver plunged into Scrawny’s torso, burying halfway up the silver shaft. Alex pried the gun from Scrawny’s hand before he could get another shot off.

Scrawny’s face twisted in pain, eyes shut and brows slanted inward. Blood ran from his nose and mouth. He whimpered and gnashed his teeth.

Slim charged around the passenger side of the Impala to the trunk, carrying a small, black pistol in both hands. “Jay dog. You all right?” The gun trained at the ground as he rounded the back of the lowrider.

Jay grabbed at the handle of the screwdriver that protruded from his chest. He dumped forward to the cargo hold.

Alex snagged a handful of Jay’s shirt, then pulled him down to shield his body. He squeezed the trigger, firing at will.

The gun recoiled in his hand twice.

Each report hammered Alex’s ears.

The two rounds found their mark in Slim’s chest and his shoulder. The impact from the bullets twisted him around. He howled, then vanished from sight, dropping below the bottom of the trunk.

Alex shoved Jay off of him, then sat up.

The pistol swept the alley for Slim or any other dangers. He peered at the concrete below the trunk and spotted both men, lying on the ground, dead.

Blood stained the fronts of their white, sweaty shirts. The screwdriver remained in Jay's chest. Slim's gun laid at his side, away from his hand.

Alex sighed, then shook his head. He hated taking their lives, but his hung in the balance. They'd snuffed Diego's men and he might've been next. It was a chance that couldn't be taken.

He rolled over the bottom lip of the trunk to the pavement, avoiding stepping on the two dead men.

The world spun for a second. His legs wobbled. He leaned against the car, then palmed the side of his skull.

Alex shook the cobwebs from his mind, then retrieved Slim's compact pistol. He tucked the weapon in the front waistband of his pants, slammed the trunk lid shut, then peered through the back window.

Diego's men were gone from the interior.

Both front doors hung open.

He craned his neck, staring over the roof of the idling car toward the front end and the alley beyond. The Impala crashed into a dumpster, pinning it to the brick wall of the building.

Alex marched around the trunk to the passenger side with Jay's gun trained ahead. The palm of his hand pressed to the heated surface of the Impala's body.

Hector laid on the ground, prone on his stomach. A small hole resided in the back of his skull and the passenger side window.

Alex glanced at the empty bench seat. Blood splattered the dash and windshield. The windshield wipers worked back and forth, squeaking with every motion.

Luis was missing from behind the wheel. No doubt tossed to the ground on the other side.

Alex ducked inside the car, then shut the door behind him. He scooted across the bench seat and settled behind the steering wheel. His arm stretched out, hand reaching for the door to close it. The driver's side window had two more holes through the glass. He glanced at the ground, then over toward the wall.

Luis laid on his side with arms out in front of him. His right eye socket had a gaping hole in it.

Alex closed the door, then sat the gun in the seat next to him. His foot pushed on the gas. The engine revved, responding to the command without fault.

A slight knock sounded from under the damaged hood.

The gauges showed no hints or signs of problems.

Alex turned the wipers off, grabbed the gearshift on the column, then yanked down. He backed away from the dumpster and torqued the wheel. His foot mashed the brake, stopping shy of backing over the dead thugs.

He punched the gas.

The tires screeched.

The Impala lurched forward.

Alex looked to the rearview mirror at the multiple dead bodies lying on the concrete, then straight ahead. His fingers touched the puffy skin on his bottom lip. He cringed from the contact, then lowered his hand.

Anger swept over him like a blanket. Both hands gripped the wheel at ten and two, fingers squeezing the leather.

Diego had some intel on Trey. Alex knew as much and was going to get it out of him, one way or another.

CHAPTER THIRTY-TWO

WENDY

One down, one to go.

Roy pursued Wendy through the woods, not giving her a second to catch her breath. He stayed twenty paces or so behind her, fighting to reach her or to get a clear shot through the foliage she weaved in and out of. His large body charged through the bushes and verdure like a rabid animal. He didn't seem to care if he was quiet or careful. Vengeance and anger fueled his body and will to capture, and kill her quick—if she was lucky.

Wendy's sides hurt from the constant running and the blunt strike from the stock of Jimmy's rifle beating her side. She palmed the aching ribs with one hand while clutching the stone axe with the other. Her boots slipped in the wet dirt and rocks, causing her to wobble. She needed to get to higher ground and fast.

The crackle of gunfire echoed at her back. She flinched and ducked her head.

The bullet hit the end of a log that was blocking a portion of the stream.

Roy had fired three shots that she'd avoided. He'd gotten close twice and missed wide with the other. That was a lucky break.

The wounded parts of Wendy's body screamed in agony. The muscles in each thigh stung and grew in discomfort. The injured ankle radiated pain that wouldn't let up. She fought to catch her breath. Her lungs burned red hot with every gulp of air she took in.

The palm of Wendy's hand kept her upright, pressing into the soft, mushy earth that she labored next to in the stream. A gap within the exposed dirt ahead offered concealment and a chance to catch her breath for a spell.

Green grass dangled over a scant portion of the entrance. Roots slithered down the back wall of earth like veins. Various sized rocks protruded around the lines of roots.

It didn't look too deep, but it didn't need to be. She just needed to hide for a moment.

Wendy ducked under the blades of grass. The tips of the greenery brushed over her head and face. She turned around and rested against the dirt wall as the heavy footfalls and rustling stomped the ground above her.

Roy moved about, looking for Wendy. Each step he made at the edge of the high ground resonated below. "Where are you, girl? You're not going to get away from me. You're going to die in these woods. A slow, painful death awaits. I'm going to make sure of it and will enjoy every single second."

Her gaze flitted to the dirt above. Small particles fell to Wendy's face. Her hand muffled the panted breaths attempting to push from her mouth.

Be. Quiet.

A hissing noise loomed from her feet. The beating of her heart ramped up. Panic swarmed her.

She dipped her chin and looked to the ground at the entrance.

A snake slithered past, gliding through the moist soil and over the stones. The grass curtain hindered her vision, making it difficult to gauge the size and type of snake crossing her path.

Wendy remained still and waited for both threats to pass. She held her breath and controlled the angst from the serpent, and the hillbilly, being so close.

Roy toed the edge and scanned the ground below. More dirt fluttered to Wendy's face. She coughed and forced her hand tighter to both lips.

The snake moved on, heading away from the opening she'd crammed her frame into.

Roy stomped away. His footfalls trailed off to nothing.

She lowered her hand and breathed. The ball of stress and tension released from Wendy's mouth. Her chest heaved. For the moment, she'd given him the slip.

Wendy waited a few more minutes, then forced her tired body to move. Both legs hurt but obeyed. She passed through the veil of grass, then stopped to check the area for Roy. All looked clear with no footfalls or boisterous shouting to pinpoint his whereabouts. She tilted her head sideways, then looked to the ground above. Still, nothing.

The snake moved on as well, leaving her sight. The trail left in the dirt slithered down the bank, then vanished into the stream.

Wendy emerged from the drape of earth, then continued on along the stream. She studied the ground above, listening and watching for Roy, but also for a way up top.

The amount of ground left not taken over by water shrank quickly, leaving little room for her to walk. She'd have to abandon the creek bed, and head for higher ground.

A system of roots from a tree growing near the stream stuck out from the ground. She grabbed the wet roots and tugged. They gave some but held.

The incline to the top was much more doable than it had been. Rocks lined the face, offering places for her boots to go.

Might as well.

Wendy secured the handle of the stone axe through the back of her shirt, down the collar. She grabbed the roots and scaled the side of the dirt wall to the top.

The tip of her boots rested on any portion of rock it could find. Her grip strength waned, slipping from the wet roots. She leaned back toward the ground.

Both hands clamped around the thick system of taproots. One hand released the vegetation and clawed at the blades of grass. Her fingers grabbed at the base. She heaved her body up and over, then rolled to her back.

Wendy panted from the exertion that on a normal day wouldn't have been anything for her to bat an eye at.

She sat up, then got her feet under her.

The endless woods seemed vast and never-ending. Dangers lurked around every tree and bush it seemed.

Wendy removed the stone axe and held the handle. The rock attached to the stick wobbled. It wasn't as tight as it had been. Great.

She ventured along the side of the creek, scouting for Roy. Her tired eyes scanned the trees and bushes as she listened for heavy footfalls.

The warm breeze rustled the leafy branches above. Wendy looked up to the rays of sunshine that tore through the small gaps.

The flowing beads of sweat raced down her flushed cheeks. The sour stomach she'd battled earlier on, lingered, making her feel a bit nauseated once more.

The thick wall of bushes she passed jolted with activity.

Wendy stopped, then spun around, facing the disturbance. The stone axe raised in defense. Her hand tightened over the handle. She peered through the branches and leaves to the interior of the bushes, finding nothing more than green, leafy foliage.

The noise ebbed. Silence took hold.

She turned about and took a step forward. Roy stood a few feet from her. Wendy jumped back with the stone axe up in front of her. Her ankle buckled, and she stumbled.

"I knew you were close." The sling attached to the rifle hung across his fat body. The Bowie knife was in Roy's hand. He peered at her with narrowed eyes and pursed lips, then pointed the tip of the large knife at her. "That twig and rock aren't going to save you now. I'm going to do my worst right here and you're going to feel every inch of it."

"It might not look like much, but it did a good enough job at handling that sick, twisted brother of yours," Wendy shot back, eyeing the large ogre. "And don't worry, you'll feel every inch of this as well."

Roy growled, then lunged forward with the knife.

Wendy swung the stone axe at Roy's head. The knife slashed upward, slicing through the hot, humid air. Wendy sidestepped it. The stone axe missed Roy's skull.

The brute turned on his heels and slashed at her mid-section, catching enough of the fabric to cut it open.

Wendy's feet tangled and her ankle gave. She fell back into a tree that kept her from hitting dirt.

Roy charged with the knife above his head. His thick arm dropped, driving the tip of the Bowie at her skull.

She tilted her head out of the way.

The knife punched the bark a second later, burying deep into the trunk. The silver-tinted weapon gleamed from the corner of her eye.

Roy pressed his sweaty weight on Wendy and yanked on the handle. His tepid, odorous breath blasted her face. The yellow-stained teeth behind his dried, cracked lips and bushy beard flashed at her.

Wendy pressed both hands into the fat rolls of his stomach. She pushed with all her might, but couldn't gain any ground. Her arms buckled, unable to overpower him.

He wrenched the Bowie knife free from the tree, then lifted it over his head again.

She raised her knee, searching for the fruit between his legs. The top of her leg smashed his jewels.

Roy's eyes bulged. A yelp seeped through his clenched jaw. His backside pushed outward as he retreated. He hunched over and lowered the knife.

"Did you feel that?" Wendy asked, wielding the axe in her hand. She kicked him in the chest.

Roy shot upward, then took a step back, reeling from the blow. His hand held onto the knife, refusing to let it drop to the grass. He took a feeble swing at her with the Bowie while cupping his junk with his free hand.

Wendy hammered his forearm, knocking his arm toward the grass. Bits and pieces of stone crumbled from the sides to the ground. The rock twisted and hung by a scant bit of rope.

The Bowie knife fell to the ground. The tip jabbed the earth.

Roy palmed the chewed, bruised skin on his forearm. Spit dripped from his mouth. Beads of sweat followed. Roy tilted his head, then glanced up at her with shiny eyes. He reached for the knife, then grabbed her wrist.

Wendy smashed the stone axe across the side of his skull.

The rock busted apart even more, scattering to the grass and dirt.

Roy dumped over onto his side, taking Wendy to the ground with him. His fingers tightened around her wrist, refusing to let her go. Blood ran from the open wound on the side of his head. He muttered and tried to sit up, refusing to yield.

Wendy wrenched her arm, then dropped the stick. Her free arm stretched, fingers grabbing the handle of the knife. She took hold as Roy pulled her closer, trying to wrap his arms around her.

The Bowie pulled free. She faced the deviant and buried the thick, long knife deep into his chest.

Roy released his hold on her arm as blood broke the surface around the knife. His head dropped to the ground. He coughed and hacked with trickles of blood running from the corners of his mouth.

Wendy scampered away and watched as Roy took his final breaths. His head fell to the side, both lids closed.

She'd ended the brothers' reign of terror, and saved herself from a terrible fate. A sense of relief washed over her. The nightmare had come to an end.

CHAPTER THIRTY-THREE

ALEX

It was a high price to pay.

Diego hung in the forefront of Alex's thoughts, as did Ava and her family. He couldn't help but worry for their safety, and what Diego had in store for them. It gave him more of a reason to get back to the Villas in a hurry and kill two birds with one stone.

The Impala raced through the crowded, powerless intersections and streets scattered with cars of various sizes and types. What few people walked the sidewalks watched the lowrider pass by, staring and pointing at it. Others shouted to the heavens and sought to stop the working vehicle by any means necessary.

An assortment of items hurled at the car, slamming its body and windows. The dense thuds punishing the Impala loomed large inside the vehicle. He swerved to miss what objects he could, seeing as it was his only salvation at the moment.

Alex took the next street at full speed, cutting the steering wheel hard to the left. His foot mashed the gas pedal, feeding the hungry beast as much octane as it wanted.

The Impala made a wide arch in the road, skirting past a small, blue car toward the curb. The tires hugged the pavement, keeping the lowrider from eating a steel pole.

The villas came into view. Not much longer and he'd be back to get his answers.

The anger built with each passing second as did the worry that Diego might've already left and taken what knowledge he had with him. Alex couldn't remember where Trey lived but knew of a few hangouts that he could try if it came down to it.

Alex slowed the Impala, then wrenched the wheel, pulling into the back entrance of the low-income apartment complex. He cruised through the parking lot, passing the blind corner of the bottom units and cars lined in front of the dwellings.

Please still be there, Alex thought, craning his neck and looking for the caddy that was parked next to the Impala earlier.

He spotted the vehicle parked in the same spot as before.

Alex slowed to a crawl, then stopped next to the fence encompassing the perimeter of the parking lot. He shifted into park, killed the engine, and removed the keys from the ignition. He tossed open the door, grabbed the pistol from the bench seat, then stepped out.

The keys went into his pocket. He'd need them later. The gun hung at his side, out of view. His finger rested against the trigger guard.

Alex shut the door and advanced on the apartments, passing through the space between the parked cars to the sidewalk. He moved quickly, leaping over the curb and heading for Lucy's residence.

The caddy came into view. The gun sprung up and trained at the windshield. Alex checked the interior from the sidewalk, finding it to be empty.

He paused at the corner of the bottom units, then peered to the second-floor entrance leading to Lucy's place. The door was shut with no armed goons standing watch. Diego had only one other man with him. He hoped that was still the case.

The gun trained at the closed door of Lucy's apartment as he rushed the landing in front of the staircase. Alex took each step with care, glancing at the shut blinds of Lucy's residence for hints of someone watching. He approached the front door with cautious footing, reducing the chances of alerting anyone inside.

Alex turned his head and listened, but heard nothing coming from the interior. He wondered if Ava and Lucy were okay or if Diego had done something to them.

He grabbed the doorknob and twisted, testing to see if it was unlocked. The knob turned freely. Someone had forgotten to secure it, or they'd left it unlocked for Diego's men when they returned. In either case, he'd take the lucky break.

His sweaty hand repositioned over the grip as he pushed the door open. The hinges remained silent.

Light poured in from behind Alex, erasing the darkness. No footfalls stormed his way. Raised voices loomed from the dark hallway—a mixture of male and female. Ava and Diego.

Alex shut the door, then swept the apartment from the entryway. The kitchen and small dining nook had no movement within the murk. Just the cabinets on the walls and junk littering the top of the bar. No shadowy figures lurked in the low light of the hallway either.

A muffled voice shouted from the living room. Alex glanced at the couch, training his gun at the source.

Lucy laid on the cushions on her side. Her arms and legs had rope around them, restricting her movement. A piece of duct tape covered her mouth. She stared at him, jerking her arms, and thrashing her legs.

The shouting continued down the hallway, increasing in volume.

Alex advanced toward the couch and watched the hallway for any movement. He gripped the corner of the tape covering Lucy's lips and ripped it off. "Are you all right?"

Lucy whimpered and nodded. Tears streamed from her eyes. She panted. "Diego has Ava in my bedroom in the back."

"Lower your voice," Alex said in a whisper, placing his finger to his lips. "Does he just have the one other guy with him?"

"Yeah. He'll be back any second. He went to check on Miguel," Lucy answered, pulling her arms. "Can you untie me?"

Alex lowered the pistol and looked over the knotted rope around her wrists and ankles.

A creaking hinge alerted them both.

Lucy gasped, then glanced past Alex to the hallway.

Light shone from the blackness, then went away.

Alex turned and crept to the corner of the couch, his pistol trained ahead.

A shadowy figure materialized from the hall. He spotted Alex and reached for his waist.

"I wouldn't do that," Alex said in a low tone, pressing the muzzle to the side of the man's skull. The man raised his arms and kept them up. "Here's how this is going to go down. We're going to get Diego out here and you're not going to try anything stupid because if you do, they'll have to mop up your brain matter and bone from the floor. You feel me?"

Juan groused, then cut his narrowed gaze up to Alex.

"I'll take that as a yes." Alex pressed the pistol to his temple a bit harder. "Now turn around and move."

Juan turned about, facing the hallway. He marched forward, venturing farther into the darkness.

The door leading to the room Miguel was in stayed opened.

Alex shifted his attention to the little boy standing in the doorway of the bedroom.

Juan lowered his arms and spun, knocking the gun from Alex's hand. He rammed both forearms into Alex's chest, driving him back into the wall of the passage.

Miguel retreated to the bright light of the bedroom, then slammed the door shut. It hit the jamb with a dense thud.

Alex raised his arm wielding the pistol.

Juan grabbed Alex's wrist and pushed the gun back toward the floor. His forearm pressed into Alex's throat, choking him.

"What the hell is going on out there?" Diego shouted from the closed bedroom door around the bend of the hallway.

"Miguel." Ava called out to her son, yelling loud.

Footfalls stomped the floor from Lucy's room.

Diego shouted at Ava in Spanish.

Alex kneed Juan's side, then shoved him back into the wall. He lifted the gun and pulled the trigger without having a clear shot.

A brief flash of muzzle fire lit up the darkness. The sound hammered their ears. The bullet hit the drywall next to Juan's head, missing the mark.

The smaller, but nimble goon batted the gun from Alex's hand. It clanged off the wood floor. Juan speared him in the gut, then drove him back into the living room. His fists pummeled Alex's side, causing him to wince with each blow.

Alex punished Juan's spine with his elbow, then kneed him again in the mid-section.

Juan's arms dropped from his waist.

Alex wrapped his arms around Juan's side, lifted, then threw him into the wall.

Juan slammed the unforgiving corner, then crashed to the floor. He groaned on his side, then tried to stand.

"Stay down." Alex pulled the backup pistol from his waistband, then trained the weapon at Juan's head.

Footfalls rushed Alex from behind. He spun around and found Diego standing at his six with the Browning pointed at his skull. He smashed the side of his face with a heavy backhand, sending him to the wood floor.

Alex hit with a hard thud. The pistol slipped from his grip and clattered off the ground.

"You've got to be kidding me. How and why are you here? Where's Hector and Luis?" Diego asked, towering over him.

"Dead, but not by my hand." Alex spat a wad of blood to the floor. "Things are shit in the city, and they're about to get a lot worse in here."

"Is that so? You're becoming more trouble than you're worth," Diego said, moving the Browning up to Alex's head. "I don't need this headache right now."

Ava approached Diego from behind, gun in hand. She pressed the muzzle to the back of his skull. "I'll fix that headache if you don't drop the piece."

Diego froze, keeping an eye on Alex. "You're bluffing. You ain't got the stones to pull the trigger. Besides, you're no killer and you hate guns. Drop it now, and I'll consider not beating you senseless."

"I hate you more than any gun," Ava replied in a cold, stern voice. "If you want to find out if I'm bluffing, go for it."

"All right." Diego lowered the weapon, smirked at Alex, then spun around, slapping the gun away. Ava didn't fire. He ripped the gun from her hand, then pointed it at her forehead. "I knew you didn't have it in you to pull the trigger. You're weak and pathetic."

Alex swept Diego's legs out from under him, sending him to the floor. His arms flailed as he hit flat on his back.

Ava rushed to the couch where Lucy laid.

Diego turned and sat up, snarling.

Alex decked him in the face, smashing his nose with his balled fist.

Diego fell to the floor. His arm lifted. Each hand wielded a pistol.

"No, you don't." Alex straddled his chest and pinned his left arm to the floor. He grabbed the barrel of the Browning, tore it from Diego's hand, then trained it at his head.

"Ah, shit, Ryder." Diego groaned with his eyes shut and teeth gnashed. His hand palmed his bloody nose.

Alex glanced at the ladies on the couch. "Are you all right?"

Ava finished untying Lucy, removing the rope from her arms and legs. "Yeah. We're good."

Juan stirred on the floor near the doorway. He looked at Alex while holding his side.

"Now, I'm only going to ask you this one last time and you better shoot me straight or so help me God, you and your homeboy over there will regret it." Alex placed the muzzle on Diego's wrinkled, sweaty brow.

Ava moved from the couch and retrieved the gun from the floor. She stood near Juan, pointing the weapon at him. "Can you go check on Miguel, Lucy?"

"Yeah." Lucy sprung from the couch and raced down the hall.

Diego removed his hand and peered at Alex. "Let's just calm down, all right?"

"I'll calm down once you tell me where Trey is?" Alex kept the Browning pressed to his skull. "Tell me what you know and perhaps I won't paint the floor with what little brains you have in that thick head of yours."

"Last I heard, he was staying at some cabin near Artesian Lakes. Unit 4b or something like that. It's about an hour from here," Diego answered, shaken. "The source who told me isn't always reliable and is normally doped up, so take it how you will."

"You seemed pretty sure of it from the way you spoke earlier." Alex applied more pressure to Diego's trapped arm under his shoe. "Talking how Trey would be joining me soon at Mr. Vargas's."

Diego shrugged. "I was just busting your balls and all."

Alex shook his head. "I don't think so." He glanced at the Browning, then back to Diego. "I'm keeping this, by the way."

"Sure. It's yours."

"Thanks. I wasn't asking." Alex punched him again, then climbed off of him.

"Oh, come on." Diego groused, then rolled to his side cupping his busted nose.

"What do you want to do with them?" Alex asked Ava, standing next to her.

"I'll deal with them. You should go." She kept the pistol trained at Juan who stayed on the floor.

"You sure?" Alex asked, covering Diego.

"I am. Me and Lucy can handle it from here." Ava glanced at Diego. "There's some things that we need to hash out once and for all and now is as good of a time as any."

Alex lowered the pistol, then moved around her toward the front door. "Take care of yourself and that little boy."

“You too,” Ava replied as he opened the door. “Thanks again for everything. And don’t worry, we’ve got your back.”

“I appreciate that. See you around.”

Alex gave a warm smile, then shut the door behind him, leaving Diego and his homie to the mercy of the two bitter women.

CHAPTER THIRTY-FOUR

WENDY

The homestead had never looked so good.

Wendy followed the stream, arriving back at her grandparents' place hours later, just as she'd hoped. The familiar woods and open plot of land behind the property made her rejoice, and breathe a bit easier.

The arduous journey had come to an end, and now she could let her guard down. The threat of the Dukes was no longer an issue, but what had happened over the past few days chewed at her mind. She'd have to tell her grandparents what went down and what she did to save her life, and the lives of others.

Wendy made her way down the small hill and past the bushes and trees to the open field. She trudged through the pasture, lost in thought, trying to find the right words.

Tears streamed down her cheeks from the emotional rollercoaster ride. A heavy toll had been taken, both physically and emotionally. The impact of the days' transgressions and what she did weighed heavily on her shoulders, more so than she ever thought it would.

The price for such vengeance was high—a lesson she was learning all too well.

Wendy wiped the sadness away, cleared her throat, then passed through the white farm fence. She made her way toward the rear of the house, anxious, yet scared to see familiar, loving faces. Her body ran on fumes, exhausted to the point of a total shutdown. Each step felt laborious, like trudging through quicksand.

A bit farther. Almost there.

The brutal sun overhead trailed Wendy the entire way, baking the land and her without regard or thought. Not a single cloud sought to shield her from the intense rays.

She licked her dried, crusty lips, savoring a drink of water. The emptiness of her stomach beckoned for some food to stay the nausea that refused to leave her be.

A cold shower drifted into her thoughts, as did some clean clothes. All in due time.

Wendy crossed the patio and approached the back door. She paused, took a deep breath, and mustered the courage to face the battery of questions she knew waited for her.

She turned the knob and opened the door.

A wave of stifling heat greeted her. Odd.

The ominous sound of silence filled both ears. No news broadcast blared from the television as she had grown accustomed to. The air conditioning unit sat idle with no signs of running.

That's strange, Wendy thought, pushing the door open all the way. She'd never known her grandparents' home to be so quiet, especially in the middle of the day, or hot for that matter. The thermostat stayed in the upper sixties during the hottest parts of the days. Had they lost power or something?

"Hello?" Wendy ventured inside the house, looking over the living room and her grandfather's empty recliner. "Is anyone here?"

The silence remained without a hint or whisper of them being home. She scanned the living room, then kitchen, but spotted no hint of her grandparents. The blinds around the house had been drawn as well, darkening the interior.

Wendy backtracked outside and glanced at the driveway. Her grandfather's truck sat parked in the same spot in the driveway from when she left the other day. They had to be there, but where?

Did one of them get sick and have to be rushed to the hospital by way of an ambulance? Perhaps they'd ventured out into the woods looking for her and something happened. She'd given no hint or clue to where she and Clint were going. Hell, her grandparents didn't even know he was there. They would've been beyond frightened not being able to find her, given what happened with her father and the dangerous men he crossed.

Damn you, Dad.

The mass of guilt eating away at her built from the stupid decision she'd made. It compounded with each second she didn't find them.

Wendy walked back into the low-lit home and scoured the bottom floor. The soles of her shoes squeaked off the wood planks. The noise sounded louder without the TV shouting the latest news and her grandparents' playful banter.

Every room was checked for any sign or clue to their whereabouts. All seemed in order with nothing she could spot to give any cause for concern. The space they kept the guns and other such gear remained in proper order with nothing missing except for the guns she took to the range.

The second floor. She hadn't checked there yet and prayed they were just busy with something and hadn't heard her call for them.

Wendy rushed down the hall and past the kitchen to the landing. Her hand glided along the banister, gripping the wood tightly. She took a single step, then paused, noticing a discoloration on the carpet.

Is that...

Blood stained the steps. Her heart sunk. She knelt and probed the droplets with her finger. The fluid had dried and matted to the carpet fibers, meaning it had been there for some time.

"Grandad? Grandma?"

Wendy tromped up the steps, rushing to the second floor without thought or care about what waited for her. Each footfall grew louder, echoing through the home as she reached the landing at the top. The blood drops trailed toward her grandparents' closed bedroom door.

She rushed down the hallway, panting and consumed with angst. What waited on the other side of the door frightened her, but she had to look.

The door was cracked open. A thin bead of light shone through the gap. She rammed the door with both hands, tossing it open.

The doorknob slammed the wall, denting the sheetrock.

Wendy skimmed over the spacious master bedroom for her family but didn't locate them. She checked the bathroom, then the closet. Both were empty.

The trail of blood led her to this room, but nothing inside hinted at an issue that would be cause for concern. She stared at the dresser on the far wall, then the large, oak poster bed and noticed something odd.

The comforter was missing and so was the top sheet. Another hint that didn't seem right. Her grandmother made her bed without fault each and every morning. It was a habit she'd tried to instill in Wendy.

Wendy took a closer look and spotted splotches of more blood on the white sheets. Her arms lifted into the air. She turned in a circle, confused and unsure of what to do next. Something bad had happened and she needed to get a hold of the police, and fast.

The phone next to her grandad's side of the bed caught her eye. She reached for the cordless handset and yanked it from the base. Her fingers mashed 91 before noticing the device didn't have the typical green glow behind the numbers.

Damn it.

She growled under her breath, then threw the phone to the sheets. Wendy hurried out of the bedroom and raced downstairs.

The police station in town was her next stop. She needed to get there quick to report what she'd found, and hopefully, it wasn't too late.

CHAPTER THIRTY-FIVE

ALEX

Trey better be there, or else.

The journey out of Houston took longer than Alex wanted. He made his way through the treacherous city streets and chaos that blistered at every corner. Vandals ransacked department stores and grocery shops, rushing from the buildings with arms full of stolen merchandise and carts full of food.

The Impala received a grave beating from the stranded people hurling a vast array of blunt objects at the car to stop it. The constant dings against the body and windows kept him on edge. He held the steering wheel with a taut hold, trying to avoid the incoming threats while pushing through the turmoil of a city consumed by fear and violence.

Alex traveled I-69 north toward Artesian Lakes. The upheaval stopped along the open road that had little to no pedestrians lurking about.

A sigh of relief left his parted lips. He remained steadfast, though, watching for any further dangers that could spring at any second.

Time ticked by in a blink. The barrage of thoughts, and the days' past events leading to where he was, skated through his tired, tattered mind. He was now a fugitive on the run and a man with a bullseye on his back. The world was against him, or so it felt like.

Alex found his way to the cabin Diego had told him about. He coasted through the wooded area and snaking roads, creeping toward the hidden drive.

The cabin came into view through the wall of trees and other greenery. The leafy limbs offered snippets of the log home. He turned down the rocky sloped drive and made his way to the bottom. His hand grasped the grip of the Browning as he scanned the front of the secluded cabin.

The windows facing him had all been drawn.

A red Dodge truck poked out from the back right corner of the cabin. He didn't recall Trey having such a vehicle, though, he could've stolen it, or worse yet, spent the money on the ride.

Alex stopped at the far end of the log home, away from the porch. He shifted into park, then killed the engine. His hand tugged on the handle, opening the door.

He left the car and stood, taking in the dense vegetation. The wooded grounds surrounding the cabin looked vast and endless with no other buildings in sight.

Birds chirped.

The hint of pollution from the city melted away, leaving only fresh air.

Alex closed the door with a soft touch, then crept toward the porch. He tried to peek through the windows, but couldn't see past the shut blinds.

The Browning stayed out of sight, held in his hand behind his back. His finger pressed the trigger guard, ready to slip inside at a moment's notice.

He stopped at the entrance of the porch, then checked the front door. It was closed.

Alex advanced up the rickety stairs that creaked from the added weight. His gaze shifted to each window, watching for movement of the blinds. He stepped to the side of the door and tested the knob. It opened.

No footfalls or rustling inside the cabin sounded. All remained silent and still.

Alex took a deep breath, pushed the door inward, then moved through the doorway with the Browning up. He crept into the dark interior, sweeping the open space for any movement.

Something blunt smashed against the side of his head, sending him to the floor. He rolled to his back, facing the entrance with the Browning still in hand.

A figure lurked next to the doorway, wielding a gun. He pointed it at Alex's head. Trey.

Alex blinked and kept the Browning down at his side, unsure if he'd pull the trigger or not.

"I'd think carefully about doing—" Trey studied his face for a second, but didn't lower the gun. Both brows raised, eyes opened wide with shock. "No freaking way. It can't be you. You're supposed to be in prison. How? What?"

Alex sat up from the floor, keeping any sudden movements to a minimum. The Browning hung in his hand, forearms resting across both bent knees. "We need to talk about Mr. Vargas, and the money you stole, now."

Trey shook his head, then smirked. “Money? Brother, that money is gone. No longer in my possession. If that’s why you came looking for me, then I hate to say, you wasted your time. The only thing I’ve got for you is this Springfield Hellcat and eleven of his friends that want to say hi.”

Great. Now what do I do?

ABOUT THE AUTHOR

Derek Shupert is an emerging Science Fiction Author known for his captivating dystopian storylines and post-apocalyptic-laden plots. With various books and anthologies underway, he is also the author of the Afflicted series and Sentry Squad.

Outside of the fantastical world of sci-fi, Derek enjoys reading, exercising, and watching apocalyptic movies and TV shows like Mad Max and The Walking Dead. Above all, he is a family man who cherishes nothing more than quality time spent with his loved ones.

To find out more about Derek Shupert and his forthcoming publications, visit his official website at **www.derekshupert.com.**